HOUSE OF FURIES

HOUSE
OF
FURIES

MADELEINE ROUX

An Imprint of HarperCollinsPublishers

HarperTeen is an imprint of HarperCollins Publishers.

House of Furies
Text copyright © 2017 by Madeleine Roux
All rights reserved. Printed in the United States of America.
No part of this book may be used or reproduced in any manner whatsoever without
written permission except in the case of brief quotations embodied in critical articles
and reviews. For information address HarperCollins Children's Books, a division of
HarperCollins Publishers, 195 Broadway, New York, NY 10007.
www.epicreads.com

Library of Congress Control Number: 2016960403
ISBN 978-0-06-249861-8 (trade bdg.) — ISBN 978-0-06-266853-0 (int.)

Typography by Erin Fitzsimmons
17 18 19 20 21 CG/LSCC 10 9 8 7 6 5 4 3 2 1
❖
First Edition

*For Jane Austen, who definitely doesn't get enough books
about the occult dedicated to her*

For Smidge, who is almost certainly a hellhound in real life

And for Ren, who pulled the sword from the stone

Those who play

with the devil's toys

will be brought by degrees

to wield his sword.

—R. BUCKMINSTER FULLER

I am Wrath.

I had neither father nor mother:

I leaped out of a lion's mouth

when I was scarce half an hour old,

and ever since I have run up and down the world,

with this case of rapiers,

wounding myself when I had nobody to fight withal.

—CHRISTOPHER MARLOWE,
THE TRAGICAL HISTORY OF DOCTOR FAUSTUS

My name is Louisa Rose Ditton. I work and live at Coldthistle House, a house for boarders and wanderers. A house owned by the Devil.

The usual reaction, and my own once upon a time, is to give a gasp of outrage if you are of one moral persuasion, a guffaw of skepticism if you're of another. But I assure you—promise you—that it is so. The Devil owns this house and all of his who live and work within it. The walls are his, and the gardens. The food we eat for sustenance and the sweets we have for pleasure—everything belongs to him, and he gives it to us at his leisure.

It is not so hard a life when you happen to be someone like me. An outcast, a foreigner, and, some would venture, a Changeling. We are all of us odd and cursed in Coldthistle House, and growing more cursed and odd by the day. The only requirement of employment here is to do your job thoroughly and without complaint. My particular post is that of host and maid. I welcome our guests. I tidy their rooms. And when they meet their untimely and certain demises, I see to the mess.

He takes care of us, the Devil, and in return we do as we are told. Cook, clean, sweep, mend, and frighten to death the rogues, villains, and crooks that ever darken the door of Coldthistle House.

Chapter
One

Malton, England
Autumn, 1809

The road to Coldthistle House was dark and dangerous. So said the woman taking me there, the English rain driving as slow and steady as the wagon.

She found me at the Malton market, where I told fortunes and read palms for pennies. It earned me clucked tongues and black looks from passersby, God-fearing folk who would alert the local parson and see me driven out of their town. But pennies, even ill-gotten ones, will feed you.

Telling a fortune is no easy thing. Indeed, it appears simple, but to tell the future convincingly, one must make the deed all feel as natural and wending as a river cutting its path. Truly, it comes down to reading what resides in people's eyes, how they breathe, how their glance shifts, how they dress and walk and hand over their coins.

I was on my last fortune of the morning when the old woman stumbled upon me. The market day would happen rain or shine, and this was another day of rain in a long, drizzly spell of dreary days. Nobody lingered. Nobody but me, it seemed, and I lacked the respectable reasons of the farmers and craftsmen selling their wares.

The girl in front of me blushed and kept her head down under a thick woolen scarf. It matched her plain, sturdy frock and the coat buttoned over it. Little bursts of tufted yellow-and-gray wool peeked through the weave. She had a fanciful streak. A dreamer. Her ruddy cheeks grew redder and redder still as I told her future.

"Ah, I see it now. There is a love in your life," I said softly, echoing her expression. An old, cheap trick, but it worked. She squeezed her eyes shut and nodded. The teachers at Pitney School had all but beaten the accent out of my voice, but now I let it come back, let the soft Irish lilt color the words the way this girl wanted them colored. Pinks and purples as vivid as her cheeks. "But 'tis not a sure thing, is it?"

"How did you know that?" she whispered, her eyes opening on a gasp.

I didn't.

A dreamer. A reacher. Truly girls of this age—my age—were as open to me as a map. I'd traded such fortunes for sweets and books at Pitney, risking the rod or worse.

"His family dislikes the match," I added, studying her closely.

Her expression fell, her gloved hands in mine clutching with a new desperation. "They think I'm low because of the pig farm. But we never go hungry! So much snobbery and over pigs!"

"But he is your true love, aye?" I could not help myself. Just as I needed the pennies to eat and that eating to live, I needed this, too. The power. Did it work every time? No. But when it did . . . The girl nodded, wetting her lips and searching out my gaze.

"I would do anything for him. Anything at all. Oh, if you

could only see Peter. If you could see us together! He brings me apples at luncheon, apples he buys with his own coin. And he wrote me a poem, the sweetest poem."

"A poem?" Well, then they were practically married. I gave her a secretive smile. "I sense a future for you two, but it will not be easy."

"No?"

"No. 'Tis a hard road unfolding ahead, but if you take the greatest risk, you will reap the greatest reward." Her mouth fell open a little, the desperate thing, and I let my smile dwindle to deliver her fate. "An elopement is your only hope."

Running away. A choice that would likely end in the two lovers being disowned and shunned. He might get another chance at a life and a wife, but she would not. The words burned a little in my throat after the fact. *Why tell the girl such a thing, Louisa?* It felt different, even wrong, when in the past, tricking my snobby schoolmates at Pitney had felt like a personal victory.

The young woman's eyes widened at me in alarm. "E-Elope?"

It was as if it were a curse, so hesitantly did she say it.

"Or find another to love," I hastily added. There. Well enough. I had offered an alternative, and that made me feel less the cur for taking the girl's pennies. The casual way I offered the substitute made her grimace. She did not believe true love was a thing to throw away, as I do. "But you knew that already."

"Surely I did," the girl murmured. "I only needed to hear you say it." She placed two pocket-warmed pennies in my palm and looked up at the gray, sinister clouds. "You have the gift, do you not? You can see the future, tell fates. I see it in your eyes. So dark. Never have I seen eyes so dark or so wise."

"You're not the first to say it."

"I hope I'm the last," the girl said, frowning. "You should find yourself a better path. A God-fearing path. Maybe it would brighten those eyes."

How fear would brighten my eyes, I could not say. I doubted she could, either, really. I closed my fist around the money and took a step back. "I like my eyes just the way they are, thank you very much."

The girl shrugged. The bloom on her cheeks had faded. Sighing, she hunkered down into her scarf and fled the market, her well-worn boots splashing in the puddles between cobbles.

"She won't soon forget ye, and that's a fact."

The old woman's voice, thin as a reed, didn't have the intended effect. I had seen her lurking, after all, and expected her to pounce sooner or later. I turned slowly at the waist, watching the crone emerge from the soaked overhanging of a market stall. Fewer than a dozen yellow teeth and pale gums flashed at me, a pauper's smile. Her hair sprang out from under her tattered bonnet in dry bunches, as if it had been lightly scorched over a fire.

Still, there was the skeleton of beauty behind the sagging flesh, an echo of wild loveliness that time or misfortune had tried to quiet. A complexion as dark as hers meant a laborer's life in the sun or else a foreign heritage. Whatever her birth, I doubted it was anywhere near North Yorkshire.

"Do you make a habit of following little girls?" I asked primly. My true accent vanished. I hoped my arch schoolroom voice sounded half as severe as those of the teachers who had forced it upon me.

"Thought you might need assistance," she said, lowering her head down and to the side. "A little cheer on this dreary day."

I might have known she would reach for my hand and the money in it; thieves were as common as merchants on market days. My hand snapped back and behind my skirts, to obscure the coin in the dampening fabric.

The crone sniggered at me and drew closer, staring up at me with one good eye. The other swam with milky rheum. Her clothes, such as they were, reeked of wood smoke. "I've no interest in robbing you."

"Leave me be," I muttered, eager to be rid of this nuisance. When I turned, her bony hand flashed so quickly toward me it seemed a trick of the eye. Her grip on my wrist was crushing as a blacksmith's.

"Would it not be better if that paltry sum was more? Not coin enough for scraps and a flea-ridden bed but a real day's earnings . . ." With that same unnaturally strong grip, she wrenched open my fingers and placed her hand over mine. The space between our palms grew suddenly hot, a lick of fire passing between us, and when she took her hand away it was not pennies but *gold* in my grasp.

How was it possible?

I sucked in a gasp of surprise, then remembered myself and remembered her, too. If she led a life on the road telling fortunes, then I should not be shocked at her penchant for sleight of hand. No doubt the coin had been hiding up her sleeve, ready for just such a dazzling purpose.

"You must want something from me," I said, narrowing my eyes. "Else you would not be so generous to a stranger."

"Just a gift," she said with a shrug, already wandering away. Such moments of luck never sat right with me—surely such riches came with a price. "Keep warm, girl," the crone added as she hobbled away. "And keep safe."

I watched her disappear behind a cheerfully painted fish stand, the tattered ends of her coat trailing behind her like a shroud. There was no reason to wait longer. If this fool of a woman was so interested in being parted from her money, then I would not refuse her the pleasure. At once, I ran with the hint of a merry skip to the shop window I had passed on my way into the town. Meat pies. The smell was intoxicating, dampened not a jot by the drizzling rain. Lamb, fish, liver, veal . . . With the coin in my fist, I could afford one of each and be spared the pain of choosing. It would be a feast the likes of which I had not tasted in, well . . . In truth, I had never been faced with such overabundance.

The man tending the shop window pulled up the rain shade

as I approached, leaning out and stacking his immense forearms like ham hocks on the sill. Ham. Yes, I'd have one of those as well. Beady blue eyes regarded me from under a cap. His must have been a profitable trade, for his clothes were new and not mended.

"One of each, please," I said, unable to keep the smile out of my voice.

Those eyes staring down at me shifted to the side. Then they slid over my face, my bedraggled hair and muddied frock. His fingers drummed on the sill.

"Beg your pardon, my girl?"

"One of each," I repeated, more insistent.

"'Tis five pence a pie."

"I can well read the sign, sir. One of each."

He simply grumbled in response and turned away, returning a moment later to face me and my growling stomach, handing across six kidney-shaped pies in piping-hot paper. They were released to me slowly, as if he were allowing me plenty of time to rethink my recklessness and run.

But I received the first pie and then the next, handing over the gold and feeling very satisfied with myself indeed.

The satisfaction did not last. The instant he set eyes on the gold, his demeanor changed from one of reluctant cooperation to rage. He snatched up the coin and kept behind the rest of my food, knocking most of it off the windowsill and back into the shop.

"What's this? Don't think a drowned rat like you would be flashing around this kind of money. Where did you get it?" he shouted, turning the gold this way and that, trying to determine its authenticity.

"I earned it," I shot back. "Give that back! You have no right to keep it!"

"Where'd you get it?" He held it just above my reach, and like an idiot I tried to scramble for it, looking every bit the desperate urchin.

"Give it back! You can keep your bloody pies! I don't want them anymore!"

"Thief!" he thundered. From inside the shop, he produced a silver bell as big as his fist and began ringing it, screaming at me above the clanging din. "Ho, men, we have a thief here! Look lively!"

I ran, dropping pies and abandoning the gold. The bell rang hard in my ears as I pelted through the market square, feet splashing in puddles, skirts growing muddier and heavier by the second as I tried to vanish into the dissipating crowd. But all eyes turned to me. There was no escaping the mob I could sense forming in my wake, the ones who would come for me and throw me in the local jail or worse.

Up ahead, the buildings cut away to the left, and an alleyway sliced a narrow route toward the outskirts of the village. I had time, but only a little, and this might be my only chance for escape. It might also lead me toward more men who had heard the cry of "Thief!" but I dashed off a hope for the best and slid on mud-slicked feet into the alley.

I collided with a brick wall and paused, catching my breath, screaming when a hand closed around my shoulder and yanked.

Spinning around, I came face-to-face with the rheumy-eyed crone and her yellow grin.

"Changeling eyes, that's what the girl saw," the woman croaked, as if there had been not a hitch in our previous conversation. "But a sturdy good frock and boots only mended the one time. Soft hands. Not a maid's hands." That one eye focused to a slit. "A runaway, eh? An orphan on the run. I can see it. The life of a governess wouldn't be for you."

"What does that matter?" I spat out breathlessly. There was no time for idle chitchat. "So you do what I do—you're a traveler. You tell fortunes and the like, so what?"

"I do, and with more discretion than you, girl," the woman said with a croak of a laugh. The laughter made the echo of her lost beauty glimmer, almost truly visible. Still gripping my shoulder, she dragged me to the opposite end of the alley and pointed. I looked toward the church she indicated and the crowd meant to come for the thief, for me. A mob. By now the girl I had told the fortune to would have repeated the story, and they would be hunting not just a cutpurse but a witch, too. It would be her father and her brothers, the priest, and whoever else felt like driving a starving girl out of the village and into the menacing cold.

I had suffered and survived this banishment before. Perhaps this time they sought graver punishment.

"Repent," the old woman hissed.

"I beg your pardon?"

"That's what they want from you, surely. Oh, they'll take you in," she said, laughing again, the sound whistling through her broken teeth. "Show a little contrition. Works, doesn't it?"

The mob expanded. It wouldn't be long now before they felt bold enough for a confrontation. Thief. Witch. No, it wouldn't be long now. The crone had conjured gold to give me, and if she gave it so freely, then there was more where that came from. She might be clever, but I could be cleverer. I could make that gold mine.

"I know a place, girl," the crone said. She paid no heed to the riot forming just down the street. She only had eyes—one eye—for me. "Soft hands now can be hard hands soon. I can find you work. Dry. Safe. Plenty of food. Got a spot of pottage and a hunk or two of pork in my wagon. It will last us the ride, if you're keen to ride, that is."

Not the choice I had hoped to make that day. Rather, I simply wanted to decide where to spend a few coins for a hot meal and a bed for the night. But that dream was dashed for the moment. A new dream formed in its place—me with pockets full of gold and a way to start a new life. The crowd spilling out from the church, however, was a vastly different story.

She latched on to my fidgeting. "Hanging is no end for such a pretty, pale neck."

"How far?" I asked, but I had already turned to follow her, and she led me away from the view of the church, toward another muddy alley running between an alehouse and a butcher's. "And what would the work be like? Are there any children to teach? My French is passable. My Latin . . . Well, I know a bit of Latin."

"Nothing like that, girl. Just scrubbing, sweeping, seeing to some easy guests. It can be hard work but honest, and you won't want for a thing."

Not ideal, perhaps, but better than begging or thieving, or spending a full morning at work only to come up with a few lousy pennies.

Or swinging from a noose.

And the gold, I reminded myself; there could be more *gold*.

"Where is this place?" I asked, hit by the smell of the butcher's and the sourness of a fresh kill being gutted somewhere inside.

"North, just north. Coldthistle House, they call it, a place for boarders, my girl, and a place for the wayward and lost."

Chapter Two

We followed the road north as long as daylight persisted. My rump ached from the bouncing of the wagon wheels over broken cobbles. The crone spoke of comfort at this Coldthistle House, but there was none so far to be found on the journey.

The horses began to plod as the last orange ribbons of dusk faded on the horizon. I sat huddled next to the old woman on the driving bench, soaked through from the leaky canvas roof of the wagon. Shivering, I listened to her singing a nonsense song, random snatches of words put to a familiar tune.

"My mother sang a song like that, but those are not the words," I told her through chattering teeth. "Are you from the island, too?"

"Sometimes," she said. The cold and the rain did nothing to drive the odd twinkle out of her good eye, and she flashed it at me now.

"What could that possibly mean? One is either from a place or not."

"So sure of that," she whispered, giggling. "You like to be sure of things, don't you? What else are you decided on, girl? That there is a God in the heavens and a Devil down below?"

I turned away from her, staring straight ahead as the road climbed, a steep hill carrying us higher and higher, as if we could reach those last golden bands of daylight. "Of course."

"For a teller of fortunes and fates, you are not a very convincing liar."

"I was taught the Bible," I said shortly. "That should be answer enough."

"It's not as simple as that. Nothing is. I thought you were cleverer than this, child. I only take clever children to Coldthistle House now."

"Now?"

She giggled again, but it was not a mirthful laugh. "The dull ones never lasted all that long."

"What does that have to do with God or any of it? No, forget I asked at all. You'll only offer more riddles and half-speak." That drew another gurgle of laughter from the crone.

"Lighter talk, then, to make the journey less bitter and damp," she said. A sudden squawk from behind us drew my mind from the cold. It came again, louder, and then another bird chirped, and another, until an entire chorus of tweets and chirps and calls erupted from the covered wagon bed.

"Is this . . ." I swiveled, drawing up one of the tethered corners of the canvas, tugging until the hooks in the wood gave. Behind the sodden covering were a dozen cages or more, all roped together, a different bird in each home, perched and alert, filling the road with song. "Birds? What are you doing with them all?"

"Why, eating them. What else would they be for?"

Yet I spied a finch and a pleasantly rotund little wren, and exotic creatures with feather plumes that I couldn't possibly name. "Monstrous. How could you eat such lovely things?"

"It's all meat and gristle under the finest wrappings," she replied. "We're no different."

"So you wish to eat me, too?"

Her nose wrinkled up at that and she shook her head, snorting. "They are pets, child. I am delivering them to their new master, who—I assure you—has no intention of doing them harm."

Gullible. Foolish. I blushed and tucked the covering back down, listening as the birds gradually calmed and fell silent. The old woman returned to her singing, and perhaps it was what kept the creatures so still and quiet during the bumpy ride.

We crested the hill as night came on in earnest, the rain slowing and giving us momentary reprieve. The two hunched and plodding horses took the descent haltingly, hooves clattering unevenly as they tried to keep purchase on the slick ground. I could feel the tension in their bodies, the reins jerking in the crone's hands as the beasts ignored whatever pulls and whistles she gave.

"Come now, steady, ye nags!" she shouted at them, snapping the reins.

It had the intended effect, but too much of one—the horses bolted, finding some last burst of energy to send us flying down the hill. The wagon bounced madly, the birds coming to life again. That drove the horses faster, as if they could outrun the piercing cries of alarm from the birds. Rattling and rattling, the wheels making only occasional contact with the road, we thundered toward the dip at the bottom, where the foul weather had left an enormous ditch of standing water.

"Slow them!" I screamed, barely louder than the birds. "Slow down!"

The crone clucked and called and heaved backward on the reins, but the horses ignored her, carrying us at reckless, mortal speed toward the bottom of the hill. I felt the wagon list before I heard the spoke crack. Then the wheel spun off into the darkness, vanishing over the swell of the hill. I scrambled to hold on to the seat, both hands braced on the wooden lip near the crone's knee.

The horses checked at the loss of the wheel, slowing, but it was too late; the momentum of the heavy wagon was already too great, carrying us at top speed toward the watery hole not ten yards away.

I closed my eyes and clenched my teeth together, holding every sinew in tightly as impact loomed. The crone gave a sudden yip, and then a rousing, trilling sound like *Alalu!* and we were weightless, in the air, soaring over the ditch and to a rough but safe landing on the other side. The wagon stuttered to a stop, the horses snorting and stamping, refusing to pull us another inch. I stared at the ground below, ground that should have shattered the old wagon to pieces. Slowly, the horses nosed toward the grass on the right side of the road, angling us away from the ditch and toward a valley clustered with wildflowers.

"How did you do that?" I breathed, shaking. The splintered remains of the wheel spoke dripped with mud and rainwater, and I could only tear my eyes away from them gradually and back to the crone. She shrugged and collected her dry bush of hair, smoothing it back from her ears.

"You drive this stretch of road long enough, you learn to master its miseries."

The woman dropped the reins and vaulted with surprising vigor out of the seat to the ground. Her boots sank into the mud, and she high-stepped around to my side of the wagon, sighing and shaking her head as she inspected the damage.

"And no spares with me on this trip," she said, more to herself than me. "Perhaps I have not mastered *every* misery."

"So what do we do now?" I asked, still trembling from the shock of the landing. From the ancient wagon to the ancient woman to the ancient, weak horses, I could not imagine how we had jumped the ditch and come away from it in one piece. Judging from the quiet, lazy way the horses munched their grass, this was an everyday occasion for them.

"We cook one of the birds," the crone replied at once.

Before I protested, she rolled her eye and beckoned me down. "I jest. We make a fire and eat a little porridge, and then, my girl, we hope for a miracle."

Chapter Three

he old woman built a serviceable fire in the gravel-and-mud clearing on the other side of the ditch. She worked quickly, efficiently, the crookedness of her hands no hindrance as she unrolled a bundle of kindling from the back of the wagon and stacked the sticks into a tidy pyramid.

"Are you just going to stand there gawping?" the woman barked.

"I am likely to freeze unless you employ me," I replied, pacing to demonstrate as much, trying to stamp feeling back into my icy feet and ankles. The blankets she supplied did little to banish the cold, even though the crone forwent them all herself and piled them on my shoulders.

"In the back," she said in that same short way. "Gather the crockery and oats. There should be a can of grease and a pair of wooden spoons."

A part of me chafed at the idea of taking orders from this stranger. She had offered me an escape from the crowd at Malton, but what power did that give her? To respect and obey one's elders, they taught at Pitney School, was the responsibility of every educated young woman. The idea seemed as laughable then as it did now. What did the teachers at Pitney School know, for all their advanced years? How to slap and scold, how to make a child stand in the freezing cold as punishment for dirty fingernails, how to deny bread, water, and sleep when it pleased them?

Naughty children please no one but the Devil.

I had heard it a hundred times or more from Miss Jane Henslow at Pitney, and recalling the phrase sent a shiver down my spine. Miss Henslow, cold, mousy, and fragile, gave a beating like nobody else at the school. I could feel the ghost of her rod smacking my shoulders as I hurried to the back of the wagon. The crone's eyes followed me. I didn't need to look at her to feel it; they were as real as a pinch.

"You travel this road often," I observed, eager for some distraction.

"I said as much. What of it?"

"You stoked that fire handily enough. It's damp as a duck's backside and yet it gave you not an ounce of trouble. Are you accustomed to cooking in the rain?"

The wagon covering, drenched with icy rain, stung my fingertips. As she'd said, a handful of baskets heaped with necessities were crammed into the back. They seemed almost an afterthought, the numerous birdcages the clear priority. Those cages were quiet now, soft blankets masking the din of the birds within, but not their pungent smell. The boards of the cart glowed, slick and white with droppings.

"I might have known you would be a nosy one," the crone said with a sigh. "Did that serve you in the past? That sharp eye of yours?"

"Sometimes, yes," I said honestly, gathering the ingredients for supper. "And oftentimes no."

Naturally, my teachers at Pitney grew weary of my vigilance. And so did my grandparents. They were the ones who sent me off to school, happy to pay for it as long as I was none of their concern. From mother to grandparents to school, they all fancied a hard, stinging lesson when I happened to do or say the wrong thing. It was better to take a beating and forget the pain and humiliation at once. But I never forgot such indignities, and the compounding misery made me constantly shy, like the horse that knows only the whip and never the faintest touch of affection.

"I cannot change your nature, girl," the old woman said. She huddled by the fire while I returned with laden arms. "But I can recommend you keep what those sharp eyes see in that sharp mind, and not let it out with a sharp tongue. The master at Coldthistle House has no time for busybodies and gossips. Hard work is all he asks, and your opinions are not required."

Again I felt a pang of doubt. An actual roof and regular meals sounded attractive, but now I wondered at the cost.

"I have never much enjoyed obedience."

"And so it is a miracle you yet live," the woman said with a harsh laugh. "Now, quick, set the grease in the pot. I think another wagon approaches, and I do not intend to share much."

I turned away from the fire and squinted into the distance

both ways—darkness and clouds and the very edges of far-off trees but no sign of travelers. "I hear it not."

"As you said, I travel this road frequently and I've learned to bend my ear a certain way."

It seemed unlikely that a woman of her advanced age would have keener senses than I, but I crouched and arranged my skirts politely, then dropped a knob of grease into the pot. When it was hot and nearly spitting, I added the dry oats and a bit of what looked like sheep's milk. The crone produced a small packet of brown powder from the many folds of her cloak and tipped it into the food. At once, the glorious scent of cinnamon swirled around us, and my stomach roared with approval.

No sooner had the crone slopped a portion of cooked oats into my bowl than a low, rumbling sound came from the road behind us. I stood and chewed, slowly, watching a wagon far finer than the old woman's crest the hill. The horses slowed, and the carriage—for in truth it was such, and not a mere wagon, with a team of two matching chestnut beasts—descended safely. A driver in all black shrank inside his coat, the collar flapping around his face as the wind and rain picked up.

"Eat what you want now. If they stop, I will have no choice but to share," the crone muttered. Her portion was already gone. "A carriage that fine, their man will have what's needed to fix our wagon." As she predicted, the driver caught sight of our meager little camp and pulled over, hefting a rain-spattered lantern and shining it toward us.

"Greetings now on this mild, seasonable night," the crone said with a friendliness of tone I'd not heard from her before. She seemed less formidable suddenly, meek, hobbling toward the road with her head bent and shoulders hunched.

"What's the fuss up there?" I heard someone call from inside the carriage. It was the voice of an older man, not a rich accent but certainly not a poor one either. A Midlands accent with the roughness polished down.

"Two women, sir," the driver called back. He was of medium height and stocky, and even his heavy coat could not hide his muscled frame. The crone was right—we could use such a man's help righting the wagon. He looked the old woman up and down and then glanced at me. "An old woman and a girl, sir."

"A broken wheel has left us stranded," she explained. "We could be persuaded to share our humble meal with you all if you aid us."

The door of the carriage swung open. It was dark inside. I could not see the eyes of whoever studied us from within.

"I do so hate to beg," the crone continued, her voice trembling. Even I was briefly convinced of her desperation. "You would not leave two defenseless womenfolk on a cold and rainy road, would you?"

"Turn off, then, Foster. Let us see this broken wheel for ourselves."

The driver obeyed, cracking a short whip and urging the

bowed-head horses off the road. The animals looked as drenched and exhausted as I felt.

When they had stopped, the driver leapt to the ground and muttered his way to the carriage door, kicking down the stand and opening the door for his charges. He had taken the lantern, and I watched two men descend, their collars flipped up against the deluge.

It was an old fellow with thick gray hair and a heavy brow, and behind him came a young man so bright of face, curious, and golden, I forgot all about the hunger in my belly and the rain soaking my hair.

Chapter
Four

"Y ou've dropped your spoon."

"Sorry?"

"There's no need to apologize, only—"

"Oh. Yes. There it is, isn't it?" The spoon had landed scoop down in the mud right next to my shoe. A tiny glob of porridge dotted the leather toe, as if to punctuate this gloomy introduction. I knelt to retrieve the spoon, not anticipating that the young man would do the same. His far larger hand closed over the handle and then we both stood at the same moment, and he produced a handkerchief to wipe both mud and porridge from the wood.

"Rawleigh Brimble," he said, giving me the spoon. "Which is my name. Bit of a mouthful. Usually just go by Lee."

"Louisa," I replied. My surname held so little value, I almost never offered it in these situations. The shock of his appearance had worn off, and I managed to grasp the spoon and deposit it safely in the bowl. I turned to put it back near the fire, where the crone was slopping out a meager portion into a bowl for the older gentleman. The driver strode off with his lantern, interested foremost in the state of our wagon.

"Are you often in the habit of rescuing maidens and their spoons?" I asked.

His smile widened at that, a feat which seemed impossible

given how widely he already beamed. "I'm afraid not, but I should be! I do feel awfully gallant now." His turquoise eyes squinted into the darkness. "Have you been stranded here long, Louisa?"

"Not very. With any luck we're on to Coldthistle House soon. Do you know it?"

Those very turquoise eyes widened in surprise and perhaps delight. "How extremely funny. Yes, in fact. That is our destination, too. What a chance this is! Uncle, did you hear? These ladies are destined for Coldthistle also!" He perched one fist on his hip and laughed, turning back to me. He wore a fine suit under his overcoat, but the wool had worn through in places and been artfully mended. "Are you boarding there as well? Uncle and I have business in the area."

"Oh! No . . ." I could feel the crone's eyes on me. They burrowed. Nothing but the truth would suit, and it felt strangely embarrassing. Somehow my destitution, my anonymity, felt suddenly harsher. "I'm taking a position there."

"In the scullery," the old woman helpfully finished.

I did not glare. I had no idea yet if she was to be my employer, and perhaps I had annoyed her enough for one journey. "Exactly so," I said softly.

This did not seem to bother or offend Lee Brimble, whose smile dimmed not a jot. "Then you will know all the secrets of the place," he said in a whisper too bright to come off as conspiratorial. "And you are honor-bound to share them with me, hm? Now that I have so bravely rescued your spoon."

"Magnanimous of you," I said drily, but without irritation. "Somehow I feel I am gaining the more advantageous side of the bargain."

"Without a doubt," he said, taking a few steps away from the fire. "Ho there, Foster, what do you see?"

"A simple job," the driver called back. He stomped back toward us, appearing like a yellow ghost under the lantern light. "We should all be back on the road in an hour, perhaps two. What the devil are all those birds doing in your wagon, old woman?"

"Foster, manners," Rawleigh Brimble corrected him sharply. Then he cringed. "And here I've forgotten mine—introductions! This is my uncle, George Bremerton, and that of course is Foster. We never call him anything else."

The driver snorted.

"And what do we call you?" the uncle asked, staring with bold suspicion at the crone. His coat buttons flashed in the lantern light, gold, an intricate Celtic cross pattern worked into the metal of them.

"Why, me?" Her voice, still softened, quavered like a plucked harp string in the gloom. "You can just call me Granny. Now eat up and get to work. It's still a long way to Coldthistle House."

"Shall I call you 'Granny,' too?" I asked, helping her dish up what was left of the porridge for the men. The tattered sleeve of her coat slid up her wrist as she stirred the pot, and, though but an inch was revealed, I saw several strange markings. Tattoos, perhaps; symbols I didn't recognize. She quickly fixed her coat, but she had seen my wandering eyes.

"Not with that attitude," she muttered. "There are hungry travelers to feed and a wagon to fix. Vexing me should be the last of your priorities this night."

"Yes, Granny," I replied, still with a smirk. Let her keep her secrets, I thought—as long as she delivered on her promise to give me employment and shelter, I would count her as a friend. Or an ally, at least.

A shiver ran through the buckthorn and birch crowding the road. Trees shaking at night always filled me with dread—it was a sound that made me long for a warm bed and thick walls. The others heard and felt it, too, shrinking down into their collars. Foster had left the safe yellow ring of the firelight without eating, choosing instead to rummage in their coach for tools.

"It's a spot of luck that we found you," Lee said, taking his bowl of porridge from the old woman and tucking in. He ate precisely, with a nobleman's neatness. For a stranger, he stood close to us, a mark of a trusting nature. His uncle, by contrast, ate apart. The boy didn't protect his coat pockets well, and even a fence less proficient than I would have no trouble swiping the coins from him in a wink.

"A spot of luck," his uncle spat, shaking his head. "This will put us back by hours now. 'Tis folly to linger here on the side of the road in full dark. We are easy fodder for cutpurses." At this, he gave me a cold, hard stare.

God help me, he wasn't wrong. The old woman and me, we were the thieves, the threat.

"All that jostling in the carriage has made him grumpy," Lee cut in with a chuckle. "I apologize on his behalf, and not for the last time, I'm sure."

"The cold makes curmudgeons of us all," the crone said, almost politely. "Do not fear overmuch. I travel this road frequently, and it is safer than most."

She had served up the last of the porridge and now gathered her threadbare clothes close around her, moving away from the fire and toward the cold, dark emptiness of the fields and forests beyond. I watched her go, only half listening to the men discuss the state of the wagon and the most expedient way to mend it. There was an odd sort of deliberateness to the way the crone strode away from us, as if she had suddenly heard something out there in the field.

At first they seemed a trick of the eye, the little lights that began to dance in the dark. But no, they persisted and grew in number and brightness. The others did not notice, only me, and I watched what seemed like a hundred glittering eyes gather in front of the old woman, as if she were consulting a hidden cabal of yellow-eyed minions. A single, sharp hoot came from that direction, and it occurred to me that these were birds, owls, many of them flocking to that one spot near the old woman.

I hadn't heard them arrive, but I did hear them go. Facing

away from me, the crone gave a solitary nod. There was no telling if she had spoken to these birds or not, but then suddenly
they all lifted into the air at once, and I knew it was no hallucination; I felt the buffeting wind of their wings as they departed,
and saw the dusting of feathers like snow that drifted down and
down and settled softly around the crone's torn hem.

Chapter Five

t was silly, of course, to look for traces of the owls in full darkness. Still, I fought exhaustion, staring out the window of George Bremerton's carriage.

The wagon rumbled along ahead of us, driven by the crone, and we followed along closely. The carriage driver, Foster, had suggested they lighten the wagon's load as much as possible, and keep the back end of it unburdened to avoid further damage to the wheel. The crone would not let them touch a single item under the coverings, and instead ordered me to ride with them in the carriage. I did not see how the loss of only my small frame would be enough to ease the strain on the wagon, but the men were too cross, wet, and tired to argue with her.

"You can sleep, you know," Lee said quietly. His uncle snored across from us on the opposite bench. The carriage smelled of pipe tobacco and whiskey, a comforting, warm scent I had not experienced in many years. It reminded me of leaving Ireland, of the dock workers who congregated on the waterfront, drinking and smoking, the ones who hooted and called at me and my mother when we boarded the boat for England.

"Nobody here will harm you," Lee added.

It is not you I fear, oddly enough.

I didn't take my eyes away from the window and what might

be in the sky over the woods. "Did you not see a preponderance of owls?"

"Owls?" He laughed a little. "When?"

"Before we left," I replied. *Or ever.* What a stupid question. But I had seen the feathers. I had felt the power of those wings beating the air. "In the field not far from the fire . . . I thought I saw dozens of owls."

"I must have been too focused on the porridge," he said. I looked over at him then, and he was blushing by the weak light of the outer lantern. It bobbed along, making tricks of our faces and of the shadows. "I would have liked to see such a thing."

Belief. It was a strange feeling. He *believed* me. Miss Henslow would have beaten me for fibbing. She always thought I was spinning wild tales, even when I was certain I saw or heard a thing. Maybe it happened too often for her liking. Maybe it seemed as though I was somehow different, gifted or cursed with the ability to note odd reflections in mirrors or footsteps in the attic at night. I often felt others cringe away from me, even just strangers, as if they sensed something about me not even I understood.

But to be believed? I decided to forget the owls. It was enough that this near stranger did not question the event.

"Where are you from?" I asked, now more than curious about this earnest young man with the startling eyes.

"Canterbury, but I should be in London now," he said, sounding forlorn. It was his turn to look away and toward the window, those eyes less bright and more inscrutable. "Uncle thinks something went funny with my inheritance. It all went to my cousin, you see, when my guardian died. John Bremerton. He's a proper lord, raised me, but just as a ward." He leaned toward me and lowered his voice, casting a wary eye in his uncle's direction. "Uncle George thinks I'm a Bremerton. A bastard one, but still . . ."

"So the money could be yours," I finished. How intriguing.

"Or part of it, at least. Some sort of entitlement."

"Precisely. I loved my guardian. He was always kind, always fair, and the money doesn't really mean all that much to me. The stipend he left me seemed quite generous, in fact."

"Then why come all the way to Malton and beyond?"

"I suppose the answer is twofold. Uncle wants to visit the spring near Coldthistle for its curing properties. He has an old wound in his ankle that still bothers him. That, and he thinks my mother is working near here, and that she will have proof of my parentage." He shrugged, and his shoulders sank with a burdensome weight. "Vast wealth does have a certain appeal."

"A certain appeal?" I couldn't keep the steel edge out of my voice. *A certain appeal.* Looking harder at this young man, I began to question my initial perception of him. Had his lovely golden hair and bright eyes stupefied me? Perhaps he was dull; dull and flippant.

He had the good grace to look shocked and then ashamed. Of course I had no business raising my voice to someone so obviously above my social rank, but it hardly mattered—once he was done staying at the boardinghouse, we would part ways, and I doubted very much the crone would mind if he told her of my impropriety. She knew what she was getting with me—a thief and a runaway.

"Heavens, I'm sure that sounded foolish," he said. One could practically see his collar constricting and choking his voice. "I never wanted for much, and clearly that's made me careless. Lord Bremerton would be furious. He did not raise a cur."

Mollified for the moment, I folded my hands in my lap and glanced at his snoring uncle. He had the look of a man who had once been handsome, but age or hard drinking or a combination of the two had turned him soft and red around the edges. His hair was thinning. A perpetual rosiness splotched his cheeks and nose, a beak that reminded me distinctly of an aubergine.

There was an air about the man I did not like, and an urge to turn out his pockets and steal from him at the first available opportunity rose sharply, like a hunger pang. Even if I were alone, I would think better of it. Under his seat, behind his shins, I saw a number of sabers sheathed in fine leather scabbards. The men were prepared for robbers.

"Have I offended?" Rawleigh suddenly asked. "It would be too like me to do so. And this soon! I really should learn to shut my mouth sometimes. I have the greatest respect for servants. It's a thankless position, truly; I wouldn't last half a second!"

Stop talking.

"Please say I haven't offended you," he added with a sheepish half smile.

"You have, but you're forgiven." There was no point in coddling him. It was obvious to me someone else had done plenty of that already. "I never expect consideration. It's the easiest way to avoid disappointment."

"What a very sad way of looking at things . . ."

A soft, fluttering noise at the window drew my attention. "And yet it keeps me alive." The glass was ice cold when I pressed my nose to it, watching, rapt, as a barn owl flew lower over the carriage, so low that it grazed the roof. "There! Did you see that?"

Lee scrambled to get closer, ducking his head to follow my pointed finger. "Astonishing! One of your fabled owls!"

It flew on ahead, but what was more, it glided toward a rising hill. Dawn broke apart the horizon, wide painter's strokes of inky blue turning lighter by the moment. A tall, two-towered manor rose as if from the hill itself, a stark, black silhouette that grew only taller and more improbable as we neared it. No woods surrounded the manse; the birch and rowan stayed well back, as if reluctant to grow on the house's grounds.

I had lost feeling in my nose, and the cold of the window spread through to my fingertips and toes. Coldthistle House. Aptly named. It looked thorny with warning, tall and spindly and precarious, and, with the sun at its back, not a building of stone and mortar but a place of pure shadow.

"Turn the carriage around," I whispered. But my voice was lost and it was too late. We had started up the hill, and feeling returned to my fingers for an instant. I looked down and shivered; Lee had gone pale and perfectly still, and he clutched my hand in his as if in dread.

Chapter
Six

xhausted, I stumbled out of the carriage and onto the desolate grounds surrounding the manse. Even with Foster helping me down, I was unsteady, clumsy, unsure if perhaps the lack of sleep was responsible for the hard pit forming in my stomach.

"How cozy." Lee had landed on much sturdier footing behind me, surveying the drive with a wobbly smile. "Or, hmm . . ."

I was struggling for words, too. Coldthistle reminded me, horribly enough, of Pitney House. My old school had been more like a dungeon than a place of learning. The pit in my gut widened, and I winced, feeling at once relieved to be away from there but also guilty for leaving behind one tolerable peer. Very well, *friend.* It was easier not to think of her as a person I liked, because now I was free of Pitney's grasp and she remained.

Jenny. Poor, sweet, trusting Jenny. Well, she was far away from me now and there was nothing I could do to help her.

And she might be better off, I mused, taking in the tall, narrow towers that perched like stony fraternal twins on the top of the mansion. It was one of the old, great houses of England, stoic and angular, with a number of yawning windows that looked dark and hollow in the dawn light. A few neglected topiaries lined the path up to the door, their shapes more like gargoyles than circles or squares. A barn peered out from behind Coldthistle House. It looked to be newer and less cruelly appointed, and one's eye went immediately back to the mansion.

My new home.

No, I corrected myself with a grimace, moving slowly toward the wagon to see what the crone wanted of me—not a home but a place of employment. Simple employment. It would be a waypoint, just a place to stop over while I worked out what to do with my life. If I could save up a little money, then I might be able to make it north and take a ship to Ireland. Or to the Americas. Both options felt equally distant and dreamlike, especially with Coldthistle House looming before me. Without a family to return to or a real home to recall, the future never felt important. After Pitney, most girls were either absorbed by the school to teach the next generation or they were picked out for governess positions by families in need.

Even scullery work sounded preferable to teaching some rich lord's brat.

The gravel drive crunched under my shoes, and the crone climbed down from the driver's box just as I approached. I glanced back at Lee and his uncle, who waited on their driver to collect a modest amount of luggage. Lee gave me a little wave and then started toward the house, his uncle clearly in no mood to dawdle.

They would have warm rooms waiting for them, even baths. Looking at the crone's sour expression, I doubted there was anything but toil in my very near future.

"Don't go falling for that boy," she muttered, skewering me with her one good eye.

The suddenness of it caught me off guard.

"Of course not," I replied. "He's a guest and I'm the help. I'm not stupid, you know."

She considered that for a moment, her jaw working back and forth in concentration. "Hmm. That remains to be seen. Not like his uncle would let you have anything to do with each other. That one cares for coin and only coin."

"How do you know that?" But I had suspected the same.

Hobbling toward the back of the wagon, she rubbed at her hip. "You've met one miser, you've met them all. Now what are you doing following me about?"

"I thought you might need assistance with, um, with the cargo."

"You're no use to me hungry and tired," the crone said with a snort. "And besides, Chijioke will be along once the house stirs. Go along inside. Take the stairs up to the second floor and go right. Your quarters are at the very end of the hall."

My quarters? I hadn't imagined I would get a room to myself. That hadn't been the case for so many years, I wondered if it would be lonely to fall asleep to just the sound of my own breathing.

"I'll send someone to wake you in a few hours," the crone added, waving me away.

"Thank you," I said reflexively, but in truth I probably did owe her a great deal.

"Don't thank me yet, child; the day is young."

I refused to indulge in such cynicism. The house was a bit shabby, certainly, and those monstrous topiaries did not make me feel welcome as I passed beneath them, but for now I had a place to rest my head and earn money. That was more than most runaways could hope to have. I shuddered as I stepped gingerly over the threshold, the massive doors opening just at the middle, enough for me to slip inside. There were darker alternatives to scullery work . . . I might have easily ended up in a women's prison or working in a brothel, which was precisely what my father had foreseen for me just before my mother ripped me from the house.

Prospects were low, very low, for a lone Irish girl with no connections, no money, and no means to fabricate those things.

The foyer of Coldthistle House was blazingly hot. A sitting room through an open arch to the left glowed with rosy color, a fire crackling away and heating this ground floor. There was no trace of Lee or his uncle—they must have been settled already. Yet I saw nobody about, and the place was unnaturally silent.

It's just after dawn, you idiot girl, of course it's still.

I crossed a tattered carpet to the staircase on the right of the foyer. It was grand but austere, and the walls around it were clustered with paintings of birds. Ornithological studies and sketches, though the painter did not have much of an eye for artistry. Those odd, stringy creatures glowered down at me from every angle. It was almost enough to make me miss the oddest feature of the room—a large green door directly opposite the main entrance of the house. There was no way it was original to the mansion; no wealthy family would have wanted such an awkwardly placed door. Perhaps it was an addition; added storage or a pantry of some kind.

My exhaustion lifted for a moment, almost as if new life had gusted into me. And the green door called to me.

It *sang*.

Not a song anyone else could hear, I'll wager, but it was as if thin tendrils leaked out from under it, speeding toward me, entering through my ears and coaxing me through whispered melody. Even the words to this song were completely unknowable, some odd, guttural language that sounded like nonsense, nonsense that resolved into guidance. It filled my head with thunder, like a headache but thicker, crowding out any of my own thoughts that might seep in and bring reason.

And like a fool, I listened, drifting toward the glossy green paint of the door, reaching out for the ornate, golden knob . . .

"I wouldn't if I were you."

A high, tiny voice came from behind me. I froze, turning to find a girl of perhaps eleven years staring at me from an open doorway. The kitchens were visible behind her. She wore a simple, white frock that was starkly clean, almost glowing. Her hair was parted at the middle, severely braided into two plaits that dangled over her shoulders. Half of her face was covered in a purplish port-wine stain, a hideous mark on an otherwise lovely child.

A dog wagged his tail next to her. It was a little brown dog composed mostly of ears and wrinkles. He made a soft *boof* sound at me, either a warning or a greeting, I couldn't tell.

"Nobody goes through the green door unless they're invited," she added. Her matter-of-fact manner had cut through the song in my head and I felt, thankfully, like myself again. But also, again, tired. "I'm Poppy. This is Bartholomew. Who are you? You're not a guest."

"How do you know?" I bit back impertinently.

"I just do," she said. "Did Granny find you?"

"Yes," I replied. "She brought me from Malton. I'm to work here now. My name is Louisa."

"Hello, Louisa," she said, kneeling and taking the pup's paw, waving it at me in greeting. "Bartholomew says hello, too. He likes you. He doesn't just like anybody."

"That's very generous of him." *And very premature.* "Do you work here, too?"

Poppy nodded, her pigtails bouncing off her shoulders. "I help Granny with whatever she needs. Some days it's cooking, and sometimes I sweep or clean the chimneys or bring food 'round to the guests. My favorite days are when I get to help Chijioke."

"And he works here also?"

"In the barn, he tends to all the animals and the grounds. You look so tired, you should sleep. Granny will want you to work as soon as you're able. And we don't call her Granny in front of the guests; it's Mrs. Haylam instead."

She had a point. My eyes were drooping and I'm sure I looked dreadful. "Mrs. Haylam it is then. Could you show me the way?"

Poppy sprang forward, obviously pleased to do so, and came to take my hand, tugging me away from the door and toward the stairs. The dog followed at her heels, wagging his slender tail and looking up at me with huge black eyes. He was an attractive creature, if perhaps of indistinguishable breeding. *A bit like me, then.*

The girl's hand was cold and soft, and she tugged harder when I gave a single glance back toward the door. "Not unless you're invited," she reminded me. "And you *don't* want to be invited. I hate going to see Mr. Morningside. He's just a cross old man with too many birds."

I chuckled and followed her obediently up to the landing. "Then I will hope to be spared an introduction."

We stopped on the second floor and turned right, but I felt a cold prickle on the back of my neck. Having lived under the vigilant gaze of the teachers at Pitney, I knew the feeling well— someone was watching us. I dropped my chin and slid my eyes to the side, trying to find the source without letting them know I was keen to their presence. A shadow flitted across the corner of my vision, tall, too tall. Inhumanly tall.

"Don't dawdle," Poppy said, pulling me down the corridor. "And don't speak above a whisper in the halls."

"There are a lot of rules here," I replied, trying to ignore the cold unease of being watched.

Poppy stopped suddenly outside a gray painted door and nodded, letting go of my hand. "Yes, there are, Louisa, and you should follow them."

Chapter
Seven

here was thunder at my door. The floor and bed rattled, shaking me out of a deep, dark slumber.

No, not thunder. A fist.

"I'm awake! One moment!" I called, scrambling to make sure I was decent, and to rub the sleep out of my eyes. It had been a long time—too long—since I had slept that well. At first, I'd worried that being alone would be intimidating, but the solitude proved blissful. Nobody fidgeted in a creaky bed next to me, nobody snored all through the night, and no teachers stalked the room, checking for naughtiness or truancy.

Now, the pounding at the door ceased, and I managed to pull my stained woolen dress over my head and rake both hands through snarled hair before the door opened on a tall figure, a young man of African descent with dazzling olive-green eyes and a furrowed brow.

Either he or someone else had hauled up a steaming basin of water and a bar of soap. Both sat next to the door, and my relief was palpable. After so much waterlogged travel, I smelled like the bottom of a foot.

"Ah!" he rumbled. "A new lamb for the slaughter!"

"I beg your pardon?" He wasn't much older than I was, hale and strong. A soft paper package was tucked under one of his massive arms.

"Only jesting. You are the new scullery girl, aye?" he clari-fied. "Mrs. Haylam wanted me to fetch you. Ach, and to give you this."

The package was warm, and it gave under my hands. Cloth. Probably freshly laundered, given its subtle heat. That made sense. I couldn't begin my employment dressed in traveling clothes. "Thank you," I said. "I'm certain she told you, but my name is Louisa."

"Chijioke," he said. His voice was deep and pleasant, with what sounded like a faint Scottish brogue. It reminded me of one of the students at Pitney. "I work the grounds."

I nodded, emerging at last from the bleariness of a sudden jolt awake. "Poppy told me as much."

"Ah, yes. She mentioned you. Several times, actually. I believe she's quite enamored." He chuckled and then pointed to the room behind me. "Why don't you prepare for the day? Afterward I can show you to the kitchens."

"You're very kind, thank you." I retreated to my quarters and unwrapped the package. Chijioke shoved the basin and soap in behind me and shut the door.

The package was not finery, obviously, and I had expected nothing but clean, simple garments. That's precisely what they were: a long, charcoal-colored skirt; a homespun blouse the color of bone; a cap; an apron; and the sturdy, corseted under-garment to be worn underneath it all.

It was rude to speak through the door, but I wanted a

distraction while I scrubbed myself and wrestled my bony frame into the corset. And I wanted to make a good impression, for once, and perhaps even stay in good standing with my fellow workers at the house. This was a new start, after all, and while I had no idea what the crone—Granny—truly thought of me, I could at least remain civil with this young man and Poppy.

"The Orkney Islands," I said, loudly enough for him to hear in the hall.

"What was that?"

"Your accent. At my old school there was a girl from there, the Orkney Islands." Of course, the teachers had made the girl suppress her natural brogue, encouraging instead a general English dialect that would be more pleasing to potential employers. The gentry had no interest in governesses who would impart a "low" voice to their children. "It's quite distinct."

I heard him laugh again. "It's where my father settled after retiring from the navy."

"What are you doing here, then?" My person decidedly sweeter smelling after the wash, I reached for the corset and laced it. Then I pulled on the skirts and then the blouse.

"You're brimming with questions."

"I didn't mean to be rude," I called back. "Might we discuss the house instead? Do you like being employed here?"

It was hard to gauge his responses without seeing his face, but he paused and then said, "I didn't like the navy. No sea legs. The whole thing made me ill. I prefer fresh air when my feet are on solid ground."

Now *that* I definitely understood. Sea travel always unbalanced me, too, and I had spent most of the voyage from Ireland bent over the railing, hurling my guts into the waves.

My hair, thin and black, never took to plaits very well, but I braided and pinned it the best I could and covered it with the simple white cap. A small, round looking glass sat on the table in the corner, and I checked my appearance in it—not a look that would win me accolades during the London season, but it more than sufficed for scullery work. I had never grown to be a great beauty like my mother, though I had inherited her large, dark eyes and black hair. In such garb, she would have looked voluptuous and even tempting, but not even the most artful corset could make a shape out of my spoon-handle figure.

Upon opening the door, I found Chijioke beaming down at me. He smiled as if I had just made some tremendously clever joke. "Dublin!"

"You can hear Ireland in my voice?" I asked, pulling the door shut behind me. "My tutors would be so disappointed."

"Ah, you should embrace it. Nobody here will chastise you for your heritage," he said. I followed him down the hall a half step behind, for the corridor felt narrow if we went two abreast. It was obvious that keeping the grounds was strenuous work; he had the build of other workmen I had met before leaving Ireland. "I don't hide the Orkney in my voice one jot. It causes so much confusion. What is a Nigerian boy doing with that voice?

Where does it come from? You should see their eyes cross."

"I suppose it is rather disarming," I admitted. In the kinder light of day, the corridor looked less foreboding, but still those odd bird sketches surrounded us. "Your father was Nigerian?"

"Aye, and he didn't hide that, either," he said. We reached the stairway and turned, descending. I could hear the muted chatter of guests in their rooms and similarly faint conversation from the kitchens below. "That's why I like it here. Whatever you were or are, the master expects you to be nobody but yourself. The harder the work, the more honest the man; he said that to me once."

"What a relief." I didn't mean for it to sound so sarcastic, but truly I had my doubts. Life with my mother in Dublin had begun well enough, and when she could no longer care for me and my grandparents took over, they appeared kindly at first. And then they, too, decided to give me up, and Pitney came into my life like a blessing.

All new beginnings, I'd learned, started off brightly and ended in shade. If something felt too good to be true, it invariably was.

"Mrs. Haylam will have tea for you in the kitchens," he said, directing me to that door near the entrance.

"How long did I sleep?"

"Through the day and night and on to the next morning," he replied.

"*What?*" Utterly impossible. I had slept for an entire *day*?

Had I really been so exhausted? "Why did no one wake me sooner?"

Chijioke shrugged his great shoulders and grinned. "Ach, well, the work here is not easy. Mrs. Haylam took pity, mm?"

"That was gracious of her, but unnecessary. I'm accustomed to harsh living. Granny, I mean Mrs. Haylam, found me scrounging for pennies in the rain, doing low carnival tricks." There was no use lying to him—the truth about me would certainly come out. He didn't give any signs of revulsion. "Just about anything would be an improvement."

He waved me off and nudged open the kitchen door with his hip. "You'll be up at dawn to help bake from now on. I wouldn't be too grateful." Chijioke paused midway through the door and lowered his voice, saying with a wink, "And now you know you must show me some of those low tricks later."

"Of course," I said with a laugh. "I won't even ask for your pennies."

"Good, because I have none!" He chuckled with me and led the way into the kitchens. They were clean and stark, in perfect contrast to the overcrowded and colorful foyer. Immediately in front of me was a near floor-to-ceiling range with an old-fashioned oven. Several blackened pots bubbled away on the heat. Preparatory tables and a deep basin lined the opposite wall, and to the left of those was a door opened to the outside. A cool, soothing breeze swept in off the fields, cutting through the intense heat of the stove.

In the middle of the kitchen stood a large, tall table, white and unstained wood, where a china set with tea waited. I smelled scones laced with orange and cardamom, and my stomach tightened with hunger. A day since that roadside porridge. It took all of my physical restraint to keep from flying toward the food.

"Poppy, get out some of last night's ham for the girl. Quickly, if you please, and steal none for yourself or that infernal hound."

I knew the voice, even if it came with an unfamiliar accent and unfamiliar face. No, I knew the face, too, though it couldn't be . . .

"Granny?" I blurted out, altogether forgetting Poppy's instruction. My eyes had trained so intently on the food, I almost hadn't noticed the others in the room: the little girl and her dog, and what looked like Granny, with two or three decades shaved off her presumptive age. Her one eye was still milky, but clearer than before. Her steel-gray hair had been combed and rolled into a neat bun tucked under a housekeeper's cap. She wore a prim, clean blouse and skirt, with a flour-dusted apron tied around her trim waist. There was a sharpness to her stance, a rod in her spine, and the same withering intelligence in her gaze.

It was her, the crone, and the shock of her appearance nearly made me forget my hunger.

"Mrs. Haylam will do," she corrected me. Her voice now was by no means elegant, but certainly not the same croak it had been on the road. She bustled toward the table and the tea set, pouring out a neat measure into one of the cups. "I trust you are adequately rested, Louisa?"

"More than adequately," I said honestly. "Thank you. I . . . I confess I haven't slept that soundly in years." Or ever.

A thin smile spread across the crone's—Mrs. Haylam's—face. Even her skin looked less leathery, though it was still a rich ocher in color. "Guests and help alike find the deepest sleep here. It must be the positioning of the windows or the calming influence of the spring."

"I need to see to that rickety old wagon," Chijioke cut in, dodging around me and striding toward the door leading outside. "It won't survive another trip to town."

Mrs. Haylam nodded, and he turned just before leaving, studying me closely before giving a brief wave. The pigtailed girl Poppy had retrieved a plate with smoked ham from the pantry. Her head just barely reached above the table, and she went on tiptoes to slide the pork up next to the tea.

Her hound, Bartholomew, waited behind her, sitting, his tail wagging furiously as he anticipated any dropped morsels.

"Well? Tuck in, Louisa," Mrs. Haylam said, exploding into a flurry of activity—seeing to the pots on the range, wiping her hands off on her apron, returning to the central table to turn the teapot just so. . . .

I approached the scones tentatively, still unnerved by the crone's sudden change in appearance. The food tempted me, naturally, but it was all so strange, so off-balance. Poppy waited quietly, swinging her arms back and forth, gently coaxing me toward the table with her eyes, and then less subtly by mouthing, "Go ahead!"

"The scones smell lovely," I said, a bit lamely.

"An old family recipe," the housekeeper replied, coming at last to a standstill. I had not yet taken a bite of the food nor a sip of the tea. "Something the matter? Do you take your tea with more sugar?"

Did I dare broach the subject? Chijioke and Poppy had been kind enough. I pressed my luck, lifting the teacup with trembling fingers. "You obviously look different."

She laughed, and the croak in her voice returned for but a moment. "Congratulations, girl, it appears you have eyes in your head."

"I only meant—"

"I know what you meant," she interrupted, wiping her hands yet again on her apron. "Sometimes it is best to look your worst. If everything was exactly as it seemed at all times, we would live in an awfully dull world, don't you think? Now eat up, girl, and fast. The master fancies a word with you."

At my side, Poppy gasped.

"Mr. Morningside wants to greet his newest employee."

Chapter
Eight

o I was to go beyond the green door. And so soon.

I felt Poppy's eyes on me as I left the kitchens. The thought of meeting my employer—someone the girl had warned against—had made the scone in my mouth all but ash. Authority figures and I never quite got on, for obvious reasons. I chafed at their superiority and they likewise chafed at my insubordinate attitude. But adults never actually had it figured out, did they? My mother certainly hadn't. And it could not be said of my grandparents that wisdom came with age; they had grown wizened but not wise.

The teachers at Pitney? I suppose they were adults in the sense that they were grown versions of us, former students who gorged themselves on power and self-righteousness, taking out their frustrations on the younger girls who could do nothing but shrink and obey.

Still, even if I had no intention of respecting Mr. Morningside, I didn't like the uncertainty that surrounded him. Poppy had made his company sound cold, even frightening . . .

She's just a little girl.

"Are you deaf?" Mrs. Haylam followed me out into the foyer and hurried me along, swatting at my backside with her apron. "He wants to see you. Now, girl, not later."

"It won't be so bad!" Poppy called from the kitchen. I could hear her cleaning up the tea, and most likely sneaking bits of ham to her hound.

"Don't be ridiculous," the housekeeper said. She bustled me to the green door, and, with company and in the warm light of day, I didn't hear the odd song coming from it that I'd heard before. "It's just a formality. I expect you to be quick, yes? We have so many guests this week, I can't imagine how we're supposed to manage them all with this skeleton crew."

Mrs. Haylam skirted around me and opened the door, ushering me through with now familiar impatience. What felt like a warm, tropical breath rushed out to meet me.

"Off you go, and show the master more respect than you show me, child."

With that warning, I nodded and began down a set of stairs. I had expected an office right on the other side of the door, but instead I found a kind of cellar passage leading underground. It ought to be cold, I thought, taken aback by how overly warm the corridor felt. The green door shut behind me, and either I hadn't noticed them burning before, or a series of candelabras lining the walls leapt to life. Yellow flames danced on either side of me, illuminating the gradual descent that turned, spiraling, leading me down into a kind of tall antechamber.

I paused at the bottom of the stairs, appreciating the paintings hung in the grand, vaulted chamber. The walls were plaster painted the color of mint, and when I put my hand on the plaster it felt warm to the touch, like it was somehow lit from within. Alive. The paintings were a series of portraits, all of solitary men, all in different stages of life and different locations. Here was a boy, perhaps of ten, posing proudly with a hunting rifle and a dead pheasant. And here was a middle-aged man with a heavy black beard, his boot propped on the railing of a sailing schooner. And there an elderly gentleman in repose in his library.

Down on this subterranean level, I could hear no hint of the goings-on above. It was as if the boardinghouse had ceased to exist.

There was no mistaking it—I was stalling. A familiar sense of panic welled in my throat. Mrs. Canning, the headmistress at Pitney School, had called me before her too many times to count. My fingernails were never clean enough; my gait was too arrogant or too sly. My spelling was too improbably correct. I was always cheating or dawdling, sleeping too late or waking too early, being too helpful or not accommodating enough. She singled me out as her adversary, her project, and from my first day at Pitney she and the teachers had colluded to make my life unstable. I never knew what, precisely, was expected of me. The rules constantly shifted, and therefore I never performed at an adequate level.

My friend Jenny always said they were just jealous because I already knew some French and Latin, and because I took to lessons readily and with a quick mind. But Jenny was always charitable that way. The far more likely explanation was that they simply hated me.

Jenny didn't believe in such things. Every bad reaction, every act of malice, needed to be justified. But I knew better—some people were simply mean-spirited. The world could be evil and unfair, and the sooner one accepted this idea, the sooner one could get on with the business of surviving. Surviving this time, I thought with a sigh, meant playing the part of a good little scullery maid.

No doubt I would face the same random cruelty from this Mr. Morningside. I tried to resolve my posture and face into the correct combination of obedient and simple. It was always best to be underestimated, and who wouldn't want a docile, dull, but determined employee?

The vaulted antechamber narrowed toward a hall and another green door. As I neared this door, flattening down my apron, I heard nothing on the other side but the scratching of a quill pen.

I breathed deeply, stilled, and knocked twice on the door.

Go in, be pleasant, leave, return to work. You can accomplish this, Louisa. You can just be normal. You can disappear.

"Come in."

It was not the voice I expected—not old and gruff but mellow. Perhaps a bit nasal, but not at all mean. I opened the door, finding a round room that reminded me of some kind of cistern.

Though I saw no leaks, the place felt warm and wet. Perhaps the spring on the grounds was responsible for the clamminess. I was at once struck by the number of standing birdcages filling the large office. They decorated the place in a semicircle around a long, tall desk. The cages stood at varying heights, each filled with a different bird. Some were simple English things I had seen myself in the country; others wore riotous colors, great crested plumes spilling over their heads. Strangely, it didn't stink at all of animal, and stranger still, each and every bird was utterly silent, as if . . . commanded. Controlled.

Some noticed me; others groomed themselves, or slept with pointed heads under their wings. The master himself, Mr. Morningside, had noticed me, too. He stood tall and straight behind his desk, his pen down and at rest on a stack of papers. His right hand was tucked into his coat. It reminded me of something Jenny had said at Pitney, that her French aunt had shown her an illustration of Napoléon Bonaparte in the *Times* and bragged about how handsome and regal he was, standing there with his fingers hidden in the flap of his jacket. A flashy gold pin studded his cravat. And he was young. Disarmingly young. Older than myself or Lee, certainly, but not very.

"Tea, of course," he said. His voice was deeper now that I heard it without the barrier of the door. There was already a lovely pot and set of cups prepared on his desk. As I approached, I saw the fine painting work on the porcelain was scenery of birds in flight.

He certainly has a theme.

He moved nimbly, smoothly, pouring out the fragrant tea with balletic grace. His coat was one of the most expensive I had ever seen, the lapels decorated with tiny vines and leaves. Hair as black as mine had been brushed back from his forehead, the ends curling under his ears. He wore it longer than was strictly in fashion, but the style suited him. His face was long, lean, with a prominent chin and equally prominent nose. Small golden eyes flashed up from the teacups, and I marveled at the thickness of his lashes, as lustrous as little raven feathers.

The silence felt suddenly heavy and awkward. I cast about for something to say, but it didn't seem appropriate to bombard him with questions, despite my desire to do so.

"I trust you've eaten," he said again with that low, calm voice. He was not at all in a hurry, though he moved efficiently enough, sliding the saucer across the desk toward me and indicating that I should drink. Unlike Chijioke's, I could not at all place his accent. It sounded neither low class nor high, but bang in the middle.

"Yes, sir, Mrs. Haylam saw to that." This tea was better than the stuff upstairs, richer, with a luxurious hint of bergamot. "I would like to thank you for offering me a place here."

"Yes, yes." He waved away my thanks impatiently. Then, placing his palms flat on the desk, he fixed me with a direct stare. "Do you fancy birds, Louisa Ditton?"

I sputtered a little over my tea. "Birds, sir?"

"It might be a *bit* of a fixation," he said with a wry grin. "You *have* noticed the birds?"

"There's no need to insult me," I replied. God, impertinent already. I needed to learn when to clamp down on that. "Rather . . . I've seen the birds, sir. Gra—Mrs. Haylam and I delivered some just yesterday. Did they arrive safely?"

He nodded, ignoring his own cup of fresh tea. A single black curl fell over his forehead, swaying roguishly as he continued. "The green-breasted pitta from Africa survived, which was my only real concern. Golden feathers, a black mask like a highwayman. Magnificent creature. Much like you, I imagine."

Me?

"You must be mistaken," I said. No, my only ambition here was to work and go unnoticed. I simply needed to toil and save up some pay, then leave when I knew where it was I wanted to go. Ireland. America. Anywhere. *Disappear.* "I swear I've never been a highwayman."

His smile deepened. "No? I seem to collect criminals and strays. Which you should know is not an insult."

I flinched. "I was at Pitney School outside of Leeds before this, and I left because of how cruelly we were treated. Forgive me, I don't mean to be so petulant, but I'm not accustomed to kindness."

"A rare glimpse of honesty." He nodded, and his eyes flashed with interest. "However you managed to keep yourself alive before you landed here is of no concern to me."

"Even if I were hunted? What if the authorities wanted me?"

"*Do* they?" Greater interest. He leaned his weight onto his palms, easing toward me.

"No," I said simply. "I'm no one."

"Now, there you are wrong. Mrs. Haylam has long filled these halls with . . . *personalities*. She knows how to see through to what people truly are, and so she must have seen something intriguing in you, Louisa. When I took ownership of Coldthistle House, I gave her but one directive: 'Hire and fire at your will, Mrs. Haylam, but never for a single instant bore me.'"

He had a way of starting a phrase sternly and ending it in amusement. And where that Rawleigh Brimble boy showed himself to be an open book, I could sense Mr. Morningside holding something close to the vest. He might have been smiling in my direction, but his gaze remained veiled.

"How *did* you come to be master of this place?"

One severely arched eyebrow lifted in surprise. Already I was doing a poor job of being forgettable and invisible.

"That was the wrong thing to ask," I said. "Only, you seem quite young."

"And thus unequal to the task?" Mr. Morningside watched me intently, and I knew then that he was attempting to read me as surely as I was trying to do the same to him. It made me curl inward, afraid; it was never comfortable to meet someone of similar or greater intellect. He made some kind of internal calculation, biting down slightly on his lower lip, and then cut me off before I could sputter out an apology. "Before you ask, and I know you will: I am not offended. Suffice it to say, the family that once owned this great house died quite suddenly and tragically. The place lay empty, and I had the means to acquire it. Mrs. Haylam does the real work, and she leaves me be with my books and my birds."

I cast an eye around the office again, noticing now the recessed bookshelves overflowing with leather-bound manuscripts. The stack of papers on his desk was impressively tall.

"You're a writer."

This amused or pleased him, and he gave a shrug, tucking his hand back into the flap of his coat. When he leaned away from me, the air in the room felt less close. "I dabble. Not a writer, really, more of a hobbyist. A naturalist. A historian. The little domestic details of running a boardinghouse never interested me. And perhaps that's a shame. As the saying goes, idle hands are the devil's playthings."

"They are indeed. I believe they are also the privilege and provenance of the rich," I said.

Disappear, Louisa. Stop speaking and making a nuisance of yourself.

"My mother always said some such, but no doubt she spoke from a place of envy," I quickly amended.

But the young man—my employer—with the wild black hair and golden eyes immediately saw through the sloppy correction. I braced for censure or even for a firing. Even if he preferred "personalities" working at Coldthistle House, perhaps mine had proven overbold.

Instead of chiding me, he shook his head, slowly, and smiled. "I like you, Louisa Ditton. A feeling in my bones tells me we will get along just fine."

Chapter
Nine

"**W**hat did you say to him?"

Damn it all. And here the day had been going so well, too.

Mrs. Haylam was bearing down upon me, finding me kneeling next to the stove, where I was busy scouring the floor and tidying up after she had cooked the evening meals. My ears had been boxed in the past more times than I could count, but receiving as much on my first day would be new.

I stood before she could reach me and bowed my head. "I'm sorry, Mrs. Haylam. I thought . . . He did not seem at all cross with me when I left his chambers."

"*Indeed.*"

There was a world of painful promise in that one whispered word.

My shoulders hunched instinctively, anticipating the blow. But it never came. She stared down at me, and her gray, neat bun had come undone a little, wisps of silver hair floating about her face. "He says you are to serve evening tea to the guests who request it," she said. The words themselves did not match her furious tone. "Serving tea. You. Already. Unheard of."

She had been reduced to single words.

"Perhaps I made an impression," I murmured, quickly adjusting my gaze to the floor.

"You obviously made an impression, girl." Mrs. Haylam let out a long breath that fluttered the cap on my head. Even without looking, I felt the intensity of her gaze sharpen. "And he made an impression on you, too, I warrant. I wonder just what that was."

I shifted. She wasn't moving. It was a question, then. Curiously, honesty had gotten me further with both her and Mr. Morningside, so I tossed aside my previous plan and spoke my mind. It would make my mother and teachers recoil if they knew I was purposely giving cheek to my betters.

"He was younger than I expected. And . . . clever."

This gave her pause. Mrs. Haylam relaxed slightly, settling her hands on her narrow hips. "I see. Young and clever." Again she paused, as if digesting what ought to be self-evident information. Did she think him anything else? "Young and clever," she repeated. "And, what, handsome?"

Without my wanting it to, my head snapped back, and I met her eye. Was this a trick? A trap? It had to be one or both. "Some would call him that, I'm sure."

"But not you."

"Did I say that?"

"Less cheek, girl, more information," Mrs. Haylam snapped, and again I looked down at my feet. "Young, clever, and handsome. Well. You're clever, too. I know you won't get any strange ideas in your head. He is the master. Young and handsome he may seem, little Louisa, but Henry Ingram Morningside is dangerous indeed. More dangerous than you know. Now pick up that tray and serve tea and do not let me hear you were slow about it."

The second floor of the manor was still as the grave as I carried the heavy silver tea tray to the parlor. Each level had its own small area for entertaining and light dining, though the grandest dining room was on the first floor toward the south side of the house.

Those ghastly painted birds stared down at me as I went, the sheer number of framed paintings on the walls making the corridor feel airless and narrow. I had thought the day a good one—a long rest, a decent meal, and what I assumed was a positive first meeting with my employer had all led into hard but honest work. Scrubbing floors. Washing pots. Slicing potatoes and boiling them. Learning where they kept the laundry and where the soaking vats were.

Idle hands are the devil's playthings.

My hands would not be long idle here, but I welcomed the endless chores and duties. So far, as long as I did as instructed and with few mistakes, I was left to my own thoughts. Those thoughts wandered from the curious Mr. Morningside and his menagerie of birds to Lee Brimble, to Poppy and her hound, and finally to the greatest questions of all: How long would I remain here, and what, if anything, could I do with myself afterward?

Mrs. Haylam had said nothing of payment so far, though Chijioke mentioned having a few coins saved up. These first days might be a trial, just to prove that I could manage the work and take direction.

The Pitney teachers would choke on their biscuits with laughter if they could see me now, my prospects plummeting from governess to mere maid. *How predictable!* they would crow. *All that pride and arrogance and Louisa Ditton made nothing of herself in the end!*

No, I could not stay at Coldthistle House forever. Fortune waited on the edge of some horizon, and I would chase it. I thought again of the gold coin that had gotten me chased out of the Malton market, and that thought led me to consider the value of the silver tray in my hands. I began calculating the cost of the fine china set and the paintings on the walls, the Turkish rugs, the gilt cages for keeping birds. . . . There was wealth in this place and few people to look after it. I could pocket small treasures and sell them elsewhere, and see if that suited me better than bowing and scraping to guests.

It was a thought, anyway, and one I felt coalescing into a plan. Mr. Morningside could hardly notice a few tiny objects going missing, and the risk seemed worth it if the stolen goods bought me passage to America. To a new life.

But until then—tea.

Mrs. Haylam called the third-floor parlor the Red Room, and it lived up to the name. The door had been left slightly ajar, and the light spilling into the hallway was tinted scarlet. The wallpaper, a leaf motif of red and darker red, had faded with time but lost little of its luster. More paintings crowded the walls, but even those were also predominantly finished in different shades of crimson. My eye caught on an ornately engraved writing set in the corner. Those quill pens looked like real silver.

Lee and his uncle sat on a low sofa, the window dressings behind gathered and folded like immense theater curtains. His uncle was having an animated conversation with a woman dressed all in black. I hadn't seen her in the house before, but she looked comfortable enough on a fraying chair. A huge emerald sparkled on her finger, the only hint of color on her otherwise sober mourning costume. Her ebony hair, shot through with gray, had been tied in an elegant chignon at her nape.

"I really must protest, Mrs. Eames," George Bremerton was saying. Red-faced, perched on the edge of the sofa, he bristled like a porcupine. The long cut of his sideburns emphasized his mastiff-like chin. "A woman of your means traveling without a chaperone? Preposterous. I insist you remain until we can accompany you at least as far as Ripon."

The tea tray rattled as I struggled to ease inside the door, close it behind me, and then hurry to the table. Lee noticed the tremor in my arms and leapt to his feet, at once helping me maneuver the tray safely to the table. He flashed me a smile and then just as quickly returned to his seat. George Bremerton and this Mrs. Eames ignored my presence entirely.

"I manage passably well on my own," the woman said. "A widow must. The waters of the spring here soothe my nerves and lessen the burden of grief. You ought to give them a try, you know; this is the best kept secret in all of England. Why deal with the *marmaglia* in Bath when you can enjoy the little spa here?"

She had a beautiful voice, a singer's voice, melodious and accented. Italian, maybe, or French. From this angle I could better see her face, and that, too, was beautiful. She sat primly, her hands folded in her lap, her chin tilted back; it felt like I was watching a portrait sitting. I tore my gaze away from her and back to Lee, who subtly flicked his eyes toward his uncle and then rolled them.

Ah. So George Bremerton had noticed her distinct loveliness, too.

"I'm sure the waters are just fine, but that is beside the point. A widow must accept assistance when necessary," George replied. "What of your sons? Could they not join you?"

"My sons are indisposed at the moment. They know their *mamma* is more than capable of handling herself. And now it is my turn to protest, Mr. Bremerton. This interrogation has rather exhausted me." At last she noticed me bending over the table, pouring the tea and setting the service. "You will of course be a gentleman and let me take tea in peace."

Peace appeared to be the last thing on George Bremerton's

mind. He had begun to sweat, and tugged at the ends of his sleeves. "Mrs. Eames, for heaven's sake, please—"

Mrs. Eames silenced him with one hand, like an orchestra conductor finishing a song with a flourish. "You must not vex yourself, *mio caro*. It is not good for a man's heart, something I know all too well. Visit the spa as soon as you are able; it will have a calming effect."

"My condolences again, of course," he said. "To lose a husband so suddenly. Simply awful."

Mio caro. Italian then. I watched her dab at the perfectly dry corner of her eye. She sipped her tea and ate precisely one corner of a biscuit, all the while avoiding George Bremerton's gaze. "Loss can be very oppressive," she said finally. It had taken her a full moment to come up with a reason to escape his leering. "And this room, too! A lady must breathe. It is time I took some air; a turn about the grounds is just the thing, then of course a drink of the waters."

Mrs. Eames stood, towering over me, and stared down her nose at me before turning with a flounce and gliding toward the door. Her plan did not go off quite perfectly, and George Bremerton was on his feet and following, giving his nephew a hasty nod good-bye before trotting to catch up with the widow.

"Please allow me to escort you, madam. The gardens are riddled with field mouse tunnels. I all but snapped my ankle in one yesterday. I will guide you safely on your walk."

Her reply, positive or otherwise, was lost to the muting effect of the hall.

"Thank God that's over." Lee blew out a breath and sprang up from the sofa. "Uncle is such a dreadful flirt sometimes. He's going to drive that woman mad with his badgering. It's like he's forgotten all about why we came here."

The three of them had barely touched the tea, and I quashed an urge to nibble on what they'd left behind. Such waste. Mrs. Haylam would not approve, naturally, and so instead I knelt again and gathered the used cups and saucers onto the tray. At once I felt tension rise between me and the young man—there he stood, idle, while I scrambled to do my job. I took hold of the service to clear it completely, but Lee put up a hand.

"Don't go just yet."

"I have a long list of chores," I replied, chewing the inside of my cheek with agitation. *Perhaps you have nothing to do, fancy boy, but some of us must sing for our supper.* He would be a nuisance if I had a mind to steal something here and there; I didn't need him watching my every move. "My position here is so new, I wouldn't want to give the impression that I'm lazy."

"Just a moment or two?" he insisted. "I'll take the blame if you get in trouble."

"Well? Here I am." I took a step back from the tray. The silver writing set winked at me from the corner. "Should you not be off on your grand adventure? I thought you were here to uncover the mystery of your parentage."

Lee turned a dark shade of red, matching the room itself, and wandered to a bookcase in the far corner. He picked up a glass jar containing a few bird bones posed among moss and pretended to study it. "I would be, but Uncle George has fallen into distraction. Can I be totally honest with you, Louisa?"

"Yes." As if I could stop him.

"You must indulge me. I *did* rescue your spoon!"

My sarcasm wilted in the face of so much exuberance. "Mm. I all but owe you my life."

"Precisely! Ha!" His cheeks had faded to a pink color, his smile inconveniently charming. "You see, the plain truth of it is, I'm unbelievably, unbearably bored."

"Bored?" I had to laugh at that as I joined him near the bookcase. Shifting aside the heavy draperies at the nearby window, I watched George Bremerton deliver the Italian widow to the garden, both of them stumbling over the holey ground. "You've not been here two days . . ."

"Yes! Yes, I know, but I have nothing to do here. I could not possibly care less about the stupid spa and its smelly waters. This was all Uncle's idea, and there are precious few books of interest in the library, and no other guests of my age." He hung his head, snorting softly. "Ah, perhaps I'm no better than he is—chasing you around, desperate for diversion."

Lee had a point. Before evening tea, Mrs. Haylam gave me a quick list of the guests currently staying at Coldthistle. Besides Lee and his uncle, there was Mrs. Eames; a physician from

London called Dr. Rory Merriman; and a retired military man recently returned from India. Hardly stimulating company for a young man of Lee's age. Now his uncle and Mrs. Eames arrived more or less unscathed to the gardens and I shut the curtain on them. "Can you not conduct this investigation on your own? Surely your uncle brought some kind of evidence of his hunch. You could find this supposed paramour of your guardian's. . . . Even if you fail, it won't be boring."

Lee's face exploded with excitement, and he went so far as to reach for my hand and squeeze it before spinning and striding toward the hallway. "I *knew* you would have the answer, Louisa! I'll just have a look through my uncle's papers and see what's what, and then we can begin unraveling the mystery together."

At first I thought I had misheard him. What could I possibly offer, and how in heaven's name would I find the time? I took a few halting steps back toward the tray that still needed clearing. He was already out the door and too far to hear my one whispered word.

"*We?*" I turned and repeated myself, this time louder.

"Well, who else would help me?"

Our disagreement—well, really, my protests and Lee's stubborn refusal to entertain them—spilled out into the hall. We both immediately lowered our voices, as if shushed by all the birds staring down at us.

The tea tray had not gotten any lighter thanks to Mrs. Eames's restrained nibbling, and I stopped at the landing and the stairs leading down. Lee breezed right by the stairs, on a steady course for his room and his uncle's belongings.

"There's simply too much I need to do." Which was true. "I'm confident you can accomplish this all on your own!" Which was a lie. "Beyond that, it's not . . . *appropriate* for me to assist you in that capacity. It would look dangerously like friendship."

"Oh, *to hell* with appropriate! Yes, I said it!"

"Mr. Brimble—"

"No, you must never call me that," he said, stumbling toward me. He blushed furiously again, to the tips of his ears. "All right, that was rude and please forgive me, but I find the expectations of society so confusing. Why shouldn't we be friends?"

"Every life has rules. Why on earth do you think I'm here? I left one set of rules I could not abide in exchange for ones I could. Is that not the very essence of existence?"

I couldn't imagine why this young man wanted so badly to like me, or why my liking him was of any importance whatsoever. It sounded like he had a family of sorts, even if it was complicated. He had his uncle, and that driver, and probably a whole host of loved ones back on his estate.

Whom did I have?

My little speech cowed or embarrassed him, and he nodded, curling his fingers into fists. "You're so right."

Somehow being right didn't feel nice at all. "I'm just a servant here," I said in a weak voice. "Good day, Mr. Brimble."

He turned and strode away before I could even make a polite

curtsy. Mrs. Haylam would have me thrown out of the manor if she knew I was speaking to guests this way. My only hope was that Lee took my words to heart and rededicated his attention to his uncle and his inheritance.

I hefted the tea tray into a higher position and turned to descend the stairs. A girl had been watching us from the lower landing—a girl my age. A girl I had seen many, many times before, but not for years, and only ever in my imagination.

The tray fell to the floor with a deafening clatter.

Chapter
Ten

On the Shadowmancers of Babylon and the Elusive Da'mbaeru

The shadowmancers of Babylon developed a technique for capturing and controlling unusually dangerous spirits. Employing an aetherial force that can interact with the physical world would make a man almost incomprehensibly powerful. Shades once considered uncontainable could be persuaded to work in service to masters they deemed worthy. Arduous trials of strength and intellect were posed by the shades, trials only a handful of shadowmancers ever managed to complete. One such shadow-mancer, called Aralu, is said to have dashed their infant son's head against a wall and cut out their own tongue to satisfy such a shade. Still, the possibility exists that these unruly shades, dubbed Da'mbaeru[1] *by the scholars of Babylon, remain harness-able through ritual and examination.*

Rare Myths and Legends: The Collected Findings of
H. I. Morningside, *page 66*

---

1. I must assume this is a portmanteau recognized only by specific sorcerers of Baby-lon. This combination of the words *darkness* and *hunter* appear nowhere else in known Akkadian documents. The name *Da'mbaeru* occurs a mere dozen times in the Black Elbion and, according to my research, nowhere else.

I only ever had one true friend in my entire life. Her name was Maggie, and a girl who looked exactly like her was gazing up at me now with wide, curious green eyes.

Then she scrambled to help me pick up the fallen tea service. Luckily the teapot itself had dropped straight down, only splashing a little onto the carpets but otherwise landing right-side up. The girl proved she was no hallucination and not my imaginary friend at all, snatching up a wayward sugar spoon and two saucers.

"Oh, heavens!" She had a sweet, high voice (unlike me) and

an Irish lilt (like me). Just like I remembered. "These carpets are so slippery as to be treacherous. I've fallen a good bit myself."

She paused, spoon and saucers clutched to her apron, and beamed. "I'm Mary. I heard you might be needing help with the service, so Mrs. Haylam sent me along."

Mary. But Maggie was the name of my friend. Imaginary friend. Yet there was no mistaking the likeness—the same wild bunches of brown hair tied up with a ribbon, the same mass of freckles over her nose so thick it looked like she had a smear of red paint across her face.

I had to stop staring.

"I'm sorry," I muttered, stooping to help pick up the mess and gather it all back onto the tray. "You just . . . You look like a girl I once knew."

"Is that so?" She laughed and handed me the rogue spoon.

"It's . . . just a very striking resemblance," I said, still dumbstruck. "I don't mean to be rude."

"Never mind that; I only hope you have fond memories of her."

We had recovered the tea service, and she helped me lift it all back up; then she joined me as I walked carefully down the stairs. "I do, actually. She was dear to me. A good friend."

"In Ireland?"

Of course she would hear the remnants of the old country in my voice. I nodded, taking the stairs gradually, sneaking looks at this uncanny creature who could be a living sculpture of a girl

I knew did not exist. But I could feel the warmth of her when her sleeve brushed me; this was a real person. "I had to leave her behind when I sailed for England. That was a hard day. How did you come to be here?"

"My mam did a bit of tailoring and sewing for the master, and he liked her work so well he brought us here from London. It was a good thing, too. She was a proud woman and hated charging pennies for her work. She taught me the needle, and I took her place when she passed last year."

"What a shame that she's gone," I said, feeling unnervingly as if I was once again confiding in my imaginary friend. It felt easy to talk to her, maybe because of how much they looked alike, or maybe because her sorrows were familiar. "I'm sorry."

"She liked it here, I think, and died happy enough. The master promised to look after me when she was gone, and so far he's kept his word."

"I met him briefly." We lingered outside the kitchen door. I could tell she didn't want to go in, either, knowing we'd find ourselves faced with new chores that would separate us. How could I feel an affinity for someone so quickly? I felt spiteful now for having chided Lee about trying to force friendships. But this was different, wasn't it? Mary was like me, abandoned and alone, far from home. . . .

Or *this* was her home, and the odd Mr. Morningside had become a kind of family. She seemed comfortable. She belonged. Something ached in the back of my throat. Belonging somewhere would be nice. I didn't know if that place was here, but if so, it would make life simpler.

"He's ever so kind," Mary said with a forlorn smile. "And I owe him so much. He pulled us out of the worst part of Shoreditch. It's not the kind of debt you can ever repay, I think."

"Nonsense. Every debt can be repaid. You earn your keep, don't you? He must understand the difficult position your mother left you in."

Mary shrugged and opened the door to the kitchens for me. Her green eyes were suddenly cold. Far off. "No," she replied simply. "For, you see, I owe him my very life."

"Is that so?" I asked, craning my head back in surprise. "I had no idea he was so heroic."

A little warmth returned to her gaze as she shook her head. "'Tis not too gallant a story, only he made certain I had a place to go and a purpose to bend my thought toward. I couldn't survive without a place to belong or a kind of family to call my own."

And here my new purpose was to steal from the house for my own gain. It almost made me feel ashamed. My old imaginary friend Maggie would understand, I knew. Could this girl Mary do the same?

It was a great comfort to retire in my little room at the end of the day. Others might have thought it lonely, but I knew the refuge to be found in the company of only one's own mind.

An hour or so after supper, Mrs. Haylam had relieved me of my duties and dismissed me. After scurrying under the watchful eyes of the birds hung in the halls, I'd washed up and changed into a simple nightgown, then gratefully fallen into bed. Exhausted though I was from a full day's work, I had trouble falling asleep. The evening meal had been relaxed, pleasant even. All of us had sat down at the large kitchen table—Mrs. Haylam, Chijioke, Poppy, Mary, and myself, with the hound Bartholomew waiting impatiently under our feet for scraps.

I'd barely spoken, but the conversation had been animated. Chijioke had caught a hare for Mrs. Haylam to cook, and he'd recounted its harrowing capture for all of us, to applause and laughter. Apparently the creature had startled Bartholomew and Chijioke so badly, darting out from under his workbench, that both man and hound had fallen over on their rumps in surprise.

Even Mrs. Haylam had cracked a smile.

And by the end of the meal I'd found myself wishing Mr. Morningside had joined us. I wanted to know more of this unusual young man who pulled seamstresses out of slums and kept hundreds of birds for fun and owned a boardinghouse that he apparently never saw the topside of. It was both sad and easy to imagine him taking all of his meals alone in that office of his. Did he ever keep company? Did he occasionally leave for town?

Now the more I considered him, the stranger he became. In all my reading and experience, I'd learned that the masters of anything tended to live aboveground; not only aboveground but above their servants. Above everything. The rich and the landed were of higher stuff. Loftier. Closer to God.

Surely he must keep quarters of his own somewhere on the higher floors. After all, even the most eccentric of men needed a place to sleep.

I sat up in bed, thinking then that I had done little wandering on the fourth story. Mrs. Haylam had not yet sent me there for any reason, and it occurred to me that it was probably because the master of the house kept his rooms there. And suddenly I had a mind to see for myself. I had stirred myself up with questions, and now I was painfully awake.

It would just be a quick look, I assured myself, a peek around a corner or two to verify that everything in Coldthistle House was operating as expected. There would be some huge, intimidating door with a valet waiting outside. I would feign ignorance of the layout of the house, and then be shooed off back to my own chambers. Curiosity satisfied, sleep would come easier.

And if I got lucky, there would be no valet and no one about. There would be rooms filled with pocket-size trinkets for me to snatch and hide under my bed until the collection grew big enough to fund an escape.

The rich could afford to amass possessions they had no time or reason to count, and then there was me, with everything I owned totaling less than my fingers and toes.

The hall outside the door was so cold, quiet, and dark I could hear a faint ringing in my ears. The corridor stretched out as a pure black tunnel before me, and I retreated to my room to gather the stub of a reading candle I had left burning. Shielding the flame with a palm, I tiptoed out into the hall, shrinking under the watchful avian eyes. Even from the second floor I could feel the tug of the green door down in the foyer. At once, it began singing to me again.

The language of the song filled my head with unquiet thoughts, and my hands trembled, threatening the flame. What strange tongue was this in my mind? Guttural and sharp, both sinister and alluring. . . . It took concerted effort to focus my attention away from the door downstairs and instead travel lightly to the end of the hall and the stairs leading up. Underneath the song I heard quiet footfalls, just a gentle pitter-patter that sounded like it came from over my head, perhaps on the floor above. Was Poppy's hound loose and wandering, too?

No, it was not the light tread of a pup but something heavier. Dragging. Still, I pressed on up the stairs, gazing behind and ahead, confirming that nobody followed. The third floor was silent, and I peered down into it to see what might be making those footsteps. I saw nothing but more shadow. More darkness. Good. These were the perfect conditions for a bit of light thievery.

The air grew colder as I ascended the next set of stairs. My nightdress did little to ward off the chill. Up and up, higher and colder, and colder, until I became convinced there was no way anyone at all would choose to live in such frozen conditions. And I was right—as I rounded the corner on the topmost level of the house, I found nothing.

Nothing.

It was neither attic nor corridor, but what looked like one immense ballroom. There was no furniture, and there was nothing on the walls. The windows looking out onto the grounds were covered in a dusty film, and the moonlight penetrating that grime made the room glow an unearthly blue.

The flame on my candle dipped. The wick would soon run out. I hurried deeper into the cavernous room, casting my eye about, desperate to find some clue as to what this place might have been or might still be. The dragging footsteps came again—distant, but there—and there was no telling whether they were below, above, or in front of me.

Then I noted a small lump on the floor. It sat lonely and apart, the area around it free of dust. At a distance, I thought it might be a jewelry box of some kind. The thought piqued my interest. Again that unnerving song rose in my head, and I knew it was now guiding me toward this object. I grew closer, closer, and felt suddenly ill. It was like seasickness, but it arrived abruptly enough to steal my breath away. My vision blurred and my thoughts threaded into one another, tangled. Yet I could not stop my feet.

My candle sputtered out, but I saw a little with the moonlight. It was not a lump on the floor or a jewelry box but a book—a huge black book. A simple drawing of a red eye with a cross through it glowed faintly on the cover. Certainly I could not trust my eyes, for it seemed to release an aura, thin wisps of purple rising from the cover like a dusky steam. I knelt and gently touched the cover. It was not warm to the touch but hot. *Scalding.*

I pulled back with a yelp, shaking out my burned hand. And I stood, ready to flee, the book's hold over me breaking a little after the shock of the burn. But before I could turn and run, a huge hand closed over my wrist. It felt like nothing, yet it crushed down on me hard enough to make my bones creak.

A black hand, not human; too slender for that, too strong, *and not quite corporeal.*

I had been discovered, and by no creature of flesh and blood.

Chapter
Eleven

asping, I reared back, trying to fling off my attacker, but that only brought me face-to-face with the thing. A thing. My mind reeled. I had no words for this, no experience to match what I now saw bearing down on me. A creature of shadow, eight feet tall at least, and I could not tell where its body ended and the swirling black mist began. Yet certainly it touched me! There was no mistaking that, or the pain shooting up my arm.

Its bulbous, round head neared me and suddenly split in the middle to reveal a too-wide set of teeth. Fangs. Every tooth was longer and sharper than the last.

"Not for yoooooou," it growled, and it spoke with a cold scrape of a voice pulled from the lowest pits of Hell.

And it was not alone. The room, I saw now, was filled with these things.

I screamed horribly, calling out for help, twisting myself this way and that until at last the demon creature released me. If only I could wake someone and rouse help. . . . *This is what you get for trying to steal.* My heart leapt with each bounding step I took, pushing my way through the crowd of shadowy things that seemed only to smirk down at me as I ran. The stairs! I had to reach the stairs! When I did, I took them two and then three at a time, holding on to the banister so as not to fly and break my neck.

They were behind me. Scraping. Dragging. *Pursuing.*

My fingers throbbed where the book had burned them and my wrist ached where the shadow creature had crushed it, but terror drove me on. I had no idea where to go. . . . Were these things all over the house? How could they be real? How could a nightmare not only touch me but *bruise*?

Panicked, gulping for breath, I fled to the lower halls, to pound on doors until someone answered. But I ran too recklessly, and on the last few stairs before the second-floor landing I lost my footing, tumbling to the bottom and hitting the carpets with a thud. Sprawled out, candle lost, I tried to climb to my feet, wincing from the pain in my wrist.

I did not need to turn and look to know the creatures were advancing. I could hear and sense them coming, their heavy, scraping footsteps growing nearer. Fear picked me up, put me on my feet, and I sprinted for my open door at the end of the hall. When I was inside, I spun and slammed the door, locking it, holding my weight against it as a brace.

Not that it would matter. Those things were huge and uncannily strong. They would make short work of the door, I thought, if they even obeyed such obstructions. Perhaps they would simply walk right through and snatch me up, rip me limb from limb . . .

My face was wet with tears as I pressed it to the wood.

Nothing could be the same again, not after what I had just seen. By the moonlight filtering into the room I inspected my wrist. There were no marks. When I turned my hand, however, there were two angry red burns exactly where I had touched the book.

Footsteps. They were light and soft, but that was assuredly some deception. I held my breath, shaking as a tiny knock came at the door.

"Louisa? Louisa, are you quite all right? Bartholomew and I heard a commotion."

Poppy. I could barely make out her mouselike voice through the thick door.

"Open up, please. There's no reason to hide."

I slid down the door and squinted through the keyhole. It was just a girl there, waiting, in her prim, frilled nightgown.

Had it been a nightmare after all? Why else would those shadow creatures not attack the girl? Carefully, gradually, I eased open the door. The hall behind Poppy was empty. She had retrieved my candle and lit it, the dancing flame illuminating her marked face and a sympathetic smile. Her eyes traveled from my tearstained face to my burned hand.

"Were you wandering? You mustn't wander. Mrs. Haylam should have told you it isn't good to leave your room at night."

There was no use lying, not after she had noticed my hand. Did she know about the odd room with the scalding-hot book? Did she sense my true intentions? "I went to the top floor.

There w-was a book and these . . . I . . . saw something startling and I ran. I stumbled on the steps."

That was all I could manage to whisper.

Poppy nodded sagely, as if this all made perfect sense and was not in any way alarming. What on earth had I gotten myself into? Summoned by my screaming, Mrs. Haylam drifted down the hall toward us, her gray hair in a long braid. It made her look more like the crone I had met at Malton.

She stopped behind Poppy, sighing as she inspected me.

"Louisa saw the book and met the Residents. They gave her a shock and she tumbled down the steps."

It was so cold in the hall, and all I wanted to do was turn around and crawl into bed, yank the blankets over my head, and pretend this night was and continued to be nothing but a bad dream. But Mrs. Haylam pursed her lips and motioned for me to follow.

"I see. Very well. She will need to speak with Mr. Morningside, then. It appears it's time to explain."

Chapter
Twelve

"How can you be so cavalier about this? There was a giant creature crushing my wrist! It spoke. It's completely unnatural!"

Mrs. Haylam put up her hand, demanding silence. "Lower your voice, girl. Or have you not learned your lesson this night?"

The threat of seeing those awful things again was more than enough to shut me up. And so I followed, numbed and stunned, afraid that she could somehow control those beasts of shadow and use them against me. But she'd spoken quietly and was now completely silent as she led me down toward the green door. Perhaps she feared rousing those things, too.

I could tell by her quick pace and cold shoulder that she had lost her patience with me. And perhaps that was understandable—getting caught wandering the manor at night when I had been employed not even a week? A reasonable housekeeper might assume I was wandering the house for nefarious purposes, planning to steal from guests. Especially if that housekeeper had heard the maid called a thief in Malton just days ago. But I was not stupid enough to let her know that such assumptions were completely right.

"You will have many questions for him, I imagine, but try not to speak too much and simply listen," she said, visibly irritated. She opened the green door for me and waited, examining me with cold slits for eyes. "Listen," she repeated. "Listen carefully to him, and make your choices even more carefully."

I wiped impotently at the tear tracks on my cheeks. I required no mirror to know I looked a frightful mess.

"My choices?" I replied. So she *did* suspect me. If they didn't turn me out that night, I would have to be more careful going forward.

Mrs. Haylam nodded exactly once. "I hope to see you again, Louisa Ditton. I think I am growing a little fond of you."

Mr. Morningside stood behind his desk with his back to me, a fanciful bird with a blue head and red bill perched on his wrist.

My own wrist still throbbed. Hot blood pulsed behind the burns on my fingertips, and standing there, watching him coo at an exotic animal, was utter misery. If there was punishment to come, then I wanted to confront it now and be done with it. And if I was lucky, he might let me return to my room and sleep out the night before kicking me out in the morning. I shivered; the thought of sleeping even one more night in a house where those shadows prowled chilled me to my marrow.

At least his study was warm, and fragrant with the tang of sunflower seeds and the earthiness of feathers.

"Parrots are remarkable things," he said at last. The riotously colored bird on his hand shifted, pecking at his sleeve. Mr. Morningside was fully dressed, and at this hour, I assumed it was only because he'd been forced to have a word with me. "So beautiful. Look at this one's plumage. Indigo and scarlet, yellow and green as bright as summer grass. But such beauty can be deceptive."

Mr. Morningside turned and faced me, though he did not take his attention away from the parrot.

"Did you know, Miss Louisa, that parrots will eat other animals? Oh yes; they do not simply gorge on fruits and seeds all day. They will eat meat, too, and I've heard tales of some that attacked full-grown sheep. All that loveliness, and it conceals savagery." Finally he looked at me, and his golden eyes were unexpectedly gentle. Kind, even.

I did not like it.

"I was attacked in your house this evening," I said. My voice trembled, the fright of the ordeal still coursing through me like lightning. Mrs. Haylam had demanded that I listen, but I could stay quiet no longer. "What manner of creature are you keeping here? Obviously not only the birds."

Smirking, he stroked one finger over the parrot's breast. "I understand you've encountered the Residents. I admit, they can be an unsettling sight for the uninitiated."

I stammered. I fumbled. My wrist ached and ached and I glanced down at it, fancying I could still feel the iron grip of that monstrous shadow. "I understand all of those words separately, but not in the way you arranged them."

"Do try to keep up, Miss Louisa."

That tore at me, and so did his breezy tone. "I have been burned and chased and terrified, and now to face this conde-scension—"

"Calm yourself," he said. He took the parrot to a wooden stand and urged it to leave his hand, then he returned to the desk and poured tea for both of us from a waiting service. "Sit."

I had little desire to stay, but there were too many unan-swered questions for my liking. I wanted to know what I had seen. The creatures, the book, even the singing door . . . The tea did help, though. It usually did. I sipped slowly, wincing when my burned fingers grazed the china.

Mr. Morningside noticed, lowering his own cup and saucer and frowning at my injured hand. "You found the book."

"Yes."

"And you felt compelled to touch it?"

"It . . . I know it sounds ludicrous, but I had no control over myself. So, yes, I supposed I was compelled."

He nodded through this response and opened one of the drawers on his desk, taking out a small glass pot of a snowy-white cream that looked like ointment. When he opened the lid on it, the scent of astringent cut through the air. "Your hand, please. It will do nothing for the marks, but it will at least ease your discomfort."

I hesitated, and he saw it, closing his eyes for a prolonged blink, as if taking a moment to choose his words carefully. It was clear my hesitation had offended him. He looked *wounded*. Probably no young lady had ever balked at giving him her hand.

"Please."

Stubbornly, I waited a little longer and then thrust my arm across the desk toward him. I watched as he gently grasped my right wrist and dabbed a bit of the ointment on the livid, burning marks. Warmth blossomed at the point of contact, and I commanded my cheeks not to blush. This person lorded over a veritable circus of dark curiosities, and it did not matter that he had glossy black hair and golden eyes; I would not give him the luxury of my blushes. It helped to remember that I wanted to steal from him. He was an unsuspecting target to me and nothing more.

The pain in my fingers was already gone.

"Now then," he said, breaking the spell. He closed up the ointment jar and shoved it back in the drawer. Then he tented his fingers and studied me intently, as if I were one of his newly acquired birds. "Did you see anything in the book?"

I shook my head, cradling my tended hand in my lap and using the other to sip tea. "It scalded me. I closed it at once. What's inside of it?"

"More on that later, perhaps."

"But—"

"What is your impression of our darling Italian countess, Mrs. Eames?"

Mrs. Eames? How on earth was she relevant?

"I . . . beg your pardon?"

He took my confusion in stride, smiling benevolently. "Just trust me, please, for I am steering us toward the answer you seek, yes? What did you make of Mrs. Eames?"

The woman had not crossed my thoughts in some time. After all, having a run-in with a living shadow and an accursed book rendered all other thoughts unimportant. But I scraped up my one memory of her, of serving tea and watching her nibble a biscuit and do her best social acrobatics to escape George Bremerton.

"She's a widow," I said shakily. "And she's extraordinarily beautiful. She's here for the spa. George Bremerton fell all over himself to escort her to the gardens. I think she mentioned sons."

"All true." He resumed drinking his tea, leaning back comfortably in his chair. "Did you know, the female of the praying mantis species will often decapitate her counterpart just before or after mating?"

Now I really did blush. Never had a young man discussed anything so vulgar as mating rituals in my presence. But there had to be some purpose to the story; he did not strike me as the type to jettison all propriety at a moment's notice.

Mrs. Eames. Right.

"Are you suggesting Mrs. Eames ate her dead husband?"

Mr. Morningside snorted over his tea. "Actually, no, but she *did* decapitate him. I believe she called it an agricultural incident on their vineyard. Funny how scythes can just"—he slashed the flat of his hand across his throat—"fall from the sky."

I recoiled, nearly sloshing my tea everywhere. "That is a severe accusation. How do you know this?"

"Not all of my employees work on the premises, Miss Louisa. Maids, valets, urchins, even the occasional priest . . ."

He was being condescending again, and it made me feel very young, and made him by comparison seem so very old. But how many years could he have on me?

"One of her sons died, too," Mr. Morningside said lightly. "His boat destined for Italy sank . . ." He paused and consulted a small, leather-bound diary on the desk. ". . . two days ago."

"Good God," I murmured. "You don't think she's responsible for that, too? An entire boat?"

"When there's a fortune at stake, the greedy are capable of anything." He finished his tea and cocked his head to the side. "The world would be well rid of these vermin, don't you agree?"

I did, but it felt like I was stepping stupidly into a trap. "I suppose."

"And so I've instructed Poppy to do away with the *lovely* Mrs. Eames on the morrow."

Murder. Brazen, remorseless slaughter. *Of a woman who killed her husband and child and stood to profit from it.* Hadn't I hated rich, haughty women like Mrs. Eames? Hadn't I watched with disdain as ladies like her came to collect governesses from Pitney? Appraising us like farm animals. Choosing a human being like one would choose a pair of earrings or shoes? Why should I care that someone like her might be killed?

But it mattered that it was Poppy doing the deed. She was just a girl like me. A child. Could she really be a killer?

"Poppy . . . But she's so . . . so . . ."

"Sweet?" Mr. Morningside nodded toward the brilliantly plumed parrot.

All that loveliness, and it conceals savagery.

"Are you always this quick to murder your guests? That's monstrous!" I stood, ready to hurl myself out the door, out of the house, and into the cold. I couldn't stand to be there another minute.

Mr. Morningside stood, too, but it didn't quite seem like a threat. "Monstrous? Killing two innocent people is monstrous. I'm merely practical. Yes, I lured her. She may claim she came on her own terms to visit the spring, but that's only half true. You said the book compelled you to touch it. No doubt you felt drawn to it, and no logic or reason or burst of foresight would keep you from doing so, correct?"

I nodded, trying frantically to piece it all together. This was madness. I didn't belong here. It was time to leave.

"Ah. Well. That is how rats like Mrs. Eames feel, Louisa, only toward this place. They are drawn here. Compelled." He leaned toward me and placed his palms on the desk, his smile crooked and cocksure. "They do not know why they come, but they do, and once they step through the doors, their fate is sealed. They come here because they are evil. Irredeemable. They come here to die."

Chapter Thirteen

"Let me out of here. I want to leave. *At once.*" Panic rose hot and strangling in my throat. I backed toward the door, wrist throbbing to the erratic beat of my heart.

"I'm afraid that's not possible," Mr. Morningside said with a sigh. He did not advance on me. "You cannot leave."

So this encounter was not meant to mete out punishment, but to be a death sentence. I had to get out. If there was one skill I had developed in all my years, it was self-preservation at all costs.

I made my eyes wide and innocent, and pleaded with my hands in prayer position. "I'll tell nobody of what you're doing here. I just want to leave—"

"You misunderstand. It is not possible." To his credit, he looked genuinely upset. "You touched the book, Louisa."

That made me freeze in place. The book? What did that have to do with anything? How could a damned book stop me from leaving? Did it command coaches? Horses? The very road itself?

"Just slow down and let me explain."

"No! You're a murderer."

"A murderer of murderers; the farmer who kills the lamed animal; the laborer who throws the match on the refuse heap. What's the difference?" he said matter-of-factly. "Still, I cannot argue with you there."

I took another big step toward the door and turned, preparing to bolt. "Nor do I wish to argue. I want only to leave this place and forget all about it."

This time I did not wait for his response. The door to his study was already open and I shoved through it, feeling his eyes upon me, knowing it was just a matter of seconds until he caught up and restrained me. But he moved not, and I was at the bottom of the stairs, on the brink of freeing myself, when he spoke once more.

His voice boomed in my ears. "*You should already be dead.*"

My hand clutched the railing of the stairs, and I twisted, listening, staring back at him, afraid but unwilling to let him see it. There was nothing to say. I should be dead? Were those shadow monsters meant to kill me?

"That is why I know you belong here and why you cannot leave. The Residents—those shadows—they are there to watch over the house, but they are also meant to protect the book. You should never have gotten near it, and you certainly should not have touched it, but having done so, that single touch should have struck you dead."

"N-nonsense," I stammered. This was more madness. More bizarre lying. "It's just a silly book. How could a book do that?"

"That *silly* book can persuade a murderous widow to come to it from hundreds and hundreds of miles away." He at last advanced toward me, moving slowly around the desk, his golden eyes no longer friendly but focused and fiery, trained on me not with malice but with total concentration. There was no escaping such a gaze, no matter how dearly I wanted to flee. "That silly book calls to all corners of this world and tempts killers and criminals of all kinds, persuading them to ignore little things like distance and inconvenience, and they come. They come to it because they cannot help themselves. All that power, and you think it would be difficult for the book to take a simple human life?"

"Let me go," I whispered. Now I was frozen in earnest, sinew and bone rigid, my hand tented over the railing but unmoving. Some force held me prisoner, suppressing even a tremble. But there had to be a way out, some trick to releasing me if I was indeed caught in some invisible spider's web. "Please, just let me go."

"It's the middle of the night," Mr. Morningside pointed out. "It isn't safe."

I could control my limbs enough to flinch as he cleared the desk, passed the chair . . .

"It isn't safe here, either," I whispered.

"Now, that's not true. *You're* safe here." At that I made a sound like a sob and a laugh. The absurdity of such a statement, when he had just confessed to arranging murder, to using strange occult things to bind people to a house of death . . . "You *are* safe," he reassured me. "You weren't lured here, Louisa; Mrs. Haylam brought you. You aren't evil, but you are one of us."

Inside I was shaking my head, shaking every part of me trying to break this infernal spell as he approached. "No," I said. "I'm nothing like you."

There was something wrong with him or something wrong with my eyes; as he walked nearer, he seemed to have an unnerving gait, unnatural to humans, and one I could not have noticed while he stood still behind his desk. I looked from his eyes to his legs and felt the world spin—his feet were like any man's but they were backward, heels pointed to the front, toes to his spine.

"No." The word tumbled out again. The warmth of the room, the threat of this *thing* coming close while I could do nothing . . . My vision whirled sickeningly. "What—what are you? I'm not like you. I'm not . . ."

The world was going suddenly black, and the last things I felt were his arms catching me and his breath on my forehead.

"You are, Louisa. You will see."

On the Wailing Bairns of Ben Griam Mor

To say that I hold the honorable Zachary Moorhouser in esteem is an understatement; however, our opinions on the nature of the so-called screaming subclasses notably diverge. His work on the dervishes of Far East nations is to be lauded, but in his seminal Demonologica, *he fails to even mention, much less adequately* describe, the smallish, almost pixie-like creatures found on or about Ben Griam Mor.

It should surprise no one that the mist-shrouded summit of that beloved Scottish hill is home to fairy descendants. However, it should come as a surprise that these folk have escaped the attention of nearly all modern mythological scholars. In my humble opinion, no study of the occult, magicked, or demonic would be complete without mentioning the Wailing Bairns of Ben Griam Mor. While in pursuit of these rarefied folk, I lodged primarily at Garvault. There, after several days of useless inquiry, I stumbled upon a seriously inebriated fellow in the local tavern.

He was, as the barman helpfully told me, deeper in his cups than usual. When I approached the man, he was eager to regale me with his story, after, naturally, I supplied him with a fresh ale. In a frenzy, he told me of a macabre event he'd witnessed not far from the very mountain I searched. While gathering mushrooms in a small wooded area, he stumbled upon a cottage. As he had been out hunting fungus for some hours, his rations were depleted, and he decided to ask the cottage owners for sustenance before starting back to Garvault. He could see quite clearly into the house, as it was well lit, and he saw a large family sitting down to supper, which only made him more hopeful that he might make his return journey on a full stomach.

His hopes were quickly dashed, however, when he watched as an argument broke out at the table. The parents were attempting to quiet their child, an odd, gangled youth who seemed to the *drunkard unnaturally pale. The child then stood on the table, stamping her feet, and threw back her head, unleashing a piercing scream. He said he heard it so clearly and painfully through the shut windows that he was knocked off his feet. When he stood and gained his senses, he saw a most horrible image: the family, all but the screaming child, were dead, their heads gone completely, erupted into gore, as if their skulls had been lanced like boils.*

The girl saw him watching through the window and bolted, coming, he realized in a panic, for him. He fled.

With a spotting of these creatures at last confirmed, I eagerly took out my notebook to scribble down his story. When I asked for greater detail of the child, he began to waver. Perhaps she was not so young, but closer to ten and five. No! Ten and seven! Older! A young woman, practically an adult, he said. In his drunkenness he made these corrections clumsily, and I quickly surmised he was embarrassed that he, a grown man, had been fearful of a little girl.

I have concluded that most sightings of the Bairns are likely altered in a similar fashion, the tellers hesitant to express fear of a child. It is likely the Bairns are thus often confused with the more common banshee and harpy, and not given their proper place in the magickal order.

Rare Myths and Legends: The Collected Findings of
H. I. Morningside, *page 6*

ow did I sleep, filled as I then was with dread and suspicion?

But I did sleep, and deeply, waking to the natural light of dawn filtering through a crack in the draperies. The tick dipped to one side, and I gasped to find I was not alone. The girl, Poppy, and her hound sat watching over me as I slept.

At once I pulled the blankets to my face, recoiling.

"Don't touch me," I murmured. She seemed not at all surprised by my revulsion.

"Too many shocks, that's what Mr. Morningside said. It always happens this way, you know, when a new person joins us. Even Chijioke fainted when he saw a Resident for the first time," the girl replied with a giggle. Her hound snuffled in agreement. He gently lowered his tawny snout to my arm, laying it there as if to comfort me. Bartholomew, at least, looked normal enough, but now I knew not to trust a single thing in this house.

His feet. His feet were on backward.

"Am I dreaming?" I asked, more to the world itself than to her. "Is this a nightmare?"

"He said you would say that."

Under the blankets I pinched myself. No, definitely awake. I groaned.

"I want to leave," I said, glad that I could move my arms and legs again. "At once. You mustn't try to stop me."

"He said you would say that, too." Poppy grinned, pushing the silky hair away from her face. I had never been superstitious, never spurned a person when birth cursed them with a wine stain on their face. But were those not called the Devil's mark? How fitting that name seemed now. "Nobody will stop you from trying, but you can't go. The book says so, and that means it's final. Done and dusted, as the master says."

Not if I have anything to say about it.

Poppy ruffled the dog's ears, and he glanced up at her with his fathomless chocolate eyes before turning them back to me. I had to admit, his warm little head on my arm was soothing. It was then that I noted someone had set my wrist and bound it. The pain was distant now, just an echo. All of it—the fear, the urgency—was distant. But only for now. There was too much to think about, and I would need to be alone for a long while to digest it all.

And Lee. God, I hadn't even thought of him. Were he and his uncle here because they deserved death? It didn't seem possible.

The girl was not in a hurry to leave, humming softly to herself while she made figure-eight patterns on the blanket with her pinkie finger. This small, soft, pale child might in fact be a killer. I pulled the blanket more snugly around myself.

"Are you really going to hurt Mrs. Eames?" I asked, a tad sheepish.

Poppy's bright eyes flashed toward me. "Oh no," she said with a tittering laugh, "I'm not just going to hurt her, I'm going to kill her."

"How? How could you do such a thing?"

She shrugged, patting the dog's head. "The same way I do all the others."

"And what way is that?" Did I truly want to know? My curiosity had cost me so much already, but the urge to know more yet remained.

"With my voice!" she chirped. She grinned and opened her mouth very wide. There was nothing out of the ordinary about her mouth, just a young girl's teeth and tongue. "I can scream louder than anyone I know, so loud it really, really hurts when you hear it."

"Won't that hurt the rest of us, then?"

"No, not a bit; Mary will protect you," she said simply. "She's quite good at protecting people."

Mary. Just the evening before I had shared a pleasant supper with these people, liking them, thinking them my peers. Even potential friends. My brain now pounded with the confusion of it all—there had been signs, of course, that the house was a touch odd, but this was something else entirely.

And I would be escaping it as soon as possible.

"I would like to sleep more now, Poppy," I said with a thin smile. In truth, I needed time alone to think and plan. After all, it was just a book, wasn't it? Whatever grand speeches Mr.

Morningside made about it, it was a book, and books could be moved, or lost.

Or *burned*.

Those living shadows wandering the halls would make it more difficult to steal covertly, but they also made me want to steal all the more. This was a horrible place, and I would feel no guilt taking from it what I wanted—ensuring my freedom. America, so far away, with an ocean between here and there, was just what I needed.

"Right you are!" she crowed, hopping down from the bed and scooping up Bartholomew. "Come along, little pup, Miss Louisa has had a bad night, but we're all going to help her, aren't we? We all get on so well together here. Soon she'll be our best and truest friend."

Chapter
Fourteen

When I emerged from my chambers an hour later, I half expected to be met by one of those foul shadow creatures. Residents, Mr. Morningside had called them. Residents indeed.

The hall outside my door was empty, but that hardly made me feel safer. I felt watched now, marked, a bright red poppy in a field of white daisies. Every choice available to me became equally urgent. If I was going to be stuck here, then the least I could do was warn Lee before he became stuck, too, or worse, killed. The pain in my wrist was all but gone, the sturdy splint around it expertly applied. I wondered at who had fixed me up, and I wondered at the fact that murderers could treat me, a relative stranger, with such tenderness.

It didn't matter, in the end. Only a fool would linger in Coldthistle House once they'd learned its secrets. And I was no fool. I decided to tackle the problems in order of simplicity: food would be easiest, and so I made my way slowly to the foyer and then the kitchen, watchful for any signs of the Residents.

Nobody bothered me. I heard the muffled chatting from morning tea coming from the downstairs parlor, and I heard Lee's laughter as he found some anecdote or another uproariously funny. I didn't necessarily like his uncle, but I struggled to imagine what Lee Brimble might have done to be drawn to the book and this place. He seemed so kind, so well meaning . . . But then again, so had my fellow employees, and perhaps he too possessed some dark secret.

I had a few of my own, of course—truancy, magic tricks, and stealing, for example—but those vices now struck me as tame, even silly.

The stoves were still warm from baking, but the kitchen was otherwise quiet and abandoned. Where had everyone gone? Were they deliberately hiding? I hurried to the pantry and swiped a piece of brown bread and a few slivers of dried apple. When I escaped Pitney, I had done so on an even emptier stomach. Life there had made me no stranger to hunger. Our punishments often involved going for days with only crusts and water.

I bolted down the bread and took more time with the apple slices, pocketing one or two for a later emergency. For now, Lee would have to wait—I had no earthly idea how to tell him about all that I knew. We were only just acquaintants, and there was no reason at all for him to trust me or the outrageous stories I might tell. Instead, I took the back exit out of the kitchen and into the brisk cool of morning. My clothes were just heavy enough to ward off the chill, and if I made an escape in earnest I would need to bring the blankets from my bedding for extra warmth. I had escaped Pitney with help from my sort-of friend Jenny, who caused a distraction while I slipped out a window and into the night. Unless I could convince Lee that my stories were truth and not madness, I would be escaping completely on my own.

This venture out would serve only to survey. If, by some stroke of luck, Lee's driver was about and going to town on a stagecoach when the post approached, I would seize the opportunity. First, I needed to test the word of Mr. Morningside.

The grass outside was thin, scraggly. Trees grew on the perimeter of the grounds, and there only tentatively. The house itself was the only thing allowed to be tall and imposing. The barn stood off to my left, the gardens farther beyond that, and more behind the manor. I walked straight out from the door, feeling completely exposed. There was no bush or tree to hide behind, and anyone enterprising enough to glance out a window would see me striding out toward the fence at the far edge of the property.

I call it a fence, but in truth it was merely a few withered planks that seemed to be held aloft by sheer coincidence. The thought made my heart clench. If Mr. Morningside and his merry band of murderers really worried about escapees, they might bother to build a proper fence, tall enough to keep people in and trespassers out. Instead, it looked like a stiff wind might topple the whole structure, and anyone in moderate physical health could scale the beams and hop right over.

Six crows sat on the fence, regarding me, then scattering and reconvening on the roof of the house behind me.

A greater barrier than the fence was the unbelievable number of holes dotting the ground. They were bigger than any field animal might make, everywhere and of varying depth. One, obscured by a clump of grass, nearly made me fall flat on my face. I picked my way across the field, wary now of all the pits. What on earth had torn up the ground so? It was almost as if someone had shoveled down a foot or two, searching frantically for something. . . .

At last I reached the fence, noticing that as I neared it the scars on my fingertips began to ache. Initially I thought little of it, chalking it up to a sort of phantom pain, but the discomfort persisted and intensified. It was like hearing a voice in a faraway room, and then hearing the person who spoke move closer and closer, their voice amplifying. The pain amplified that way, and with it, a voice.

It was just a whisper at first, in that same unknown language I'd heard when I'd passed the green door and found the book. This time, however, I knew it was not the fence calling to me; nor was it the door or even the book.

This voice, this whisper, came from *inside* me.

The pain and the voice reached their peak as I laid my hand upon the bleached timbers of the fence. I clenched my teeth through it, determined to endure. If this was all that kept me from freedom, I would be stronger. But strength meant nothing when I pushed my hand out a little farther, beyond the fence, and felt a heat like lightning scream from my fingertips to the base of my skull. It brought me crashing to my knees with a scream, the voice echoing in my head almost more painful than the raw flames searing up my arm.

A pair of strong hands closed around my shoulders and helped lift me back to my feet.

"Easy now." It was Chijioke, steadying me until I had the ability to stand on my own. I wrenched out of his grip, taking a huge step away from the fence. The pain in my head and body dulled at once. "Ach, come now," he added, frowning. "I've no designs on ye. I won't hurt you, only you looked in distress."

"I was," I whispered. "I am."

After lurching away from the fence, I had stuck my foot in one of the hundreds of holes in the yard. Muttering, I shifted onto more solid ground. Chijioke leaned against the fence, apparently unaffected by it the way I had been. He rested a large shovel against the barrier and ran his hand over his face. Despite the cold, he perspired, the front of his white shirt damp with sweat. He otherwise wore simple workman's attire: black braces and sturdy breeches tucked into mud-flecked boots.

"Poppy's mutt is a damned menace. I try to fill in the holes as best I can, but the little blighter digs six for each one I patch."

"Perhaps you should be digging a grave instead," I said darkly. "Won't there soon be a body to bury?"

His expression hardly changed, but I saw a tension in his jaw that hadn't been there before. "So you've heard. I thought as much. Mrs. Haylam mentioned you suffered quite the fright last night. You're taking it surprisingly well. First time I met a

Resident, I ran out of the house screaming like a banshee."

Taking it well? I didn't think I was. "So why do you stay?"

It was an earnest question. Chijioke had been nothing but kind toward me, and with his sweet, friendly eyes staring back at me, it was nigh impossible to imagine him participating in the crimes of Coldthistle. I felt edgy and crazed, as if I had wandered out of reality and through some veil, stepping into another world altogether, one where up was down and bad was good.

"It just fits for some," he replied with a shrug of his huge shoulders. "I've no big speech for ye. I came and didn't want to leave. I didn't think the guests here could be as bad as Mr. Morningside said; then I met a few and had my mind changed right quick. All I know is, life isn't fair for some of us, and he makes it fairer, mm?"

I shook my head, turning to look out across the fields beyond the fence. White blobs moved on the horizon, coming closer. Sheep. If there were sheep, then a shepherd couldn't be far behind. Even so, who would believe my story? What country shepherd would hear the madness spilling out of my mouth and move a finger to help?

"I think it would be better if I left," I said softly. *After I lift a few choice shiny objects to sell.* "If that's even possible."

Chijioke studied me, then turned and faced the fields. He dangled his forearms over the wooden beam and rested one foot on a lower slat. "Do you know your Bible?"

I snorted. "I'm Irish."

Laughing, he said, "Then you know Leviticus. 'And he that killeth any man shall surely be put to death.' It's that 'surely' in there that's the rub. How many men really get what they deserve in this life? Particularly the nasty ones. . . ."

"And what about Romans?" I asked. "'Recompense to no man evil for evil. Provide things honest in the sight of all men.'"

He sighed, glancing down at the grass and then up at the clouds. "I should know better than to talk the Bible with an Irish girl," he said. "But I'll give you one more, also Romans: Leave room for the wrath of God, aye? Vengeance is mine, I will repay and all that?"

It was close enough. I nodded, convinced he had simply made my own point for me.

"I will repay," he repeated in a whisper, squinting toward the blob of sheep. "But when, I ask you? *When?*"

"I suppose that's not for us to know. It's not your job to do God's work for him, is it?" I replied slowly. We were both quiet for a moment, the wind picking up, making the grass of the fields shiver and sway, as if an immense hand had dragged fingers over a piece of green velvet. The sheep ambled closer, but they and their shepherd remained a long way off. Was it futile to wait for help?

"One of the girls at Pitney liked to steal my breakfast. She was older, bigger, had these giant teeth like a horse's. When I told on her, she waited until nobody was looking and slammed my head into a desk. I plotted for months to get back at her, and then I managed to pour ink in her tea one morning. Catherine's teeth were black for a fortnight."

Chijioke laughed heartily, slamming his hand down on the fence. It wobbled, looking about ready to splinter. "You see? How can doing the right thing be evil?"

"There has to be a better way," I replied. "I only put ink in her tea."

"Aye, and she only stole your breakfast now and then." He paused, taking the shovel handle and running his thumb thoughtfully along the grain. "You should stay. If only for a wee while, just to see if you don't change your mind."

I heard soft footsteps rushing across the grass and glanced over my shoulder, watching Mary scurry across the pitted lawn toward us. She dodged the holes with tiny, endearing hops and a flail of the arms.

How can they all seem so normal?

"What if you get things wrong?" I asked, making a note to come back here sometime and check again for the shepherd. In fact, my window faced this side of the fence. I might be able to dash out if I was ever idle on that side of the house.

"No, the master is never wrong," Chijioke replied solemnly. "Never."

I thought of Lee, of his hand grazing mine as he rescued my fallen spoon. "We shall see."

Mary reached us in a swirl of clean skirts that smelled of fresh bread. Her hands and wrists were dusted with flour, a smudge of it on her nose and cheek, too. "There you are! Chi, shame on you for tarrying with her here. There's but five of us to see to this great beast of a house!" She took a deep breath, leaning back and putting her hands on her waist. Chijioke slinked away, sheepish, giving me a helpless shrug and a grin as he went.

"Mrs. Haylam wants you in the library," she said. "It needs dusting. I was going to do it but it's one of the easier tasks, and I thought you mightn't be ready for anything more daunting."

She was having trouble meeting my eye, and it was no secret why.

"I don't know if I want to dust the library," I said. My fingers and head still crackled occasionally with the pain of having pushed beyond the borders of the property. "I'm really not keen to stay here."

Mary nodded, wiping her floury hands on her apron. "Was fretting, worried you might say as much. Do as you will, then, Louisa. I'm just the messenger. But if you're going to stay, you'll have to work like the rest of us." She clapped a hand over her mouth and hurried to add, "Not the . . . *that* kind of work, oh, bugger it!"

The curse sounded ridiculous coming from her. She seemed the type to blush after even *thinking* such a word. The wind changed directions, coming now from behind me, from where the sheep grazed out farther in the pasture. I smelled the sweet grass and the scent of bread from her aprons and drank deeply of the air. I knew now that the master was not lying. He or that infernal book did have some power over me.

I needed more time. And the library might have a few rare books. Books that would see me out of this place and on a boat to America.

"I'll see to the library," I said, holding back a sigh. "Lead on."

Chapter
Fifteen

t was less a library and more snowdrifts of books and dust heaped against sagging shelves, cramped and labyrinthine. I had to wonder at Lee's inability to find anything worth reading when I had never in my life seen so many books piled in one place.

On a better day, the room might have enjoyed clean, pure sunlight through its third-floor windows, but a troubling layer of grime darkened the place.

I stood dumbfounded and overwhelmed in the doorway, while Mary fidgeted like a guilty thief behind me. I felt that if anyone should be twitching, it ought to be me.

"The easier task," I murmured.

"I . . . may have forgotten the state of things in here," she said. "I can stay to help if you like, but only until Mrs. Haylam needs me again."

"No, that's all right." The time alone would be welcome. Crucial. There were no shadow creatures in here to notice whether anything went missing. "It's straightforward enough, I think."

"Don't put yourself out tidying the books. Mr. Morningside just keeps chucking them in here despite Mrs. Haylam's protests. Once, she sent a few of the dog-eared copies to a school for charity and Mr. Morningside was furious with her. He *raised* his *voice*. It was terrible stuff, just awful."

"He raised his voice?" I said. She looked horrified all over again by the memory. "One shudders to imagine it."

"But you must not judge him because of that. It really was not her place to dispose of his property that way." Mary began wringing her hands, puffing out her cheeks as she surveyed the messy room ahead of me. "I *can* stay. . . ."

I ignored the offer. "Does Mr. Morningside often leave the cellar?"

Her eyes flamed wide. "Oh. Oh no, no, that's very rare indeed. I haven't seen it with my own eyes, in fact. He says the air up here bothers him. The pollen, or some such."

"I see." I didn't, of course, but it was just another little puzzle piece to file away. I would need information and luck to get away from Coldthistle permanently. "Well, I had best get started. Idle hands, and all that."

God, now I was quoting *him*. But Mary was soothed, and she averted her green eyes just for a second, then glanced at me again from under her lashes. "If you do fancy help, please come and fetch me. It . . . You must be in such a state! So confused, I mean. Only . . . don't think too harshly on me, on us, before you know all, please."

I looked away from her, feeling ill. The way she spoke, her mannerisms, it was exactly like my imaginary friend, and it was too affecting. "I haven't decided what I'm going to do."

"You should stay," Mary said quietly, backing away. "I want

you to, but only if *you* want to. What I mean is, I'm hoping real hard that you stay."

She was gone, flitting down the corridor, leaving me in the dense silence of the dust and gloom. Eerie shafts of light pierced the dirty windows in places, those rare spears of silver and yellow mottled with dust motes. I almost had to laugh at the idea that I could clean all of this with just a feather duster and a washcloth. Within moments of wiping the cloth across the floor and rinsing it out in the bucket, the water turned murky brown. I pressed on, trying to scrub and dust without ruining the splint on my wrist.

The library room was situated in the east wing of the house, positioned in the turretlike corner of the building. It was subsequently round and fairly large, and some mischievous carpenter had fashioned the bookcases so that they spiraled toward the back of the room, almost like spokes on a wheel. This created a series of private reading nooks, each furnished with a divan upholstered in heavy brocade. In its cleaner, better days, the library had probably been a lovely place, a peaceful retreat, but now, with books piled and spilling and going to ruin, it felt more like a refuse heap.

And it proved impossible to tidy around all these piles of encyclopedias, novels, and histories. I made short stacks at the end of each bookcase, then cleaned what I found underneath. It was time to see what hidden treasures Coldthistle House had to offer. If I could find a way to get beyond the barrier made by the book, then I would need a few valuable items for trading. Most of the books I recognized from the library at Pitney. They were common enough collections of poetry, history, and popular stories. At last I came across a compact book of Cowper's poetry. It was in good condition despite the general neglect of the library, and when I peered inside the cover I found a faded signature on the title page.

This would fetch a pretty penny. My luck had changed for the better, at least a little; the collection was small enough to hide easily under the waist of my skirts and the apron that covered them.

The floors and shelves grew neater as a result of my meticulous searching, and after also pocketing a naturalist's field guide apparently owned and signed by Lord Byron, I moved on to the windows, scrubbing so vigorously at the hardened grime that my teeth clacked. Of course the meager staff here could not keep up the amount of work necessary to maintain a house like this, but I was beginning to suspect that this was by design. It was no doubt easier to keep the dark secret of the place with just a handful of servants. I leaned down and dipped the rag into the water, then squeezed it out. In this position I could see a handful of books scattered under a shelf, and I reached for them, greedily hoping for another good find. Sighing and then freezing, I knew as my fingers closed around the nearest book that I was being watched by a shape in the corner.

Oh Lord. The shadows had returned for me.

"Hello again!"

"Jesus, Mary, and all the hallowed saints," I swore. The rag flew out of my hand and missed the bucket, and I leaned back against the wall, clasping a hand to my chest with relief. It was only Lee. The books lay lost and forgotten where I had seen them.

Lee. Lee, who had to be tainted by some awful past or predilection or else he would not be at Coldthistle. Lee, who might still escape the clutches of the house and deliver me safely, too, or else send someone back to collect me.

My first instinct, obnoxiously, was to embrace him. Considering I had not so long ago rejected his offer of friendship, embracing was even more impossible. He was middling rich and I didn't have a single penny to my name, and we could very well be dead in days or even minutes. Those shadow beasts might be watching us. Observing. Catching us in the act of conspiracy.

I straightened, wiping my soiled hands on my apron and gesturing for him to come forward. Urge to embrace quashed, I found my voice but kept it low. There was no telling who listened in. Were there peepholes everywhere in the house? Did those shadows have ears? Did they need them?

"Just the person I wanted to see."

"Oh!" He brightened an already bright smile and sauntered into the library. "I do like the sound of that. I began to worry when we didn't see you at tea this morning, so I thought I might seek you out. Uncle was being a real bore and I was plum certain that Italian woman was going to knock him senseless with her—wait a moment, your wrist. What the devil happened to it? Are you quite all right?"

He rushed toward me, curls bobbing, all worry and care as he made to reach for my wrist, then thought better of it, his hands poised in the air awkwardly like a puppeteer's.

"Just an accident," I lied smoothly. "A slip. It doesn't even hurt anymore."

"I never knew scullery work was so treacherous."

I guffawed. That, like my clumsy fall down the stairs, was an accident. Generally I was not the guffawing type, and Lee noticed at once the violent way the sound ripped out of my throat.

"Coughing"—and this lie was far more artless than the last—"there's so much dust in here. It should be a crime to treat books in such a manner."

And a crime to murder, a crime to have backward feet, to employ shadow monsters, to hoard dark, magical books . . .

"No," Lee said softly, pursing his lips. "Something really is the matter. Forgive my saying so, Louisa, but you look . . . Rather, I am a gentleman, and being a gentleman I do not think I can properly express—"

"I look horrid," I finished for him. "I am aware of it."

"Actually I was going to say 'peaked,' but all right." That only tightened his expression. He moved to lean against the library wall next to me, crossing his arms and ducking his head slightly. "Well, I am here, you know, if you would like to discuss it."

"My looking horrid?"

"Louisa . . ."

I had to phrase this perfectly or risk alienating a potential ally. But the weight of what I needed to communicate was abruptly crushing. How did I tell him all that I had seen? Or even some of it? No sane person would believe me. *I* hardly believed me. And yet the fact remained that I needed him, his resources, his help, his driver, his carriage, perhaps even the sabers I had glimpsed under the passenger seats. I had not escaped Pitney without help from Jenny, and my chances of getting out of Coldthistle House would increase greatly with some assistance.

And standing there next to him, I confess I felt safer. Here at least was a neutral element. I was marked to stay, he was marked for death, but while we yet lived I would struggle against such destinies.

So. How to tell him. . . .

"I did go through my uncle's things," he said. When I did not interrupt—for I welcomed the chance to puzzle out my approach—he drew in a long breath to explain. "He had some very odd items in his luggage. An unusual number of knives, and a pistol! I always knew he was a bit anxious, but still, it seems excessive. There were normal things as well: a comb, some gloves and quills and so on. It's the damnedest thing. I truly thought he would have more information about my so-called mother, beyond just a single note—an address, I think. How astonishing to make this long journey based on so little."

"Perhaps he keeps those other papers on him," I murmured. "If they are valuable or confidential, he may not wish to keep them just anywhere."

Lee nodded, regarding me still with his head bowed. "That was what I came to tell you, which means it's now your turn."

Wonderful. My hands had grown pruney from the damp washrag, and I wiped them anxiously down the front of my apron, careful not to dislodge the pilfered books hidden there. There was no rubbing away the scars on my fingertips, and I kept the marks out of his sight, pressing my palms flat to my skirt.

"I think we are in danger," I said in a whisper. "But do not raise your voice or show any signs of alarm. If I am right, we must maintain the utmost secrecy."

"*Danger?*" His brows shot up, and he leaned in close. "Your wrist; did someone harm you deliberately?"

"No, no," I assured him, and technically it was the truth. After all, some*thing* had harmed me. "Mr. Morningside said some terrible things about Mrs. Eames—that she's only a widower because she killed her late husband. He claims that she murdered her son, too. I think he means to . . . to exact revenge. *Severe* revenge."

Lee's brows continued to rise, reaching their absolute zenith as I drew out the last two words.

"Good heavens."

"I think he fancies himself some sort of vigilante. A force for justice above the law. If he knows you've done something vile, he punishes you for it."

"How extraordinary," Lee whispered. He unfolded his arms and rubbed his chin, but he was starting to look pale. Guilty. "What do you make of such claims? Can he be believed?"

Here I was less certain, yet a pit in my gut persisted, a nasty, guilty pit. For some reason I could not get the image of her huge green ring out of my mind. Such a flourish of excess, such decadence, when she was supposed to be the grieving widow. . . . And if she was to inherit a fortune, why come to the dumpy, drafty Coldthistle House?

Why come here at all, unless, of course, she had been summoned.

"She does come across a bit . . ."

"Strange," he said in agreement. "So you think she's capable of murder? Of killing her own child?"

"I really can't say. The only thing I know for sure is that Mr. Morningside does not have kind intentions toward her," I said. My gaze snapped to the open door, where I could have sworn a dark shape lingered and then vanished. Palms sweating, I took Lee by the wrist and dragged him deeper into the library and behind a bookcase, concealing us in one of the room's dusty nooks.

"This is going to sound upsetting," I whispered. "But you

might consider taking one of your uncle's weapons and keeping it about your person. Just . . . Just in case. I think the proprietor is quite mad, you see, and I don't know if any of us are safe. We must be careful, quick, and quiet, and you must promise me not to say anything about this to your uncle yet."

"But if we are all in danger—"

"*Promise.*"

"O-Of course, Louisa, you have my word," he said. Then he broke into a nervous smile, glancing shyly to the side. "Lord, I did make you swear to tell me the secrets of this place, didn't I? This is all rather more than I bargained for."

Oh, my dear boy, you don't know the half of it.

"Precisely," I replied. I had no idea if I was protecting him or damning him by telling him only the partial truth, but I could always reveal more later if it seemed prudent. "But what's most important now is that you tell me something, Lee. You must be honest, yes? Hold nothing back. . . ."

"What?" he asked, searching my face. "What are you asking of me?"

"You must tell me," I said, still holding his wrist tightly. "Are there any unspeakable secrets from your past? Have you greatly sinned?" I demanded. "Have *you* killed?"

Chapter
Sixteen

ne of the most dangerous things of all is a secret hope. A secret hope is always buried deep within you, like a disease, one you have no idea lies in wait. It's always there, ready to wound you, and even if you have some vague conception of its existence, some instinct or inkling, it is ever surprising. The worst secret hope I can remember came from my mother. Her name was Alice. Alice Ditton. She kept my father's surname out of spite, because in the end they hated each other so much that she stole me away from him in the night.

Actually, I'm not certain the word *stole* is quite right. Can you really steal something that isn't wanted in the first place?

It is not a nice thing to admit, but I always knew, even as a child, that my mother was not a balanced person. There was too much of Ireland in her, old Ireland, the superstitious, fairy-believing wild Irish that my city-dweller father and grandparents despised. Once, after we had moved from Waterford to Dublin, a neighbor boy was bitten by a rabid dog. My mother convinced him that the only cure for it was to be touched on the hand by a seventh son.

She meant it. So, unbalanced. And I think that's being kind.

I can remember her eyes flaring wide as she loomed over poor, sick Danny Burton, saying, "Oh, and if that seventh son be born of a seventh son? Well then, boy, he'll bring you more than just good health, but good luck for the rest of your years!"

Danny Burton died that week; no telling if he ever found that seventh son.

The point being, I was always keen to the strangeness of my mother. Even if I only ever spoke of it to my imaginary friend Maggie, and only then in guilty whispers, I felt in my heart that my mother was odd. And by association and blood, I was odd, too. Folk rarely warmed to my mam. Tolerance was about the best she ever got. That curse passed to me, too. Excepting Lee and the curious servants of Coldthistle House, most people decided upon meeting me that I was not worth knowing. I swear sometimes I could see them recoil, even if unintentionally, as if there was some invisible black brand upon me that said: BEWARE.

It was the worst and cruelest joke of the world, and I was not in on it.

But my secret desire, always, even in the depths of my hard knowing, was that one day my mother would be different. She would change. The old-country parts of her would fall away, and like a tree shaking off winter's chill, she would bud and blossom and emerge a fine, sensible woman with a laugh that made you thrill instead of wince. I kept that secret hope locked away tight, so tight and so deep down that it wasn't until she was really out of my life for good that I recognized that wish.

Here, in the library, I recognized another secret wish even as it, too, became impossible, and this time I knew how the longing would hurt.

"Oh God." Lee was crumbling before my very eyes. He slid down against the window until he was huddled on the floor. Then he hid his face in his hands. I could tell from the tension in his shoulders that he was holding back a sob. "I killed my guardian. I'm one of the bad people, too. *I* did a vile thing. I *killed* him."

"*What?*"

There it was, the secret hope soaring up from the bottom of my gut to wallop me. Lee would be one of the good ones. He would be different. This time, a someone—a boy—would like me and want to be around me, and there would be no trick to it. I would finally be in on a joke. A good, wholesome human would desire my company, and it would mean that the black mark upon me had all been a lie. The whole rest of the world would be wrong, and Lee would be right.

But no, he could not remove the mark. He was ruined inside, too.

Birds of a feather . . .

"Louisa, please, I swear—you mustn't think harshly of me. It was an accident. I swear on my life, it . . ." He sighed, scrubbing his face with his hands. "He had this ghastly reaction to nuts. Any kind of nut in his food would make him ill almost to the point of death. I know I told the crofters no nuts, but I delivered this bread from them as a gift, and he ate it, and . . ."

He couldn't go on.

"Lee." Well, perhaps my secret hope could return to its undisclosed location in my heart and linger a while longer. "That is the very definition of an accident. It isn't your fault."

"But it is, don't you see? I should have checked the bread. It was so foolish of me, just reckless. Clumsy. The kindest and best man I've ever known slain by *walnuts*."

"He might have checked, too," I pointed out, sitting next to him on a stack of immense map books. "Being a fully grown man and all."

"As you say, but I feel responsible all the same," Lee murmured. His face had gone red and splotchy, but he no longer looked in danger of weeping. He looked at me, a small smile spreading across his lips. "You asked if I had killed. Other than a few does and fish and rabbits, that's the worst I've managed. I confessed, you know, to a priest. God never gave me much comfort in times of misery, but I thought maybe it would make me feel less guilty. Only it made the guilt more real somehow."

"You didn't kill him, Lee. If you could speak to him right now, you know he would say the same."

"Because he's generous and forgiving," he replied, glancing away. "Like you."

I shook my head, rejecting outright the praise. "You don't know me, Lee. I'm not good like you are. I haven't lived the kind of life that allows for being good."

"Which is why it's all the more impressive." We were both

silent for a moment, the dust drifting around us and settling gradually at our feet. "Do you really think I need a weapon? Should we try to protect Mrs. Eames, or, God, at least try to warn her?"

I was not generous or forgiving, as he theorized, and now he would learn it in earnest. "As cold as this sounds, I think perhaps we should stay out of it. If what Mr. Morningside said is true, she hardly deserves our help."

"But what if he's wrong? We can't very well stand aside while an innocent woman is hurt." He paused and bit his bottom lip. "My uncle has become close with her. They spend most of their time sipping that disgusting water at the spa. Perhaps he might find some proof for us that she is indeed a murderess."

"That's much too dangerous," I cautioned. "We have nothing to do with her, Lee. We shouldn't get mixed up in her affairs."

Fetching the rag, I swished it in the murky water and began washing the window behind Lee. It was easier to lie to him without having to see his face. "And if your uncle is with her all the time, then maybe she's already safer in a way. You said yourself that he is armed. It could be enough to protect her."

"But should I not warn him? He could become a target, too."

My hand stilled, the tepid, disgusting water in the rag gathering in my palm and then trickling down my sleeve. Warning the widow, we agreed, was out of the question, but what about warning his uncle? These were lives we were discussing, actual lives, and the weight of it felt too far outside my realm of experience. I had no affection for George Bremerton, but that did not mean I wanted him dead. Lee was watching me expectantly, I could feel it, and so I made my decision. If Lee could be here innocently, with no evil past to doom him, then so too could his uncle be a good man worth saving.

"Warn him," I said softly. "But be general about it. I feel mad just telling you these things. It sounds like so much nonsense spilling out of my mouth."

"Well, I believe you." And there it was again, his belief. It felt just as good as the first time, so much so that it made me smile. "I'll simply tell him the proprietor seems a bit strange and mentioned having it out for the widow. My uncle's natural chivalrous tendencies will do the rest, I think."

Nodding, I dropped the rag back in the bucket and watched Lee fidget his way back toward the door. There was more he wanted to say, obviously, and I sat silently through his hesitation, trying to look the picture of patience and understanding. It was a miracle he had believed a single word I'd said, and even more impressive that he confessed to accidentally poisoning his guardian. The least I could do now was listen.

He stopped at the end of the bookcase blocking us from the door. His bright turquoise eyes were sad but clear, and it took him a moment to screw up his courage and stand tall. "Only . . . Thank you. You did not need to tell me these things. I might have gone on in blissful ignorance here. Well, not that knowing all of this is blissful, but I think the alternative is rather worse, isn't it? You trusted me and you didn't have to, and after I behaved so rudely . . . This all seems very big and frightening, but I'm glad we can at least rely upon one another."

Lee managed a small, brave smile and bowed from the waist politely. "Did . . . Did any of that make sense?"

"All of it," I said. "Thank you, too, for believing me."

He chuckled and scruffed the back of his curly head and then backed away. "I should go, then, before we stand around thanking each other all day long. Good-bye for the moment, Louisa. I shall seek you out again soon, and that's a promise."

"Good-bye."

After Lee ducked out of view and his footsteps retreated to the door, I fell back against the window and sighed. I hated to be alone. I hadn't realized how comforting it was to have the company of someone "normal" like me.

I had done almost all I could about cleaning the library and searching it for treasures, so I abandoned the rag and did my best to straighten more of the toppled piles of books. Lee would be on the lookout for himself, and for his uncle, and maybe even for me, and his uncle would be warned, and it felt like maybe I had done a bit of good. For now, I could do nothing but plot the details of my escape, foremost being the destruction or disruption of that book in the attic and then the careful sale of the rare books I had found.

The corner farthest from the door remained to be cleaned, and I wiped at the dusty sweat that had sprung up on my brow from the effort of rearranging so many giant, heavy books. Kneeling, I spread out the books from one messy pile, tutting at the bad treatment of so many old bindings. This was a fortune in paper and leather treated like garbage. Most of the spines were still in good condition, however, and I picked the sturdiest book of the lot to use as the base of the pyramid. If my new luck held, perhaps there would be a book in this library that acted as some kind of antidote to the book in the attic. After all, if one book caused the problem, then another might be the solution. Now was the time to keep a weather eye out for any strange or arcane-looking tomes.

I swept up the last book from the heap, the littlest one, and was about to put it on top when the title, obscured by a thick layer of dust, caught my eye.

No, not the title, the *author.* With my sleeve, I wiped away the dirt, feeling a pang of fear and a spike of excitement war painfully in my throat. This tiny, forgotten thing, more like a journal than a proper book, had been hiding in this far corner of the library, just waiting for me to find it.

Was it fortune or something else? Something like luck but sinister. . . . And it could be, now that I knew such things as doors and men and books had the power to lure and trap. But I picked it up all the same and held it close to me, hoping against hope that it would tell me what I needed to know.

That it would be my salvation.

"*Rare Myths and Legends*," I whispered aloud. Well, that sounded both arcane *and* strange. "*The Collected Findings of H. I. Morningside.*"

Chapter
Seventeen

s soon as I stepped foot outside the library, I saw it. Watching. Waiting for me.

It moved like an ink spill suspended in the air, slithering back and forth, bobbing side to side as it observed me. The shadow creature took a step toward me, unnaturally long legs blurred at the edges, as if its body were somehow always on the periphery of my vision. I could see it but not see it, its boundaries constantly shifting and rearranging even as we stared at one another.

What it had for eyes were tiny, just pinpricks of light, a stark contrast to its enormous mouth, the shape of which looked permanently fixed in a delighted grin.

Closer. Prowling. The creature looked far more menacing in the daylight because it so obviously did not belong in this world. I had sincerely hoped that these monsters couldn't operate outside the darkness. I had hoped in vain. I felt its strength, its odd fluctuating temperature, as it moved around to trap me in the doorway. Had it listened in while Lee and I spoke? Did it know what lay hidden in the folds of my apron?

The shadow, still smiling that awful smile, drew up its too-long arms, tapping its fingers together thoughtfully as it looked me over. Yes, it was looking for something, searching me. . . . It must have known that I had not one, not two, but *three* books hiding under my apron. Closer it came, until I felt its icy breath on my face. I shivered and drew back, the cold so intense, so concentrated, it might burn my skin.

"Do not hide from me," it growled, each word drawn out like the creak of a rusty door hinge, setting my teeth on edge.

The cold was unbearable. My wrist began to throb, pulsing as if in response to the creature that had nearly broken it. The spindly fingers on one hand reached for me, and I cringed, shaking, silent, managing one tiny whimper of protest as I prepared for it to shake out my skirts and find the hidden book. If I ran, it would catch me; if I tried to dodge around it, its arms would be too long to avoid.

I closed my eyes tightly, and the searing cold descended on me.

And then, in a flash, it was gone. I heard the heavy footfalls in the same moment I felt the creature vanish. Peeling one eye open, I found myself staring at nothing. But I could not be alone; someone or something had frightened it away. That someone was barreling down the hall toward me, a stout man in his later years, a bushy, bristly mustachio covering half his face, as if two doves had settled in to roost on his upper lip. In my fright I could not recall his name, though Mrs. Haylam had mentioned this guest briefly. A military man of some kind; it had to be him, for he was wearing a uniform-like coat that may have looked smart before he'd grown too large for it. A navy-blue turban slid down his forehead, and he jammed it back into place as he hurried toward me.

Mrs. Eames followed, emerging like a bride all in black, her hands floating gracefully to her sides. She wore a fashionable day dress with an empire waist and sleeves as puffed and beautiful as paper lanterns. That same giant green emerald glittered on her hand, a single spot of color, a winking eye of envy on an otherwise austere body.

Whoever the man in front was, I was more than glad to see him.

"I say, is this place utterly abandoned? It's a disgrace. I must have rung that bloody bell for a quarter of an hour, and now I find you loitering out here, dirty and agape. I am not, young miss, paying good English coin to be ignored!" He bustled his way down the corridor, red-faced and furious, stopping in the exact, unnervingly close place the shadow creature had just been.

His breath, however, was hot, and laced with pipe tobacco.

"Hello? Hello there! Are you listening?" He threw up his hands in frustration. "Pudding-headed yahoos, the lot of them," he muttered, not nearly under his breath enough. Then he rounded on me again and I felt my breathless dread of a moment ago turn hastily into disgust. A towering shadow creature had just vanished before my eyes, and now this. Insults. I felt my fingers curling into hard, uncaring fists around the dusting rag and bucket handle.

"Do not berate the girl," Mrs. Eames said, floating toward

us and then pausing, looking down her nose at me. I stared back impertinently, wondering if these were the eyes of a scheming killer. She lifted one gloved hand and plucked at her lower lip in thought. "A servant never takes a slap without spitting in your wine," she added. Her eyes, already chilly, seemed to look through me.

And when the veneer of warmth and beauty faded, how similar she looked to the shadow beasts, I thought.

"George Bremerton's boy said something . . . Something about you being new here, child; is that correct?"

I nodded.

Mrs. Eames folded her hands together and smiled, but it was a withering look. A string of rosary beads hung around her wrist, tinkling softly. "Pray you last long enough to learn the true reward of obedience. 'Before destruction the heart of man is haughty, and before honor is humility.'"

"Your tea," I bit out through a clenched jaw, deliberately turning away from her to face her companion. "Of course, sir. Right away. Remind me of your room number again?"

"Third floor, room six, tea for Colonel Mayweather, for heaven's sake! Shall I instruct you on how to set a kettle to boil, too? Does Dr. Merriman suffer this same neglect? How about Bremerton?"

Bow your head. Curtsy. Do not under any circumstances dump the bucket of foul water on his head and watch that bushy monstrosity on his face wilt like a wet dog.

I scuttled away from them, toward the stairs, and, as far as the odious Colonel Mayweather and Mrs. Eames knew, in the direction of the kitchens. They might get their tea eventually, but not from me. I had no intention of bringing that man anything. What was the point? As I had no desire to stay at Coldthistle, it now seemed ridiculous to continue doing any of the work expected of me. My time was better spent looking into this book Mr. Morningside had written and finding a way to break the barrier so I might hawk these rare books and leave. What could they do if I failed in my duties? Throw me out?

More's the pity. I would have relished the opportunity to make their drinks bitter with spittle.

When I reached the landing, I paused, considering where I might read Mr. Morningside's book in peace. It was burning a hole in my skirts, begging to be studied, if only to shed some small insight into his personality and motives, and how the book in the attic could be overthrown. But now I was certain the shadow monsters didn't want me to have it—that made it more valuable, of course, but also more dangerous. Reading the book inside the house was out of the question.

I headed back outside for the second time that day, finding that the weather had remained chilly but not intolerable, with a heavy bank of clouds rolling in to sit like a dark thought over the manse. The rag and bucket I left in the small overhang near the door to the kitchens. Other tools and supplies were kept there on ladders leaned against the wall to form makeshift shelves. I poured out the bucket and squeezed the rag, leaving them both for some far more devoted worker to find.

Inside, I could hear Mrs. Haylam cooking supper, pots and pans clanging away. The yard between the door and the barns was empty, and I bundled my skirts and the book into my hands and picked my way quickly toward the low, dark building. The wind rose as I did, and the familiar heaviness of the atmosphere shifting before a storm made the hairs on the back of my neck prickle. Those clouds above me were no longer just a thought but a genuine threat.

The smell of hay and horses wafted toward me as I gained the barn. It was a sturdy, handsome building made of thick timbers. All of it had been painted a rich black-brown, and it looked newer and in better repair than Coldthistle itself. I peered inside one of the open doors, anxious for any sign of Chijioke or the others. But I was alone. Well, alone but for the five horses in their stalls. A few ears turned toward me with interest, but the beasts didn't seem to mind the intrusion.

I had always loved the coziness of barns, and used more than one as shelter when I ran away from Pitney. This one, too, felt almost homey, and I raced between the horse stalls to a rope dangling from the ceiling near the far wall. An open archway there led to the coach storage and Chijioke's workshop. I grabbed the rope and pulled, grunting from the effort of it, then scampered up the makeshift stairs that appeared from the ceiling.

The hayloft was exactly as I'd hoped—empty, warm, and quiet. I pulled up the stairs behind me and settled onto a mounded lump of hay. There were only two windows in the loft, one that looked toward the house, another with a view of the fields next door. I chose the one with more light to read by, watching more rain-bloated clouds roll in over the pasture.

Mr. Morningside's book had not found gentle treatment in that library. Water-damaged and yellowed, the pages felt brittle enough to crumble in my fingers. Gently, I cracked the weathered cover, finding an inscription written in an elegant hand, one I assumed belonged to Morningside.

Spicer,

This had better make us even, you miserable bastard. I know I owe you for that cock-up in Hungary, but this is getting out of hand. Szilvássy wasn't even my man, he was yours, but I admit mistakes were made on both sides. It should be in the past, as all things inevitably are. Even you cannot hold a grudge this long.

At any rate, read this or don't, but don't say I never did anything for you. Sparrow can find her own copy; she despises me anyway.

Yours in perpetuity (ha!),

Henry

I read the inscription three times. The second time because it was hard to imagine the Mr. Morningside I had met admitting he was wrong about anything. The third time because I at last noticed the little date dashed off under his signature.

December, 1799

Either the date was wrong, or Morningside was far older than my estimations. A six-year-old boy could not have written a complete book and made out an inscription in it. Even a seven-, eight-, or nine-year-old was silly to consider. By generous calculations, a person would need to be at least fifteen to manage a book of this length and apparent complexity, which would put him currently around six and twenty. That couldn't be. He hardly looked a day older than Lee or myself!

But his backward feet couldn't be, either. Nor could little girls who murder or books that lure and trap or walking, talking shadow creatures. None of it was possible, and yet . . .

And yet . . .

Reasonable, earthly thinking must be set aside, I decided. Mr. Morningside could be a youth, or an elder, or anything in between. Poppy had called him a grumpy old man. Either he had somehow located the Fountain of Youth, or there was more here that I did not yet understand. The book, naturally, might lend a few ideas. And so I began to read. The introduction spoke of world travels, of schooners and wagon rides, horseback adventures spanning months, dangerous climbs up previously unconquered mountains, and dozens of references to explorers and chroniclers I did not recognize.

It told me little. He had traveled far and wide, though I could not venture a guess at how, considering his unusual feet. That was not so surprising—he was a young (or not) man of surprising fortune and a collection of exotic birds. World explorer did not run counter to that particular persona.

Chapter 1: In Which I Meet a Child of the Dark Fae and Make an Impassioned Plea

Now we were getting somewhere.

Chapter Eighteen

In Which I Meet a Child of the Dark Fae and Make an Impassioned Plea

My most recent travels in Ireland left me with one conclusion: the Fae do not choose their victims at random, and the Dark Fae are even more particular.

While traveling to Derry, I made a brief stopover at the Crosskeys Inn, and met there a young woman, perhaps only *fifteen years of age, begging outside in the cold rain. I invited her in to dine with me, to her great surprise, but by and by she joined me, eating what can only be described as a remarkable amount of chicken liver pie. Over this harrowing feast and several pints of good stout ale, I invited her to tell me how she came to be a beggar in these parts. She reacted with hesitation at first, and that is perhaps my own fault; all this while I had been studying her closely, for the woman—we may call her Edna—possessed all the markers one expected from a Dark Fae descendant.*

The very black hair and similarly black eyes, the paleness, the thin stature and sunken cheeks . . . All of these features I had sketched before when encountering what the Irish merely dubbed "Changelings."

"My mother, she had me young and without a man" was Edna's explanation.

"You mean unwed," I replied.

"If you like," she said, visibly uncomfortable.

"You will have no judgment from me," I told her.

Edna nodded, and continued, saying, "The family liked to tell it that mother was never the same after she came in from washing at the river one day. That's the river Bann, I mean to say, and her cousins said she was gone for two whole days just to do a bit of rinsing. Two whole days! It couldn't be true! But all present swore to it, and for a long while Mother thought they were just having her on. She started to believe a wee bit more when the babe—I—came along."

And here she stopped, for she had become suddenly emotional. Some men in the inn looked at us with more than polite curiosity. More proof for my solidifying theory.

"She was taken," I said to her, calm. "This is not the first I've heard of such a thing."

Her eyes grew enormous and she nodded, reaching for my hand and squeezing it, in relief, I warrant, or gratitude. As with all descendants of the Dark Fae, I battled a disquieting feeling in my chest. Those unaccustomed to mythic and magicked creatures do not understand that they are experiencing the body's natural ability to detect Unworldly or "Dark" elements. This is almost always chalked up to "instinct" or "gut feeling" that leads to instant repulsion, but one can learn to control this response.

I did not flinch away from her, and Edna noticed this.

"You're different," she told me. "You believe me."

"Yes, and yes, but I must ask you to remove your hand, madam, as we are drawing a number of unsavory glances."

Edna complied, but her excitement was not diminished. "Changeling whore," she whispered, "that's what they call me. That's why I've no family, no man of my own. Folk 'round here just know it, can sense it. They know something is wrong with me, but that isn't fair-like, is it? I didn't do nothing to get this way, and my poor mother . . ."

"The grim reality we must all face is that the dark and different and strange among us face a kind of exile. Man desires comfort above all else. Comfort, security . . . You were born of

an unworldly creature and a hapless mortal, and if an innocent washerwoman could be stolen away to the heart of the forest and made to be a Fae bride, then no one is really comfortable and no one is truly secure. Then that bump in the night could come for them or their sister or their son, too, and that is chaos. That is ruin. You are ruin and chaos to them, but you are lovely to my eye."

"You're brave or daft, then," she said, quite rightly. "Chaos and ruin. Where does that leave me, then?"

"In the in-between, my dear, where all things magic go to wait."

I put several coins down on the table to cover our meal, then handed Edna what money I could spare. She grasped my hand again, trying to pull me back down to my chair.

"Wait?" she asked. "Wait for what?"

I did not answer her then and still cannot. Long have I suspected that the growing number of so-called Changelings among us is a sign of acceleration. We are moving quickly toward a reformation of the world, I think; the widespread proliferation of Unworldly and magicked creatures does not so much hint at this but points and stamps its feet and shouts: What has been made in darkness to serve the dark will rise at last, at last!

It is the deep, trembling drum that beats faster, ushering in an age we humble explorers and historians can only imagine. Apocalypse, cry some, but I disagree. Some of my less compassionate colleagues use their studies as a means to an end, that *end being eradication. This is foolhardy in the extreme. These creatures, these* people, *are not weeds to be pulled out and flung aside. They have been hunted and burned and driven out for millennia, and who are we to deny them their ascension?*

Does Edna not deserve a home and family of her own? Must she beg until death at the doors of those who would shun and hate her and keep her forever scrabbling in the mud, all for the sake of their comfort?

Esteemed men and women of this most curious profession, I call on you in this first chapter and in all those that follow to hear this, the closest I will come to a thesis, to see these creatures—these Changelings and priests of shadow and Wailers and all else— not as curiosities to be studied but as people to be understood.

<hr />

y mind rebelled, filled with churning, burning, horrible questions, and yet I slept. I had never begun to dream as quickly as I did that night in the barn, finding myself at once immersed in a vivid memory of my birth town.

Waterford was a place of wonder to me, of magic, of cracked, crumbling keeps and brightly painted houses lining a serpentine river. Beautiful houses filled with Waterford glint glass, homes like princesses would live in, homes that I would never have. Our house was just a shack on the edge of all this singularly

Irish beauty. In my dream it was night, and I could see from our perch on a dusty berm the boats moving downriver.

I was tiny again, no more than five, dressed in the thin dress my mother had patched beyond recognition. It could have been a rag for scrubbing dishes with all the holes and tears and dodgy seams. In one hand I held my favorite dolly, a crude thing like an effigy, just sticks and straw wrapped in scraps of potato sack. In the other hand was a cast-off piece of wood from the butcher down the lane. Only it wasn't a nasty old stick to me, it was a sword and I was fighting pirates.

And of course, Maggie, my imaginary friend, was my first mate. Maggie. Mary. They were the same even in the dream. Perhaps even more the same. Her hair was like mine, wild and dirty, bits of hay and grass stuck in the snarls. Our swords clashed. We giggled and chased each other around the outside of the house. Mother yelled at us from inside but we ignored her. We were living a life of freedom on the high seas. We were unstoppable.

When my sword slipped and smacked her wrist and she began to cry, I held her and apologized over and over again. *I'm sorry, Mary, I'm sorry, I need you. You're my best and only friend.*

She stopped crying and giggled again, the mistake forgotten. This was when we first became friends; not in the dream, but when I was five. It was around then that Father stormed out of our lives, off to start another family. I probably had half brothers and sisters scattered all across Ireland. This was when they screamed at each other day and night. This was when I began hiding in the cupboards, listening to the fights, jamming my fingers in my ears until it hurt.

That little beasty isn't mine!

She is yours too, Malachy Ditton, she has your devil in her! Your eyes!

No eyes of mine, witch! Eyes from Hell! Don't come at me with that broom, you're the one gone and fecked a demon!

Even when they knew I was in the cupboards crying and hearing it all, they wouldn't stop. When he left, she said it was just the drink that made him say all those mean things. But I knew there was truth to it, felt it deep in the place where secrets go to fester. *Eyes from Hell.* My eyes had always been strange and black, not like other children's. Sitting in the cupboard, I wished for a friend who didn't care, for someone who wouldn't beat me in the schoolyard because of the way I looked and was.

Mary saved me. No, Maggie. I called her Maggie. It didn't matter. I chased her around the house and I was happy for a while. She didn't care that my eyes were black or that my mother was odd.

Around and around we went, shrieking with laughter, smacking each other on the shoulders with our sword-sticks. Then she ran away from town and I followed her, into the wood, to the parts of the cove where I was never supposed to go. I hated listening to my mother's superstitious nagging. Her stories were dazzling but couldn't be true. Fairies and devils and all sorts in the wood. It was just a bunch of bushes and grass and trees, nothing scarier in there than a rabbit ready to startle you.

I followed Mary into the wood, up a hill, running out of breath but loving every second of it. I'd be hided for this when mother saw how dirty my feet had gotten. It didn't matter. I ran after her, giving chase, little legs working hard. We crested a shallow hill and stopped short, oohing and ahhing at the sweet fairy ring that had sprung up around a kind of natural well. I picked up a stone and tossed it into the water, laughing.

"What if a water spirit's inside?" I asked.

Suddenly it was night. The dream didn't feel fun anymore. Mary was there but she looked sad. She sat next to the fairy ring and shook her head.

"You shouldn't throw stones. That could be someone's house."

That was silly. What could live in that water but a fish or frog? I tossed another stone in, but it did not plop. Someone had caught it. Someone angry. A gray-green figure slid out of the water, its face and shoulders covered in slime. It was naked, but all I could see were its huge silver eyes.

"Little greedy child," it whispered, hoisting itself higher until it loomed above us. I heard myself scream. "You disturbed the water and now I shall take her back home. She's mine again, little greedy child, and you are alone. You are alone. . . . Alone . . ."

The thing snatched Mary by her hair and pulled, dragging

her into the water, plunging back below, her small legs kicking, thrashing, spraying murky water in my face. I toppled in after her, crying, reaching for her. . . . But she was gone. I stared helplessly into the surface, but it only reflected my face and the stars.

I heard her voice from deep, down below.

Don't cry, Louisa, I'm only going home.

Chapter
Nineteen

The first crack of thunder jolted me out of sleep.

One crash and then another. Nature's horrible fury shook the barn. I nearly leapt up off the hay bale, the book on my chest clattering to the floor as more thunder rumbled overhead. My dreams had been full of dark, swirling entities and someone crying far away, obscured by a misty curtain I could not penetrate. It was my mother's voice in the dream, calling to me, begging for something, but the words were pulled apart like tufts of yarn before they reached my ears.

Fell winds pounded the barn walls, and below I heard the horses stamping their feet in alarm. The thunder rattled in my bones, and my hands shook as I retrieved the book. It had fallen open on the last page I'd read before sleep took me—page ninety-eight: "The Enduring Mystery of the Lost Order."

The Lost Order would have to wait. Just below the howling winds and thunder, I heard voices outside. That didn't make any sense, not unless Chijioke was gathering up the last of his gardening materials before the storm struck in earnest. But it was not his voice I heard moaning in between blasts of lightning, and it seemed too late an hour for cleaning up the yard tools. Peering out the window, I saw the moon at its highest point, glittering behind storm clouds. Midnight.

At first I thought perhaps someone had become lost and

wandered onto the property, calling for aid. But when I crossed to the opposite window and pressed myself close to the cold glass, I saw instead that a solitary figure stood with arms raised in the space between the house and the back gardens. She had a woman's slender build and small hands, and she seemed not to mind at all that a tempest raged around her.

Her words carried to the barn but I could not make them out. And so I bundled Mr. Morningside's book back into my skirts and climbed down the hayloft, stepping lightly as I rushed past the pawing, snorting horses. Here it was again, my damned curiosity. I could climb back up into the hayloft and try to shut out the storm and sleep, but instead I was throwing open the barn doors, plunging out into the swirling winds, and shielding my eyes from the bits of grass and dust swept up into the atmosphere. It felt like the full weight of heaven was bearing down upon me, more than just the elements, more than just icy air and thunder.

I tumbled forward at once, foot caught in one of the yard's many holes. Sprawled out on the grass, palms wet and skinned, I squinted into the storm, crawling onto my knees and then rising to my feet, stumbling ever closer to the figure in the clearing. Who was this person, facing down the will of the sky itself, hands raised fearlessly, feet planted sturdy and strong? It felt private, like I was intruding on her intimate conversation with the clouds. Her voice rose and fell in a kind of chant, and fragments of it sped toward me on the chill fins of the winds.

Furain an t-aoigh a thig, greas an t-aoigh tha falbh . . .

It was Mary. The hood on her dark green cloak had fallen back, and her brown, curling hair tossed like wild bramble, framing her pale face. Now more than ever the cluster of freckles over her nose looked like a smear of blood. I recognized the Gaelic language but not the meaning of the words. Still, their strangeness did not diminish the haunting beauty of her voice. A lullaby and warrior's chant all in one. The refrain repeated, louder now, for I was limping closer as her song reached its crescendo.

Furain an t-aoigh a thig, greas an t-aoigh tha falbh!

The rain began not as a trickle but as one drenching downpour. I was soaked in an instant, and I wrapped the book more carefully in my skirts, desperate to keep it safe from the sudden rain. A crack of lightning struck so close to the manse's property that I was temporarily blinded. When the shock wore off, I reeled back a little, gasping, the house illuminated as if it stood in broad daylight. I saw shadows moving among the windows, their silhouettes blinking from one floor to the next, great, grasping bodies lurking wherever I looked.

Mary's voice broke through to me again, and I forced my way through the rain, watching, gasping once more as I realized the raindrops avoided her altogether. Not a speck of water darkened her cloak. It was as if a beam from heaven protected her, keeping her dry and safe.

I stumbled in one of the holes and swore, and she whipped

around to face me. Never could I have imagined a less kind expression, but it softened as soon as she recognized me. One of her raised hands dropped, reaching, gesturing . . . I regained my balance and pushed through the mud, taking her hand as the sheltering force around her blasted back the rain.

"Don't let go," she whispered. "Don't let go, Louisa, it will be all right."

But I jumped, startled by another silver spike of lightning cracking open the sky. Shadows stood in every window now, and it occurred to me that perhaps they were not up to any business inside but were in fact staring out. Watching Mary. Watching *us*.

And then I remembered—tonight was to be the night of Mrs. Eames's demise.

Mary squeezed my hand tightly just as the scream ripped through the house. No, not *the* scream—two of them, though they tore at me simultaneously. One was real and raw and present, shorter than the other, which sounded oddly muted, as if my ears had been suddenly dunked in water and the liquid still sloshed around in my head, dulling everything.

It gave me a jolt, a headache that came and went before I could even make sense of the pain.

And as both screams died, the wind rose harder and faster, and I huddled against Mary, anchoring myself to her, afraid then that we would be lifted into the air and dashed against the walls. But the rain eased, and with it the winds, and though I still shivered with the cold and wet, the storm was no longer a danger to us.

Mary squeezed my hand again, her sweet, familiar face back to smiling shyly.

"What was that?" I whispered breathlessly.

"Only a bit of shielding," she said, as if it were the most obvious thing in the world. "Poppy's scream could kill us all, the little scamp. She never did learn how to rein herself in."

"Then Mrs. Eames is dead." It was less shocking than I expected. Less affecting. I didn't know if I believed the stories about her, but I did know that there was no longer anything I could do about it.

"Oh aye," Mary replied, taking my arm. She tugged me gently back toward the house. "But she went real quick-like. No suffering but what was already eating away at her heart."

"No." I pulled my arm out of her grasp. "I won't go back in there."

"Well, you can't sleep out here," Mary said with a frown. "You'll catch your death."

Grimacing, I nodded toward the barn. "It's warm enough in the hayloft. Those shadow things . . . I'll never rest knowing they're prowling about."

"It does take some getting used to," she admitted. "Can I at least bring you tea in the morning? You have to eat eventually, you know."

She looked so sad, so . . . offended. And I suppose in a way that made perfect sense. I was rejecting her as much as I was rejecting the rest of the madhouse she lived in. Her cloak settled in the lessening wind, falling more tightly to her body, and she hugged herself, waiting for my reply.

I couldn't meet her warm green eyes. Green eyes that had peered back at me for years and years of my childhood, eyes that had sparkled to hear my jokes and shed tears when I shed tears. But this was not Maggie, it was Mary, and Mary had just helped a little girl kill someone. I would not allow myself to be deceived, even if her eyes said: Trust me, and her smile said: I mean well.

"I can manage on my own," I said, turning back toward the barn. "I don't need your help, and I don't want it."

Chapter
Twenty

Áinsprid Choimhdeachta: Guardian Angels or Guardian Devils? A Journey

In the spring of 1798, I brought a handful of gifts to Kilmurrin Cove, following a rumor of a spring sacred to the Dark Fae. There is the better known Holy Well, which is easy enough to find, but this particular spring was a long-held secret of Waterford. Mentioning the secret spring in pubs and taverns resulted in grunts and dismissals and suspiciously high bills. These inquiries *were not wanted, and thus, I was not wanted.*

It was on an unseasonably warm evening, after another failed campaign of casual suggestions in a pub, that a young man approached me as I left. He was stout and round-faced, with ruddy hair and a knowing cat's grin. The name he gave me, Alec, was surely not his own.

"If a spring's your thing, I ken one fit even for a king."

Charming though his rhyming was, I was not in the mood for games. It did, however, spark my interest, considering nobody else in the Irish town seemed willing to entertain my questions. And so I indulged him, answering in kind.

"If you know the place, I have a coin for your trouble; lead on, young friend, to the place where dark secrets bubble."

"Aye, to the spring we will go, but not without tribute. The Fae are greedy, as you and I both know."

The redheaded boy began to walk a spiraling route through the shadow-draped town, avoiding the alleys where stray cats called and dogs barked. Wood smoke filled the summer air. Whiffs of heather from the surrounding valleys tricked one into the mindset of a bright, hot day. Alec must have walked for twenty minutes with me close on his heel, taking me to the edge of Waterford and to the cove proper. The harbor air was thick with the scent of fish, making my nose twitch from the power of it. Here the winds blew harder, and I breathed deep, filling my lungs with the air fresh off the river currents.

We cut along the top of the cove, the drop down to the water stomach-churningly steep. One false step would plunge a man to his death among the jagged rocks waiting below. Alec moved swiftly, and in my mind, unnaturally, a fact that made me more certain of our destination. We moved inland for a half mile or so, to a place where the grass grew thin and the stones rose in a kind of uneven circle. This was the spring; I could hear the water bubbling nearby, and a curiously neat ring of mushrooms grew around the rocks.

"The spring is yon, but you must pay the price. For you, strange one, an answered riddle and a trinket will suffice."

I nodded and told him to continue.

Alec's smile glittered under the stars. The mushrooms sprinkled around the spring were bright red, the spots on their caps shining like a dusting of crushed diamonds. "An open-ended barrel, I am shaped like a hive. I am filled with the flesh, and the flesh is alive." He cackled, throwing his head back. "What am I?"

It was a simple riddle, one I puzzled out quickly enough. "A thimble."

Pouting, Alec seemed disappointed in my quick response. But then he smiled again and clapped his hands and pointed to the pocket on the right side of my coat. "The price is inside; now toss it in the spring. Who knows what manner of blessing the thimble will bring . . ."

I reached into my pocket, and sure enough, my hand closed around a small, cool thimble. The spring bubbled more fervently as I moved into position, and I gazed down into the roiling waters, wondering just what might come of doing as the odd boy said. But I did, closing my eyes, casting the trinket into the spring.

Alec had disappeared when I opened my eyes.

This was how I came to find the Spring of the Ainsprid Choimhdeachta, so-called Guardian Devils. The words were chiseled in half-legible script on a stone to the side of the spring. I had heard whispers of these beings before, guardian spirits of a female persuasion that could be summoned to perform all manner of spells, shielding of the spirit and the flesh principle among those skills. Curiouser still, they were said to be summoned by dark thoughts or prayers, which led many demonologists to suppose they are not guardian angels but more of a curse, a weight 'round the neck of their summoner. I've yet to find evidence of such a curse, and I participated in Alec's game with the hope of creating just such a Choimhdeachta of my own.

Alas, no amount of wishing, praying, or cursing produced a spirit. Either the legend is wrong or a soul in greater need managed to pray her out from under my nose. Regardless, I did feel a great deal of Fae energy surrounding the spring; it filled me with dread and wonder, and I sat beside the waters and the fairy ring for a long time, fancying I could feel invisible spirits dancing merrily around me in the darkness.

Rare Myths and Legends: The Collected Findings of

H. I. Morningside, *page 210*

I had only ever seen one dead body in my life.

When my mother and I still lived in Dublin, we watched them pull a man from the river Liffey on market day. He was gray and bloated, draped in a shroud of plants and muck, nothing like the body I was looking at now. Nothing like the still-beautiful Mrs. Eames, who, with her head down on her dressing table, might have been sleeping. She was still clutching her rosary, but the emerald on her hand did not glisten, shadowed as it was by her dead body.

A single trickle of blood ran out of her ear and down her cheek, underlining the eyes that stared out at me in mute surprise.

I stood in the door staring—at her, at the many open traveling trunks heaped with luxurious gowns, at the shoes lined up neatly by her dressing table, at the lacy frill of her robe, at all the trappings of a once-living person—and bile rose in my throat. It smelled like dried roses in the room, sweet enough to remind me of rot.

Nobody had yet found her even though it was midmorning the next day. I had come inside to scrounge up a bit of breakfast, and then found myself drifting up the stairs, wondering if it all was really true—if Mrs. Eames would be dead, killed by a child and abetted by gentle Mary. Perhaps I had also meant to see if there were any unlocked rooms and trinkets in them to steal, but that was all forgotten now. Here I was, the taste of toast souring on my dry tongue. It was all true. Her door had been open just a crack, and when I'd peered inside, I'd felt at once that this tableau had been left for me to find.

But maybe that was selfish. Maybe the answer was far simpler: this was not an occurrence of any urgency or rarity. If this were the first guest to be killed on the property then there ought to be some kind of commotion, but in this peace, in this silence, it felt as if this was business as usual at Coldthistle House.

Yet it was not usual for me. I took a careful step into the room, aware that my mere presence would look suspicious to outside eyes, but I had spotted something under her head on the table. A pot of ink lay open next to her, and a quill pen had tangled in her skirts as it fell. The parchment under her cheek was smudged. I dared not touch it, but I held my breath, leaning over her, scanning the letter with a growing sense of disgust . . .

My dear Enzo: The men here are so delightfully gullible—morbido come pane caldo—one or both will empty their pockets for us soon. I linger here only until their hearts are fully ensnared. Wait for me in San Gimignano, you know the spot, I will

It ended there, abruptly, with a giant ink splotch.

Good God, it was true. Everything Mr. Morningside had

said about her and everything he'd threatened to do. It was all true.

My disgust deepened to nausea. Something must be done, but what? I turned straight around and marched out of the room, smashing headlong into George Bremerton.

He had taken everything in already, I could see from the bloodless shock on his face.

"Help," I murmured, blinking up at him, feeling just as bloodless but not nearly as shocked. "Something terrible has happened."

Moments later I sat staring at the wall in the Red Room as a man I didn't know took my pulse.

I was well and truly caught now, caught between these two groups—that of the rich male guests left staying in the house, and that of the odd creatures determined to annihilate them—and I belonged in neither. The venerable old clock on the far wall tick-tocked, tick-tocked, marking the excruciating seconds. Listening to it was better than the alternative: Colonel Mayweather paced the carpet, speechifying endlessly, hands akimbo as he enumerated the horrors of not only the widow's death but my apparent part in it.

You see, George Bremerton had not kept quiet about finding me in her room, and now two old men and one slightly younger one stared at me as if I might at any moment grow a second head and try to swallow them whole.

The doctor's hand on my wrist was steady, but I could feel my blood and sinew trembling, the ticking clock growing louder and louder in my brain until it was the only thing I could hear.

"It's suspicious, I say! Damned suspicious! If this were India, I can tell you what I'd do, oh yes, I can tell you how we handled things in the company."

No. The clock was less aggravating.

"The girl is already in distress," the man holding my wrist said. He had a soft, melodic voice, one he quite obviously used to great effect on nervous patients. Dr. Rory Merriman, that was his name. Now I remembered him introducing himself before he sat down to take my pulse. The time between finding Mrs. Eames and now had gone blurry. There'd been commotion, yelling, accusations flung in every direction, but most aimed at me.

"You will only fluster her further," the doctor continued.

Colonel Mayweather thumped down on a divan with a harrumph. "That's warranted, wouldn't you say? She was found in poor Cosima's room! Practically . . . Practically leering over her!"

"If I recall, Mr. Bremerton did not say *leering*," the doctor corrected.

"Oh ho! Cosima, is it?" And now George Bremerton sprang to his feet, crossing his arms. "Awfully familiar with the dead, aren't we? I had no idea the two of you were so well acquainted, Colonel."

The two men erupted into shouts, each one puffing himself up as ridiculously as possible, threats and challenges flying fast and loose between them. I heard the doctor sigh as he released my wrist. He was young for a physician, with shaggy black hair graying at the temples, a square, unremarkable face, and a wisp of a mustache over his thin lips. His complexion led me to believe he was Spanish or perhaps from somewhere in South America. He had suffered from the pox as a child, with divots and scars now peppering his skin.

"These two," he muttered, rolling his eyes behind thick spectacles. "If they could raise the dead with the force of their argument . . ."

"It does seem impolite to fight over a woman who can't even defend herself," I replied. That made him chuckle, and he leaned closer, studying me. It was then I noticed his hand was on my thigh, the grip too tight to be incidental. I shifted, but there was nowhere to go on the tiny sofa. "This isn't my fault," I added weakly. "I only found her that way."

"She complained to me of headaches for days," he agreed. "I wouldn't be surprised if she was simply ill with some unknown malady of the brain. Even curative waters cannot help such things."

Like greed, for example, or evil.

"Then you will speak in my defense?" I asked, although really it would make no difference. Who would they report me to? The master of the house? He could hardly turn me over to the authorities, knowing, as he did, that this murder rested on his shoulders. But they might search my room and find the stolen books I had put for safekeeping under the bed. Then they would know that I intended to steal from them. What would Mr. Morningside do to a person who tried to take from his precious collections?

"Quite readily, as soon as these two fools calm down."

He smiled at me, rather intently, too intently for my liking. His hand remained on my thigh, and the heat of it there made me feel ill. Nobody had ever touched me in this manner, and while I generally trusted physicians, there was the not so small matter of this man being a guest here. What had he done to land himself in this cursed place? Now I was watching him back, and he flinched, suddenly taking great interest in the patterns on the carpets. What was inside him? If I looked hard enough, would I see whatever black mark stained his character?

The argument raging on next to us reached an abrupt peak, and Dr. Merriman shot up from the sofa, tangling himself in the two men, who had now come to blows over the widow's honor. It would not surprise me in the least if the afternoon ended with a duel.

While the three of them slapped lamely at each other I took a deep breath, watching as Lee burst through the door, Mrs. Haylam not far behind with tea. Lee spared the quickest glance at the men before joining me on the sofa. He looked as pale and drawn as I. I needed no mirror to know we had become reflections of each other's fear.

"Are you all right?" he whispered, searching my face. "You . . . You were the one to find her?"

"It's all as I said," I replied, putting equal weight on every word.

He took my meaning at once.

"How dreadfully, dreadfully awful," he murmured, the very last of the blood in his face draining away. His eyes roamed to the squabbling men, but he didn't really look at them. He was gazing beyond, thinking, and it was the same for me. What were we to do now that the scant words of warning I had given him proved prophetic?

"Gentlemen, I must insist that you stop this barbarism at once!" Mrs. Haylam bit out sternly. It was a schoolmarm's voice, a mother's voice, the sort of soft but steely tone that brought all three grown men instantly to heel, as if they were naughty children. "There is tea here, yes? Drink it. Sit down. There has been enough upset in this house for one morning."

The men broke apart, each taking a separate piece of furniture and claiming it as his own.

"Now then," she added, surveying the room and landing at last on me. She did not miss, of course, the close way Lee and I sat together. Her tight expression only became that much more strained. I had forgotten the stark, skewering power of her gaze. For a moment I remembered the crone who found me in Malton, and, as she glared at me now, I could see that spirit again within her. She had changed her clothes and hairstyle, but nothing could perfectly mask her nature. "I'm told our young maid here was the first witness to the tragedy, is that correct?"

The men piped up, but she only watched me as I nodded once.

"As such," Mrs. Haylam continued, folding her hands together and approaching me, "I must ask that she come along now and give a statement to the master of the house. He will deal directly with the village constable. And if it would not be too much trouble, Dr. Merriman, might you examine the body and prepare an official write-up of what you find? It will make the difficulties to come that much easier to face."

The doctor stood and brushed off his sober, simple suit. He was taking a deep breath as if to agree when Colonel Mayweather popped back up like a weasel jumping out of a burrow.

"Just a moment," he said, twirling the ends of his mustache, agitating them until they were perfect circles. "You cannot expect us to stand idly by while nothing is done with this girl! Not only my sense of duty but my sense of logic demands that she be questioned most thoroughly. *Most* thoroughly! Why was she the very first to come upon poor Mrs. Eames? Why did she not call for aid? Mr. Bremerton claims he found the chit *lurking*, and I for one will have this lurking behavior explained."

"For once we agree," George Bremerton chimed in. He propped his elbow up on his knee, shaking one finger in my direction. "Why, the local constable should do the questioning himself. It's intolerable to consider staying another moment in this place with a killer stalking the halls."

I couldn't feel my hands. They had gone numb with cold horror. What could I say? That they were not at all in danger? That was a lie, and while they had nothing to fear from me, I knew even now the machinery of their own demise was somewhere in motion. To lie to these men did not bother me, but in that moment, flustered and afraid, I could not conjure a single word of defense.

"There was no instrument of murder found in the room," the doctor pointed out reasonably, unbuttoning and rebuttoning his coat. "And again, I recall the woman complaining of severe headaches—"

"She said nothing of the sort to me!" Colonel Mayweather huffed, rounding on the doctor.

"Or me," Bremerton agreed.

I could feel Lee fidgeting helplessly beside me. Even Mrs. Haylam looked a little nervous, stranded as she was in the middle of the room, the Colonel on one side and Bremerton on the other. No matter how sincerely I silently implored the doctor to speak up again, he remained silent, shifting his eyes between the two men as he fussed with his coat.

"There! You see? No objections." Colonel Mayweather wrinkled his nose at me, grinning, as if accusing me gave him supreme pleasure. "The girl shall be turned over to the constabulary at once."

"And yet we will do no such thing."

The Colonel's smugness melted away immediately. He and everyone else turned to regard the tall, handsomely cut figure in the doorway. Mr. Morningside had arrived, and he did not appear at all pleased.

Chapter
Twenty-One

"When if ever did I sign over ownership of this establishment to you two gentlemen?" Mr. Morningside was dressed impeccably in indigo with a pale green cravat. The room seemed to shrink at his presence, and my eye went at once to his feet; they appeared normal, sheathed in glossy black boots.

"Really, sir, please, nobody is suggesting—"

"Anything of merit, how right you are, Colonel." Mr. Morningside waved a folded piece of parchment back and forth as he wandered into the room. "This letter ought to clear young Louisa of any suspicion. The widow Eames was not robbed, and her correspondence suggests she had every intention of fleecing both you, Colonel Mayweather, and you, Mr. George Bremerton. If there are accusations to be flung about willy-nilly, it is not in her direction." He paused when he reached Mrs. Haylam's side, lazily finding my gaze and winking. "Unless of course you fancy her some enterprising young avenger of your honor, gentlemen?"

"Preposterous!" Colonel Mayweather half exploded with the word. He blinked hard, wringing out his hands and then his mustache. "Just . . . outrageous. To insult us and the widow in one breath—"

"The insult, I'm afraid, is hers to claim," Mr. Morningside

said, handing the unfinished letter to the Colonel. "Read it yourself. I believe you will find evidence enough to quench the flames of injustice."

Before the old man could even finish reading the letter, Mr. Morningside extended his hand toward me, the very picture of calm certitude. "Now, Louisa, I think you should remove yourself from the room. There is no need for you to endure these unfounded allegations any longer. You must be exhausted."

It was not a request, that much I knew. I stood without thinking, with one last look at Lee. Never had I felt such a tearing of my desires. I had no interest in staying in the room, but I also dreaded whatever Mr. Morningside might say to me in private. Did he know I had his book? But now I was standing, halfway to a decision, and I could not linger there without seeming suspicious. I might blurt out to these men that they were going to die here, that the widow was just the beginning, but what love had I for them when moments earlier they were ready to send me to the constable and then, presumably, the gallows?

"My condolences to you all," I said softly, dipping down into a curtsy. "She seemed a very . . ."

Mr. Morningside's golden eyes flashed at me.

". . . accomplished woman."

With that, I was being swept out of the room by Mr. Morningside, buoyed on a tide I felt powerless to stop. Mrs. Haylam said one more word to the men about taking solace in the tea and then followed us. Neither of them laid a finger on me, but it didn't matter; I felt the combined force of their urgency and something else . . . elation, perhaps. Excitement.

The door to the Red Room closed with a bang.

Mr. Morningside dusted off his hands, leaning against the one blank spot on the wall without a bird painting. "What an immensely tricky knot you nearly hanged yourself with there, Louisa," Mr. Morningside said, eyes sparkling.

"And what? I should thank you for the rescue?" Tears were building, threatening to spill, hot and humiliating, down my cheeks. "You *left* her there for me to find, didn't you? A woman is dead and all you care to do is play cruel jokes!"

His demeanor shifted, that excitement I felt previously evaporating like snow in a fire. Slowly, he looked away from me, over my shoulder and at Mrs. Haylam. "Please fetch the doctor. He needs to do his examination. I want the formalities with Mrs. Eames over quickly."

Sighing, she turned back toward the Red Room, but then she hesitated. "That you let her speak to you in this manner . . ."

Mr. Morningside waved her concerns away, his golden eyes burning into the side of my face. I didn't want to look at him, or at her. I simply wanted to be away from them both. Already I was calculating where I would go next—back to the hayloft, perhaps, to search the book for more clues and some way of breaking Mr. Morningside's hold over me.

"She is but a buzzing fly. Allow Louisa her tantrum; it bothers me not."

"If that is the case, a fly hardly warrants your parading around aboveground. I've not seen you in the house proper this much in years," Mrs. Haylam replied, but her lips hardly moved, her face tight with frustration. When she was gone, I spun at once to run for the stairs.

"I should rather be the fly than the spider," I spat, hurrying away. If I was an insect to him, then my presence must be offensive. And inconsequential. *Let me go*, I silently pleaded. *I'm nothing and no one, so just let me go.*

"Back to the hayloft, little fly?" he drawled. And followed. *Damn it all, leave me alone!* I did not give him the satisfaction of my anger. Instead I kept on, gaining the top step as he called more loudly after me. "How are you enjoying the book? Take a peek at page one hundred and fifty-five. I think you'll find it most instructive."

Of course he knew. I couldn't let that stop me.

His rich voice carried down into the foyer as I ran, the words wrapping around me, tugging as surely as the horrible magic that tempted me to his green door, to the attic. It was as clear as if he were right behind me, though when I turned I saw he was yet at the top of the stairs. "The more you learn of me and this place, the more you will crave answers, and then, naturally, more answers. Disgust and curiosity are easy companions."

He was wrong. He had to be wrong. I could overcome the temptation of my curiosity; I could overcome whatever I had to in order to flee this place.

"I'm not going to confiscate the book, and I would have told you all you wanted to know and more, but you did not come to see me . . ." The pout in his voice was unmistakable. "It hurts my feelings."

Whatever man or creature or demon he was, I doubted there was even a beating heart in his chest to wound.

My hand was pressed against the front door when he called out one last time. This time it was not just in my head. "You won't find what you're looking for!"

I braced against the door, swiveling to glare up at him where he stood posed like a portrait subject on the staircase landing. He might have been young, or older than his looks betrayed. Whatever his age, there was no mistaking that he was the lord of the manor as he stood with a hand on each banister, chin tilted up, eyes gazing down on me as if I were his lowly subject.

"Then you have no reason to follow and trouble me further," I said, barely raising my voice.

"It simply pains me to see you wasting your time." He was right, of course. I knew what would happen if I made it to the end of the drive. More pain. More frustration.

He descended the stairs, coming at last to regard me from the middle of the foyer. I slid down against the door, squeezing my eyes shut.

"What happened to your feet?" I asked, letting out a choked laugh. "Did I simply imagine them strangely the last time we spoke?"

"Not at all." He lifted one foot and turned it this way and that. I watched, sickened, as the bones rearranged themselves, reverting to how his feet had been before—backward. Backward like a demon's. My mother had told stories of cursed beings with wrong-facing feet, born that way so as to confuse when their tracks seemed always to lead away when in truth they followed. A shudder ran through me. He seemed to stand more like some satyr of myth than a man now, his calves curving away, his beautiful, shiny shoes made absurd by the disjointed position.

"Better?"

"*No*," I breathed, shutting my eyes again.

"It's a glamour. Simple magicks, really, at least for me. It would be for you, too, I suspect, if you had the willingness to try."

Now I wanted to look at him even less. I pressed my forehead hard into the worn wood of the door. "You're a liar."

"Often, yes, but not right now."

My hand slipped from the knob but I grabbed it again, holding myself up, torn between running away from this thing that spoke as prettily and confidently as any fine gentleman. But he was no fine gentleman. He was . . . He was . . . "What *are* you?"

I opened my eyes slowly, but he had not moved. And his feet were normal again. Had he changed them in the face of my obvious disgust? Mr. Morningside brushed his hair back, though the perfect black curls needed no rearranging.

"Do you sincerely wish to know?"

"I don't know," I whispered truthfully. "I don't know."

"It's in the book, Louisa, should your curiosity resurface." He sighed, taking one small step toward me. "Stop cowering that way, it's upsetting."

I straightened, but slowly, refusing to shed tears and look even more the pathetic little fly. My hands were still pressed tightly to the door, and I had every intention of going that minute, to at least seek some shelter in the hayloft again, but it was then that Mrs. Haylam and the doctor emerged from the Red Room. I heard their soft conversation and watched them cross the portion of the corridor open to the foyer.

They were going to fetch the widow's body, and hers would not be the last.

"Rawleigh Brimble doesn't belong here, you know," I said, succeeding somehow in keeping the tremor from my voice.

"Who?"

My head flew up at that, and I scoffed. "Rawleigh . . . Lee Brimble. The young man. He's one of your *guests*."

"Oh." Mr. Morningside shrugged and crossed his arms. "Well, if he's one of my guests, then he belongs here and he will meet his end here; that is all but woven into the tapestry of fate."

"He hasn't done anything wrong! You've made a mistake."

He shook his head and squinted, studying me more carefully. Slowly, laughingly, he said, "I never make mistakes. He's here for a reason."

"No, no, he's a good person. It would be wrong to hurt him."
Of course Lee might have lied to me, but that seemed impossible. I had looked into his face as he told me of his guardian. The whole thing was a misunderstanding. An accident. "He doesn't belong on your twisted list."

"Why? Because you like him? Louisa, please, I implore you—be better than this."

"Than what?" I demanded, feeling bolder.

"A gullible little girl."

That only emboldened me further. "Do you know how to speak to anyone at all without being a condescending git?"

"Not really, no." He shrugged again, elegantly, and wandered closer. I recoiled, but he either didn't notice or pretended not to. A thin, mischievous smile spread across his face, and that, more than his proximity, frightened me. "But I'll entertain your theory, Louisa, and should you find proof that this Brimble boy is truly an innocent soul, then do bring it to my attention."

"You're serious. Do . . . You *will* listen to me if I can prove he isn't a killer?"

He nodded once, pressing his lips together.

"But why? I thought . . . I thought you never made mistakes."

"Because I'm beginning to like you, and because you remind me of someone I knew once. You're both bold as brass and stubborn to a fault. Not that I should be encouraging these things, but everyone has their weakness." He stopped a hand's width from me and pulled something from his cravat. It was a gold pin, shiny and perhaps the size of a shilling, and he offered it to me in his palm. "Or, of course, you could leave."

What?

"You said I couldn't! You said it was the book keeping me here!" My fingers itched to snatch the pin anyway. Even if this was a trick, I valued freedom more than I valued my dignity in that moment. And if it were true, if I could recover the books from under my bed and take them to trade . . . Only now he stood between me and my room, and the small fortune hiding under the mattress.

"That's still true. But these pins have always been used to navigate away from the binding ritual. Even those who bound themselves willingly occasionally needed to do work for us elsewhere, and this is what allows their passage." He pinched the pin, holding it up, waiting for me to extend my hand.

And I did. God help me, I did. I wanted to believe it was true, that I really wasn't tied forever to a place of murder and darkness. Even without the books to sell, I might be free. Coin could come later. The pin fell into my palm, unnaturally warm and unnaturally heavy.

"Careful; that warding pin belonged to Kit Marlowe. The Catholics didn't much care for his work for the Unworld. Stabbed in a bar fight, my right foot. He liked to eat and blaspheme. My kind of gentleman." Mr. Morningside cackled to himself, as if anything he had just said made a lick of sense. "The playwright," he clarified, arching a brow. "*Doctor Faustus?*

The Jew of Malta? Massacre at Paris? Good Lord, I thought they educated you at that girls' school."

"I know who Christopher Marlowe is," I muttered, staring at the gleaming pin in my hand. "I simply don't believe you."

"Shall I show you the foot trick again?" He chuckled, watching my expression crumple. "Believe me, Louisa, the pin was his. That I own such a pin and you now hold it is the smallest absurdity and wonder of the Unworld."

"Unworld . . . I saw that word in your book," I said, taking the pin and holding it close. "You're part of it, and so is Poppy with her screams and Mary with her spells."

"Just so."

"And this . . ." It still felt ridiculous, but I rolled the pin in my palm, studying it, looking at the small characters stamped into the gold and the serpent emblem behind the phrase. "*I am Wrath.*"

Mr. Morningside's smile deepened, a faraway look misting his eyes. "That's from *Doctor Faustus.* Quite proud of that speech—even let Marlowe use it for free. Well, for an ale, but that seems a cheap price, all told."

"You're having me on," I murmured, fastening the pin to my apron and feeling its weight more keenly. "You . . . You must be, yes? How old *are* you?"

"Still so full of questions even as you hold the key to your freedom." He sidestepped the question with a wink, eyes flitting to the door behind me and all that it symbolized. Then

Mr. Morningside leaned in, so close that I could feel his warm breath on my chin. "But what will you do? I thought your new friend was innocent. Will you stay to prove as much or take this gift and never look back?"

Chapter
Twenty-Two

ran. Hard. Fast. Testing my legs. Testing my strength. I am not proud of it, but God help me, I ran.

In that moment I flew. I flew out the door, between the topiaries, over the paving stones, across the lawn. Books forgotten, murder forgotten, Lee forgotten. Running farther, harder, faster, ignoring the stitch in my side and the twinge in my wrist as I pumped my arms, abandoning all dignity for the chance to escape. And the rush of excitement carried me far— far beyond the drive and the fence. The fence! I ran right past it, feeling no pain at all. Nothing and no one stopped me.

Nothing until I was perhaps a mile down the road, retracing the path I had taken to arrive at Coldthistle House just a scant few days ago. It felt like a lifetime had gone by, and more than that, it felt like so much had changed. *I* had changed. When the manse was simply a looming silhouette in the distance behind me, I slowed down and then walked, drinking deeply of the crisp, cool air.

I thought your new friend was innocent.

No . . . I had to push Henry Morningside's words out of my head. In fact, I had to shove his entire existence and memory out of my mind. My fingers, still scarred from touching the book in the attic, brushed the cravat pin stuck to my apron. I didn't dare remove it, afraid that without it the pain would come back. Must I wear it forever now? What would happen if it were stolen or lost?

Such thoughts—such doubts—must be eradicated along with all remembrance of Coldthistle House. What I had seen, I had not really seen. What I had felt was just the work of an overly enthusiastic imagination. What I had read was silly falsehood, a collection of dark madness written by a lunatic. None of it was real. It couldn't be. If it were, I would remember and I would hurt, and I would think of Lee's kind face as he said, "I believe you."

The clouds hung low above me, the terrible winds of yesterday now just a gentle breeze that ruffled my skirts and the long grass beside the road. I would not turn back, not now, not when I had this one chance to go. I would be better. I would be good. I would find some way to travel to America and start fresh, where not even the shadow of this place could linger in my mind. Distance would do the trick.

And so I walked. Midday came on, warming the fields. Nobody traveled the road, and the solitude felt wonderful. I wrapped my arms around myself and marched like a prisoner out of her cell.

. . . *He belongs here and he will meet his end here; that is all but woven into the tapestry of fate.*

I shut my eyes tightly, scolding myself for letting that monster's words creep back into my skull. And if he was right? If Lee's death was certain, then what could I do? How could I possibly prove what a crofter did or did not bake, or what nuts were or were not used with intent to kill? This was, firstly, none of my affair and, secondly, far outside my ability to settle.

Yet you didn't tell him everything, did you? You didn't tell him he, too, was marked for death.

None of my affair. Not my spill to clean up. I walked on, determined, trying to think instead of what I would do now that I had escaped. Food and shelter had to come first, but I was still a long way from Malton. I veered off into the fields, hopping the nearest fence, and followed the curve of the hill until it dipped back down into a shallow valley thick with violets. If I looked back I would see Coldthistle, and so I stubbornly turned my head away from it, traveling diagonally toward another rise in the landscape and what appeared to be a tiny cottage perched upon it.

As I neared, I watched a giant herd of sheep roll in from the far side of the cottage. They swarmed the house, kept in a near perfect circle by a dog nipping at their perimeter. The barking and bleating were almost soothing, a sweet pastoral counterpoint to the nightmare I had been living.

Then I saw the cloud.

Never had I seen a cloud so dark and dense before, and I stilled, watching it gather speed and size as it roared above me, all but filling the sky. Unnatural and black, it headed directly for me, coming from the direction of Coldthistle. And as it lowered itself, diving down, furious with sound and falling feathers,

I realized it was not a cloud at all but a horrible mass of crows. The noise was unbearable, thousands of shrieking, cawing creatures swooping toward my head. They gained speed, making one pass and circling over the cottage, turning, making a wide circle as they prepared to dive at me from behind.

I ran again, just as hard this time, pelting toward the cottage, saying a desperate prayer under my breath, pleading with powers greater than beasts and birds for the strength to outrun this menace. Bits of black feather rained down on me as they took another pass, so near now that I felt the beating of their wings on my head as they dived. One pecked my hair, pulling out a few strands painfully. Another stabbed at my ear, and I screamed, throwing my arms over my head, sobbing, knowing their next attempt would be the last.

How would it feel to be killed by a thousand crows? Pecked and shredded to ribbons like carrion long dead on the road. . . .

They were coming back around, but now I was so close to the cottage. The sheep dispersed in an explosion of woolly bodies, their bleats suddenly panicked as I charged through the herd. The dog yapped excitedly at my heels, then disappeared. As I careered toward the cottage door, I heard the beast turn and bark furiously at the birds.

I slammed hard into the door. It was made of sturdy wood, but it creaked from the impact. Locked. My fists pounded and pounded, sweat pouring down my neck and forehead as I glanced behind one last time to see the crows descending, flattening into a black, murderous spear.

"Let me in!"

They were coming, so close, so focused . . .

"Please, I beg of you! Let me in!"

I braced, knowing the rip and tear of a hundred hungry beaks would be upon me. The sheep had scattered. The dog placed itself in front of me as if to take the blow. Then I was soaring backward, tumbling into something soft and warm before the door slammed shut, protecting me.

The sound that came next was awful. I shook, listening to the birds not quick enough to change course crash into the wood. Some stuck like arrows in a target; others screamed before falling dead to the dirt.

"Not your birds, I reckon?"

Slowly, I picked myself up from the floor, still trembling and breathless. A snowy-haired man and a young woman watched me from the safety of a fire, their dog sniffing the door and then me curiously.

"N-No, not mine. You saved my life," I whispered. "Thank you."

"Oh no, thank you, my dear. Our pot will be full with those meaty buggers for a week," the old man said with a dark laugh. "Now sit, why don't you, and have a spot of ale. Yes, you'll sit and you'll tell us who you are and what business you have bringing ill omens to our door."

Chapter
Twenty-Three

The ale was strong and bitter and fortifying as it went down. I gulped it, perhaps greedily, both hands clamped tightly around the earthenware cup. All the while, I drew deeper inside myself, feeling crushed by the weight of their staring.

"I'm so sorry to trouble you." It was the third time in as many minutes that I had offered an apology. "I don't . . . I don't know how such a thing can happen."

Already I had told them my name but without telling them about the horrors of Coldthistle House, I could not tell them the truth and still expect to receive anything resembling hospitality.

"Strange occurrences all the time 'round here," the old man said. He hadn't given his own name, but there was something in his voice and his demeanor that made me want to trust him; he looked the way a kindly grandfather ought to, round-faced and soft, with wrinkled eyelids from smiling often. And I could hardly think ill of a person who saved me from a dreadful fate. It was then, with his face lit in yellows and golds by the fire, that I could see the film over his eyes. Blind. The speckled, furry Shetland sheepdog had gone to sit at his master's feet, and the man kept one hand always on the hound's head as if for guidance.

"Once the entire west field lay covered in those blasted crows. Couldn't sleep for the bloody racket they made. Next morning there was only a circle of them left, and not a one of them living."

"He says you grow accustomed to it," the girl said with a shrug. "But I don't think I ever will."

Her name was Joanna. She had given me the ale and a moistened cloth to clean the blood off my ear from where the bird had pierced the skin. She now sat next to the old man—who I assumed was her father or grandfather—dressed in sensible flannels, a long skirt, and worn boots. A chunky shawl the color of porridge was draped around her narrow shoulders. Her straw-blonde hair was plaited neatly in one braid over her shoulder.

"You've seen things like that before?" My ale was nearly gone, and I slowed down to savor the last few sips.

The old man nodded. He was dressed in typical shepherd's fashion, with a soft brimmed cap worn low over his eyes. "Strange omens, though we seem to get on all—"

"They say the Devil himself lives at Coldthistle House!" Joanna blurted out. She shrank when the old man snorted. "What? Swinton to Wykeham they say it. Circles of crows in the west field, serpents bubbling up under your feet in the vegetable garden, and last autumn half the pasture was naught but nightshade!"

The blind shepherd cleared his throat, turning his head toward the girl, and she fell quiet, looking down at her hands in her lap. "I only say it to warn her, Father. For no other reason."

"I know it, child, but she is already frightened enough. We aren't yet acquainted, are we? Perhaps she is not in need of a warning."

"Oh . . . Oh, indeed, I see what you mean. Did you come from there?" Joanna hopped up, hurrying to the pantry and fetching the carafe of ale. She filled my cup and then poured one for herself, sitting closer. She didn't seem to heed the little grunts of dissatisfaction her father gave. She propped her chin on her palm and leaned in, whispering, "Did you *see* him?"

Him. The Devil. She of course meant Mr. Morningside. The ale did not go down so easily on my next swallow. Surely, I had seen him, but could he really be called the Devil? And given all his evil and strangeness, would I want to risk associating myself with him in front of my hosts? I managed a queasy smile, swirling the ale in my cup.

"It's . . . true I came from there, but I had no dealings with the proprietor." What to say? And how much? "I went to take up employment as a maid, but I found the conditions untenable."

"They beat you?" the man asked. Some of the tension in his face had lifted, but his daughter remained the kinder of the two.

"No, nothing like that," I said. He could not see the bandage on my wrist, but surely his daughter could. Perhaps I could win their sympathy and subsequently their aid. It never hurt to be pitied. "I escaped such a place. A school, Pitney; perhaps you have heard of it? They favored mortification of the flesh as a means of punishment. I hoped never to return, but now I find myself utterly lost."

The blind man stood, and, hand still clutched in the dog's fur, made his way to the fire to stoke it. "Will they come looking for you?"

"Who?" I asked softly.

"Take your pick, dear," he said with a dark laugh. "The school or the folk at Coldthistle. You can stay the night and collect yourself, but I'll not endanger Joanna nor my flock."

"Father, she is half dead with fright and injured! You will be in danger from *me* if you turn out this poor lamb now," the girl said. She shot a cross look at his back.

"I can make myself useful," I murmured. "There is no need for charity."

"Nonsense! Of course there is a need!" Joanna jumped up again and hurried over to her father, touching a small hand to his shoulder. "He is a good man, my father, only he worries that people take advantage when you intervene in their lives. Indeed, he was softer once and can be again; it simply requires a nudge or two from me."

"That's enough of your nudging," he grumbled, but when he laughed it was lighter. Sweeter. I could not place their accents. Certainly they were not locals. A simple shepherd's family would speak with a stronger Yorkshire lilt. "I can speak for myself, child, and speak I will."

Sighing, but only half seriously, he turned at the hip and looked in my direction. For a moment, it felt as if he could really see me sitting there. "You can stay, but I must wonder—are you really all alone in this world? Have you nowhere to go? No family? No friends?"

Lee's name stuck like a burr in my throat.

I stared down into my ale again, and Joanna drifted from the fireside to my own, taking my good wrist lightly and squeezing. "There, now, no need to be shy. It was an honest question, and not meant in malice I'm sure."

"My grandparents bought my place at that infernal school so they could be rid of me. There was . . . one person who was kind to me, I know not if I could call him a friend . . ." *You could, but then the guilt would be too much.* "But there is little he can do now, and I am on my own. I do not seek pity. It is a fact that does not frighten me."

"Oh, but it should." The shepherd squinted at me, and I froze, aware suddenly that I was blindly trusting these folk when such mistakes in the past had cost me dearly. Had not Coldthistle seemed like a blessing at first, too? I pulled my hand from the girl's grip, but the man simply smiled at us. "A sheep far from the flock is vulnerable. Should be brought back in where it's safe. A solitary life is a meal for wolves."

"That is not our business, Father," Joanna scolded softly. "And here, you cannot see, but she has a lovely gold pin! It could be bartered for passage, I'm sure. Surely it would get you as far as London and a modest room."

I reached instinctively for the pin, closing my fist around it. "No, this pin has . . . It . . . Well, you see, it has sentimental value. I cannot be parted from it."

"Joanna." The man let go of the dog, turning and facing us directly. "Big Earl needs feeding. Take him out, will you? There's a lamb's knuckle in the smoking shed for him."

He was deliberately sending her away, and I braced, knowing whatever came next would not be good. I eyed the door, ready to bolt, watching as the young woman pursed her lips in frustration and whistled, the dog snapping to attention and following her out the door. After it closed, I could hear her kicking aside the corpses of dead birds.

"I'll go," I volunteered, standing. "I've obviously trespassed on your kindness."

"The offer to stay the night still stands, dear," he said. He took a few careful steps toward me, finding the table and holding it for balance. "But we've not the space or means for another child here. I took Joanna in after her mother met her God, and I would never call her a burden, but this is a humble trade with humble earnings." Then he paused and lowered his head, and again it felt as if he could regard me clearly through his blindness. "She said you wear a gold pin . . ."

"I do."

"Describe it for me," he said. "What sort of price would it fetch? We might be able to make a trade."

"It's gold, with a bit of filigree and a serpent symbol," I told him. The ale was loosening my tongue now and dampening my wits. Even with a hazy mind, the inscription felt too strange to share. What would this old shepherd think of a lone, wandering girl with *I am Wrath* emblazoned on her one possession of value?

"Is that all, Louisa?"

"That is the pin exactly," I lied more or less steadily. "But I cannot and will not give it to you."

The shepherd let out a short bark of a laugh. "You think me greedy."

"Not at all," I replied. I touched the pin again, holding it, feeling its unnatural inner warmth. "You may love Joanna, but she *is* a burden. So am I. All young women of no fortune and no family are. Doubly so the poor, family-less girl who is changeable and ill-humored."

"Heavens, my dear, you are too harsh on yourself," he said, pulling out a chair and sitting down slowly.

I set my jaw, resentful of his pity. "The harshness of a thing does not change its veracity."

"Something weighs heavily upon you," he said, closing his eyes. Again his face was soft and appealing, like a sun-kissed apple. With surprising deftness, he poured himself ale and then more for me. Gradually, I sat, too. The sound of Joanna's voice and the flock's bleating bled pleasantly through the walls. "Once, I had a mind to be a man of the clergy. Could always tell when a soul needed lifting. 'Tis not a gift any man should covet—sensing so much pain takes a heavy toll. A sheep far from the flock is vulnerable, and this loneliness has made you cold."

We were both quiet for a long time, and I could feel the ale muddling my thoughts, making my tongue even bolder than usual. "It was careless parents and hard-hearted teachers that made me cold, and I'll be Queen of England before I shoulder the blame for their cruelty."

The shepherd nodded, adjusting his woolen cap. "You mentioned a friend, and someone gave you that fine gold pin. Sentimental value. You have folk, I think. Even if you don't want them, might they want you?"

Being wanted. It was not a feeling I was at all familiar with. I knew in my marrow that I did not care to be wanted by Mr. Morningside, but Lee had been kind. He had believed me. Mary, too, had accepted me, as had the rest of the house. *Just because they want me does not mean I must return the sentiment.*

He waited patiently for an answer, which was good, because it took me quite a while to conjure one. When I escaped Pitney, my one and only friend there, Jenny, had been the one to create the diversion while I slipped out the window and fled into the night. She had faked a spasm, and I had convinced her to do it with a promise that I would find a way to rescue her, too.

There would be no rescue. Pitney was far behind me now. But Coldthistle . . .

"My friend . . . I think he might be in danger. He needs my help. It's not the loneliness that irks me, shepherd, it is knowing I might have aided him somehow and instead did nothing."

"Ah." He sipped his ale and touched his cap again. "Faith without works is dead," he then said. "Will you stay the night with us, dear?"

I put down my cup, feeling the weight of my worries crush down harder and then, unexpectedly, abate. "No, shepherd. Thank you for your hospitality, for saving me, but I believe I'm needed elsewhere."

Chapter
Twenty-Four

The Ferryman of Calabar

Few have had the extreme pleasure of watching an authentic Ferryman at work. Well, few are willing to pay the exorbitant price such practitioners charge for a glimpse of their craft. There are untold variations on the name, but "Ferryman" has always struck me as both the most descriptive and poetic of the bunch.

There is a natural ability necessary to do the work, of course, though the average charlatan or boastful shaman will claim they are capable of similar magicks. The Ferryman must work in darkness and secrecy, and only by the light of a blood moon. I was never given the woman's name—I found her through discreet inquiry in the outer markets of Calabar, and then only through a young Nigerian adventurer I had met some years ago on a voyage to study the canis infernalis *in distant Zanzibar. Olaseni scrounged up our Ferryman through a complicated system of symbols left on doors, then papers slipped to market runners and urchins, and then at last, after two weeks of idleness in Calabar, we received a message from the Ferryman herself. We were to find the water's edge just before midnight and follow the calls of the red-necked nightjars.*

It was a hot night, the shoreline thick with flies and swarms of bats diving for them. Tall ships swayed in the harbor, sails tied, their naked masts jutting out of the water like the skeletons of giant beasts. The sandy earth sank beneath our feet as we waited for each nightjar call, then went a little farther, then waited, then farther. . . . It was a rare and coveted blood moon, the light of which dyed the sands and the bay a deep, rusted vermillion. Olaseni was a slight young man and moved with amazing speed and silence. I struggled to keep pace, following the flash of a blue scarf tied around his waist. To our left, the water; to our right, the foreboding sprawl of so many tall and interlocked trees. We must have waited for a dozen ringing calls of ta-tweet ta-tweet ta-tweet *before we stumbled upon a dirt path that cut into the expansive coastal forest.*

Her name was Idaramfon. She complimented my Efik, and I complimented her English. She worked out in the open, sheltered by a few low-hanging fronds. A small fire had been stoked at the edge of the clearing and a child tended it, his back to us. Idaramfon wore a simple white tunic, clean and pure, a red-and-black sash twisted into a kind of rope she let hang loose around her neck. Her clean-shaven head glowed like a ruby under the blood moon.

The dead body of a young boy was laid out in front of her on a bed of grass. He was washed and naked, his expression one of peace. There were no visible marks upon the body, and I could surmise only that some unseen illness had taken his life.

"Not afraid of death or bats, I hope, stranger," she said with a smile.

"I have seen my share of death, Ferryman. And as for bats? Fascinating creatures" came my reply. I checked my notes, which were shockingly easy to read in the bright moonlight. "They are not to be feared. Are they your chosen . . . vessel? Is that the word you prefer to use?"

She nodded, and as she did, a few of those very bats swooped down to join us. They landed on one of the low fronds, two dark brown creatures that were, quite frankly, grotesquely ugly. Their faces were wrinkled and their lower jaws pronounced, giving them a hungry, feral look. Still, I smiled to see them. They were part of the ritual, after all, and that was what I had come to witness. Perhaps the hideous things were a poetic choice, given that they would serve as waypoint between life and death for the soul, until someone or something chose to set them free.

A dense, cold miasma surrounded us, emanating from the young woman. Whispers chased around us, a soft tornado of voices that vanished the instant you tried to decipher the words. Chilled beads of sweat traced down my temples, the transition from hot to cold air so sudden it left me breathless and numb.

Her brown eyes glowed scarlet, then redder than that, hot coals that pulsed white in the moonlight. Next to me, Olaseni whimpered. I looked into Idaramfon's burning eyes and a hundred lost souls stared back at me, challenging and provoking me to gaze on and on, to stay fixed in that spot and perish there so I might join them. Later, when we returned to his home, I asked Olaseni what he thought of the experience. He described it thus and with haunted eyes: it was like I could feel where my soul and body met, I could feel the seam, and then I felt that seam begin to give and tear.

In the clearing, her eyes red rimmed with silver, Idaramfon the Ferryman whispered, "When I tell you to close your mouth and eyes, strange one, do so. I intend to ferry away only one soul this night, and it should not be yours."

Rare Myths and Legends: The Collected Findings of
H. I. Morningside, *page 233*

hijioke and Mary worked side by side on the lawn, both of them filling in holes as the orange glow of dusk grew all around us. A passel of crows had apparently survived the chase and now sat grouped on the manor's roof, preening and fidgeting. By the time I left the shepherd's hut, Joanna had cleared the dead birds from the stoop, though their feathers had gathered like black snow.

It was Chijioke who saw me first, jamming his shovel into the soft earth and leaning on it. He shielded his eyes and then waved, gesturing me over. I had taken the road back to Coldthistle, deeming it safer than the fields, where more of those ravens might be hovering. Two wagons waited in the circle drive outside the manse, and one was being loaded by Foster and George Bremerton, a long wooden slat with a draped figure balanced between them. Mrs. Eames. Somehow it made me slightly gratified to think she wouldn't be buried right there on the grounds.

"Where are they taking her?" I asked, stopping near them and watching the somber men hoist the corpse into the wagon.

"Derridon," Chijioke answered. "It's a village just north of here. I expect her family will have the body sent overseas, or maybe to London." He didn't seem interested in watching the loading, instead keeping his eye fixed on me. "I heard they took a wee bit of umbrage at you finding the lady. Did you think to flee?"

Glancing between him and Mary, noticing their slumped shoulders and hooded eyes, their collective sheepishness became utterly apparent. They thought I had run because I was being blamed for the murder. It seemed simultaneously ridiculous and endearing, but I was in no mood to tease.

And even if I did not trust them, I had no intention of treating them like buffoons. "No, I ran because this place frightens me. I don't want any part in your . . . whatever it is you think you're doing."

I saw Mary's eyes settle on the pin on my apron. "Then why did you come back? You were gone for hours, lass. We thought you gone for good."

"A quite literal murder of crows chased me into a shepherd's cottage," I said tartly. "And there I had a sit and a think, and I decided to come back for Rawleigh Brimble."

"He does seem like a nice boy," Mary said, hugging her shovel and leaning on it. "Only Mr. Morningside doesn't make mistakes, Louisa; he must be here for a reason. I know it's hard to accept, but even nice people can be rotten on the inside. Haven't you ever bitten into an apple you thought looked delicious only to find out it was sour? It's horrible, and folk are tricky like that all the time."

"Rawleigh isn't a rotten apple," I snapped. "He's just . . . confused. And he's my friend."

They shared a look, one I couldn't quite interpret. Chijioke ran a hand over his square jaw and frowned, an expression that foretold yet more scolding. "Right, then."

"I'm sorry?" Where was the fervent devotion to Mr. Morningside's word?

He shrugged and went back to filling holes. "Stranger things've happened. If you're right, I'm sure Mr. Morningside will find out in the end. What's the boy supposed to have done?"

"Killed his guardian," I said, waiting for Mary to interject with support for her master. But she, too, looked thoughtful, even receptive. "The whole thing was an accident. Some violent reaction to a nut or some such. The important part is that Rawleigh didn't mean for anything bad to happen to his guardian. I think he truly loved and respected the man."

"Then maybe he belongs in the Unworld!"

I nearly leapt out of my skin, spinning to find Poppy and her hound right behind me. She did a tiny wave and then pointed at Chijioke. "You're ruining all of Bartholomew's hard work!"

"The holes are unsightly, Poppy," he muttered with a roll of his eyes. "And dangerous. I've nearly broken a leg twice this week!"

"He's practicing!" she pouted.

"What do you mean?" I asked, leaning down a little to address the pigtailed girl.

Poppy stuck her lip out and crossed her arms over her light blue frock. "He's just a little one, but he needs to practice now or he'll never get better and never get back to the hot place! I don't want him to go away, but it's what all his kind must do. And so he *needs* to practice, *Chijioke*."

And then she stuck her tongue out and blew.

"Not the dog," I said with a sigh. "About the Unworld. What did you mean precisely?"

"Oh!" She gurgled with laughter and patted her pup's head. "Lee could be one of us. Never had it turn out that way before, but Mary and Chijioke are very, very smart, and if they believe you, then it could just be a twisty-twisty sort of thing."

"He seems perfectly normal," I said, then winced. "Meaning . . . just . . ."

"Don't worry," Mary murmured charitably, but her cheeks were red. "We know what you meant."

"Normal is a funny word. I like the way it sounds." Poppy giggled again and swatted at Mary's shovel, then kicked at Chijioke's. "He could be . . . a dark Fae or a wraith or a dead caller or a Ferryman or the thing Mary is that I'm still convinced isn't real words at all or a shadow drinker or, or . . ."

"We get the idea, Poppy," Chijioke said, moving his shovel out of her reach.

"He's just a boy." This was another absurdity in an ever growing list. "A boring, human boy just like I'm a boring, human girl." They stared in oddly tense silence at me, silence that was broken only when I noticed the front door of the manse opening behind them. Lee himself emerged, hurrying over to his uncle and the wagon. Then he stopped, finding us clustered not far away on the lawn.

Nobody spoke as he loped up to us, dressed in a patched traveling coat with a light gray piping and leather gloves. He beamed at me, clapping his hands together as he all but hopped into the spot next to me. "What a delight. The housekeeper said you had departed but didn't specify a length of absence. I hadn't thought to see you again so soon."

"Hello, boring human boy," Poppy said, waving.

"Oh, um, hello," he replied, chuckling nervously. "We're headed into town briefly. Somewhere called Derridon. I don't know it, but apparently there's a rather good undertaker there. I thought you might want to come along, Louisa. I've been desirous of your company."

Softly, Mary cleared her throat, tugging the others away to give us privacy. I blushed, knowing exactly how foolish this all looked. *Desirous of your company.* If I admitted to myself what that sounded like, then I would have to accept that Lee was not just trying to befriend me but *court* me.

"I can't do that," I whispered. "How would it look? I'm just a servant here."

He leaned in and winked, and the proximity made that wink more potent and deadly. "For me? Can't you make something up? I know! You're helping with the delivery, or, I don't know, you're the clever one."

The others were watching us, and I couldn't tell if he or the audience made me more uncomfortable. Regardless, I knew what had to be done. Had I not come back to help him? He must be warned. And maybe I could go. Maybe we could get on that wagon and leave and never look back.

I took his sleeve and pulled him toward me, lowering my voice to a tense whisper. "I'll find a way to go with you, but if I cannot or they stop me, promise me that you won't come back here. Go to Derridon if you must, but then hire a coach and leave. Leave, Lee, and get as far away from Coldthistle House as you can."

Chapter
Twenty-Five

The Enduring Mystery of the Lost Order

In the vastness of my travels, in Syria, in Jerusalem, in Venice, Rome, and the catacombs of Paris, I have come across an unnamed sect that perturbs me more than murderous banshees or hounds from hell. I say unnamed, but I know that to be untrue—they have a name, and indeed it must be of great import, because at each site of their worship, the name of their order has been scrubbed. If it is not burned or painted over it is laboriously chipped out of the stone, leaving behind just the stray glimpse of a letter here and there. This strikes one as a senseless waste of time and effort, to chisel the name and spells of your order into a wall or floor, only to deface it immediately upon completion.

So wrote the bard, "What's in a name?"

Beyond erasing the name itself, they take no pains to erase the evidence of their being there—misshapen skulls used for ritual purposes, withered corpses of red-and-white-striped serpents knotted up and mutilated. Even fragments of their incantations are left behind, almost brazenly, as if to taunt. They praise Mixcoatl, Gurzil, Maahes, Laran . . . Gods of destruction and war, but to what end?

Other demonologists have suggested that these cultists are nothing more than random amateurs, unorganized rabble playing at spell work and magicks, that they have no larger purpose in the study of the strange. I must disagree. There is order to their madness, and order signifies purpose. Purpose signifies a goal.

Rare Myths and Legends: The Collected Findings of
H. I. Morningside, *page 98*

hey finished loading the wagons as the sun dipped below the horizon. Lanterns glowed on the lawn of Coldthistle, the grim-streaked glass dousing their lights until they were nothing but weak puddles in the coming darkness.

I took advantage of the shadows, volunteering to help Mary and Chijioke with filling holes until the wagons looked ready to depart. Then I offered to take the shovels back to the barn, a kindness which they accepted happily. Chijioke would be going with the men to Derridon, and Mary was needed in the kitchen. I might have simply strode off to the wagons with Lee, but I had tried a brazen approach once and had a flock of crows after me, sent by Mr. Morningside or whoever else, either as warning or punishment. This time a quiet, subtle approach suited better.

I needed to escape Coldthistle, but not before knowing Lee was safe. Even if I managed to get to America, an ocean of separation would not save me from the guilt of his death.

In the barn, I decided to stash the shovels and sneak back into the hayloft to retrieve Mr. Morningside's book. I had considered leaving it, but Mr. Morningside was right about one thing—I was still curious. Curious to know if there was any truth to what he said of the larger world and Unworld, curious to read more of his ridiculous tales even if I only half believed them. And without finishing the thing completely, I had no idea whether it might instruct me, directly or otherwise, on how to undo the book in the attic's binding power. It seemed foolish to rely forever on a mere pin.

I pulled down the stairwell to the loft and scurried up into the cozy little hideaway, stopping dead when I found it occupied.

Mr. Morningside. He flipped through his own book casually, his back to me, then slowly he turned, lifting one black brow as he regarded me over the tattered cover.

"Do you know, it's extremely rude that Spicer didn't bother even to take this with him. Cad. I suppose I shouldn't expect anything less from an Upworlder." He snapped the book shut and held it out to me, the picture of casual benignity.

I didn't reach for it. This felt, like everything else, like one of his traps.

"How was your little jaunt across the countryside? Do anything interesting? Bird watching, perhaps?"

"You sent those crows," I said, feeling the seconds tick by at an alarming rate. The wagons would leave without me if I didn't make haste. "They *attacked* me. I thought you said I could leave."

"Of course you can. I gave you the pin, didn't I? Anyway, how do you know the birds were after you, mm? Maybe they were meant for that old fool in the shed."

"You know about the shepherd?" I asked, eyeing the small loft window. It was fully dark now. I needed to hurry.

"Our dear, dear neighbor. One of his stupid sheep will wander onto the property every once in a great while. So, yes, I've dealt with him. Looks rather like an undercooked pudding, don't you think?"

"He was kind to me," I said, lifting my chin defiantly. "And he isn't harboring a house full of murderers."

"Then perhaps you should go live in that dirt hovel with him. I'm sure you would find it incredibly stimulating. Sheep! What a thrill. I hope your little heart can take the excitement." He took a step toward me, grinning his white, toothy grin, extending the book until it grazed my arm. "Take it. I have a hundred of these cluttering up my closet."

"Nobody wanted to buy a collection of fairy tales for children?" It was a gamble, but perhaps I could anger him enough to make him leave. If he stayed, there would be no getting to Lee and seeing him safely away. Yet the jab only made him snort. I snatched the book out of his grasp and crossed my arms over it.

"Gotten to the chapter on Changelings yet, Louisa?" he asked, squinting.

"No. It sounds insipid."

"Appropriate, then." He chuckled at my blank expression and bent almost in half, checking the loft window and clucking his tongue. "It appears your ride to Derridon is about to leave. You should scurry along now."

My ride? I couldn't help it; I gawped at him, the book nearly sliding out of my grasp. "Why should I go to Derridon?" I asked, even as my heart leapt with the possibilities.

"There's something not aboveboard about that George Bremerton person," Mr. Morningside said, straightening. He cocked his head to the side, golden eyes roaming the ceiling. "He came with his nephew to investigate some boring claim of inheritance, but he has done nothing but flirt with the dearly departed Mrs. Eames and poke about the house. If he's so eager to rob that boy of his money, then why not try harder to get it in Brimble's hands in the first place? No, something does not smell right, if you take my meaning. There's no good reason for Bremerton to go to Derridon this evening, and I want to know why he's suddenly so keen to go. You can help me with that."

He was moving too quickly. Of course it was a possibility, and yes, the house did seem to attract villains, but this seemed like an extraordinary effort just to swindle his nephew. And yet I hadn't liked him from the first, had I? My head began to hurt. No, no, no, I simply disliked him because he was exactly the sort of rich bastard I could steal from easily. This had to be a ploy of some kind. . . . A distraction. A way to pit me and Lee against one another.

"I won't spy for you," I said, backing away toward the loft ladder.

"Who said anything about spying?" Mr. Morningside asked. He held up his hands innocently, but I knew better. "I thought your friend Lee Brimble was innocent. If his uncle has designs on the young man's fortune, then surely you must want to protect him. I only want to know if my suspicions about his uncle are correct. You were ever so keen to prove Brimble's innocence. Has that changed?"

"It hasn't," I said, turning away from him. "Maybe he and I will just go, have you thought of that?"

"There's nothing to think about. If he belongs at Coldthistle, he will be there. Nothing short of a miracle will prevent that." Mr. Morningside shrugged and strolled toward the ladder, crowding me. His proximity made my skin crawl, and yet I could not move, his orbit as repellent as it was irresistible. I hated him, and still I wanted him to say more. Reveal more. How could he have such power over people? How could he know of books and curses and an Unworld that moved like an evil shadow beneath our own?

I glanced up at him, fuming into his catlike eyes. "Then perhaps I am that miracle."

At that, he burst out laughing. "You?" he asked when he had recovered, wiping invisible tears from his cheeks. "Are you a miracle, little Louisa, or are you a *curse*?" He lowered his voice and his head, bringing his lips close to my ear and finishing his thought in a throaty whisper. "I think we both know the answer to that."

"Sir? Sir? Mr. Morningside?" It was Chijioke calling from underneath us, his voice booming through the timbers.

"Up here." Mr. Morningside removed himself to a safe

distance and smiled at me once more. "I think that's your cue, Louisa, unless of course you'd like to stay and chat a while longer?"

"No," I said, disappearing down the ladder. I refused to look at him anymore. I refused to be snared. "I'm leaving, Mr. Morningside, and I won't be back."

Chapter
Twenty-Six

hijioke helped me into the back of the wagon he would drive to Derridon. I inched around to the right bench, fixed to the floor. A second bench lay on the opposite side of the wagon bed, and between that and me lay the body of the widow, wrapped in a heavy sheet. The floor of the wagon was caked with dried bird shit.

"I'd rather sit in the carriage with the others," I said softly, letting only my tiptoes touch the floor. Now it would be almost impossible to convince Lee to go away from Coldthistle forever, with or without me. Still, going was better than nothing. I had to make sure he didn't return to the house. Even boosted to this height, I was only slightly above Chijioke's eye level. He wore a heavy woolen coat now and a chunky knitted scarf.

"Mr. Bremerton requested privacy for him and his nephew," he replied, also in a whisper. "For now he's a guest and must be accommodated. There's no room for you on my bench, lass. With you lot and the widow's body, I barely have room for this week's supply crate up front. Just keep your head about you, aye? The doctor isn't to be trusted. None of them are."

"I trust Lee," I shot back. "He's not like them. And besides, the doctor stood up for me."

Chijioke shook his head and waited until Dr. Merriman arrived to step up into the wagon bed. The back was latched shut and Chijioke ground his jaw, waiting to speak until we locked eyes. "Think what you must, Louisa; just remember what I said. Give a shout if you need me."

He stalked away into the darkness, and for a moment I lost sight of him as he passed out of our lantern's safe glow and around to the horses. There was an old blanket on the bench, and I slipped it over my lap, trying to keep back a shiver.

Foster called to the horses in the carriage ahead of us, and I heard the crack of a whip as they started off into the night. We followed, and I thought longingly of the warmth inside the carriage. God, how much had changed since the last time I had been inside it. That was less than a week ago, yet I felt so different, as if the whole world had been tipped on its side. Innocence could die in the blink of an eye. I had been so eager to get to Coldthistle, and now I could not wait another minute to leave it all behind. I would survive the drafty ride for what was on the other end of it.

With a friend, I reminded myself. This was my chance to get us both away from Mr. Morningside and his evil plots. It would probably require leaving Lee's uncle behind. Whatever his nephew said, what grown man would believe my story? He would call me hysterical and silly, and perhaps poison Lee against me.

If he wasn't already doing that now. *Requested privacy.* That did not bode well. He was doing his best to separate us, but why? Did he sense that we were becoming close?

"You look troubled, young miss."

The wagons turned out of the drive, wheels crunching over stone and gravel, lanterns squeaking on hinges as the motion rocked them and us back and forth. I had curled up like a dead thing on the dirty bench, and I turned my head with a bleak smile for the doctor. At once, the road turned rough and uncomfortable, the rains ruining any chance at a smooth ride.

"Traveling by night always leaves me unsettled," I lied. The night did not scare me, not anymore, not now that I knew far scarier things than darkness existed.

"Fear not. I have some skill with a pistol," he said with a chuckle, "and not *just* the doctor's knives. Foster, too, must have some martial training, and Mr. Bremerton mentioned at tea that he's quite handy with fist and saber. Boxed in his youth, apparently, and spent time in the Levant and the Americas."

I nodded, pretending to be heartened. The chill under the blanket persisted, and my eye drifted always back to the wrapped bundle between the doctor and me. It seemed only a concept, that a dead woman should be so close to me. The corpse did not smell, and, wrapped up like that, she was more like a carpet or a package than a once-living thing.

"How quickly it all can change," I murmured.

It was a surprise that the doctor could even hear me over the noise of being rattled around in the back of a supply wagon.

"The beauty of life lies in its fleetingness," he said seriously, closing a hand over his heart. He was a truly ridiculous fellow, but more palatable than the Colonel at least. "I hope you are not overly troubled by our . . . somewhat unusual travel arrangements."

"I will find a way to endure," I replied. I wondered if he could even hear me over the commotion of the wheels as they clattered over the bumpy road.

I made the mistake of glancing up at him, only to find that he was regarding me intently. Intensely. His expression was one of deep fondness, as if he looked upon an old friend and not a young girl who was completely strange to him. I shifted, pulling the blanket more tightly around myself. Then I pretended to put my head back and sleep, yet still I felt his leaden gaze upon me.

"You know, you look just like an angel that way. So peaceful. Innocent."

My eyes snapped open in alarm. "I am no angel, sir, just a tired servant."

"No, that's true, you are no angel." He chuckled, running his forefinger over the dark smudges of his mustache, outlining it. "One must wonder if you really did do in the widow."

"I beg your pardon?" I wanted to disappear under the blanket, or perhaps throw him out the back of the wagon. The road flattened out, and Coldthistle became a small speck behind us. Still, I could see the shadows that flitted among the windows, the Residents coming to fervent life with the fall of night. I glanced to my right, to the drawn curtain and Chijioke beyond it.

"Oh, the others think you were jealous of her, of her beauty and wealth, but I doubt you would sink to murder over such pettiness," he said, still stroking his mustache. "You seem an intelligent girl. Did you happen upon her letter? Did you know she intended to swindle those men blind?"

"I found her exactly as you saw her," I replied quickly. "Her plot had nothing to do with me. Why should I care?"

Dr. Merriman nodded slowly, but his stare intensified. "Then you *are* innocent of her death."

"God above, of *course* I am!"

The wagon wove hard from side to side, tossed by the uneven ground. That was the wrong thing to say. The doctor smiled at me and moved, quickly, darting from his bench to mine, stepping over the widow easily with his long legs. He sat down next to me. Close. Too close. I remembered then his hand on my leg in the Red Room, and the frost of the nighttime air turned perilously cold. How long was the ride to Derridon?

"True innocence is so rare," he said, and I recoiled at the sultry note in his voice. He no longer regarded me with that odd but endurable fondness. His intent had sharpened, his breath heavy and sour on my shoulder. "My young girl was innocent, too. You remind me of her—my daughter—the same dark hair and dark eyes . . ."

I scrambled for the right thing to say. The right distraction. "What is she like?'

"Not very clever, but trusting and good. She always listened to her father. Always did as she was told." He sighed wistfully.

"Until one day she didn't. I always wondered how it came to pass. . . . How a good, loving child could change into a sullen chit too important for her father, too important for all the world."

The doctor sighed again, but now he sounded disappointed.

"It might be that innocence is a candle; it can be blown out short or it can burn down to nothingness, but it is destined one way or another to die." He shook his head and placed that dreaded hand on my thigh, and I felt my spirit wither at the touch. God, Chijioke was right—and curse him, Mr. Morningside was right. These people drawn to Coldthistle were rotten to the core. "For a long time I blamed her mother, but no, Catarina chose her own path. She chose another man above me and was never the same again."

"Please," I said in a choked whisper. "Could you remove your hand . . ."

"I don't think so." He tightened his grip, fingers biting through blanket and skirts and into my flesh. "I buried her with my own two hands, you know. Washed the body. Dressed the body. Digging the grave took much longer than I anticipated, but it was worth it, to do it all, to be the only one alone with her in the end."

I swallowed hard and looked up at the ceiling. Perhaps he was just a lost and grieving father. This moment would pass once he collected himself. I would survive it. "You must miss her terribly."

"Every single moment, yes."

"If it upsets you so, then we need not speak of—"

"It helps to talk about her," he interrupted. His dark brown eyes filled with tears. "There is sadness, yes, and bitterness. Rage. Regret. . . . So much regret."

"I'm sure you did everything a father could," I said weakly. A reliable voice in the back of my mind insisted I did not want to know how the girl had died.

The roughness of the road and the way it rattled us made my jaw ache.

Dr. Merriman rocked back and forth, his hand still tight around my thigh like a vise. His expression relaxed after a moment, and he patted my leg. It felt as if he might veer from this upsetting conversation, but then he looked at me once more and I felt my heart stop.

A feral dog looked like that. Hungry. Blind, hungry, and mad. And though he smiled, I sensed no joy in it, only fixation. "You could be like her. Like the good Catarina. You could be obedient and sweet, never placing another man above your father."

"I . . . I'm certain your daughter is irreplaceable."

The laugh he gave was indistinguishable from a sob. "You have no idea what it's like. You couldn't know . . . what it's like to make someone. To make another person! It is heaven and hell in one, for the love you bear them is painful. Every lie they tell, every scrape they incur, it wounds you. They are your flesh, but they do not act as your flesh. You cannot control them; I could not control her. You cannot understand it, young Louisa, how it feels to fail that way."

I made my face a blank mask of submission. *Do not smile. Do not frown.* Even the slightest hint of mockery or dissent felt like it might plunge him deeper into this melancholy. His hand became wet with sweat, a dampness that seeped through the blankets and my skirts to my skin. I gulped down a shake of revulsion.

"I failed her. I failed myself. I made a body with my own body and she turned wild and strange. In her last days I hardly recognized the soft, sweet girl who once sat in my lap and sang lullabies. My father beat me, oh God, did he beat me! But I never laid a finger on her, never until she became a stranger. Your own flesh and blood should never become a stranger to you."

Coldthistle was out of view now, swallowed by the night and a light mist that rolled in off the moors. Its vanishing frightened me more than I cared to admit; we traveled through the night in what felt like a sea of fog and shadow, unanchored, adrift until we reached Derridon.

If I reached Derridon.

My thigh ached, a cramp spreading out from where he squeezed my veins shut.

"Sir, you're hurting my leg."

The doctor rambled on, perspiration making his skin glisten. The wagon thumped into another crater in the road. "I created her flesh and it spoiled. There was only one way open to me: to take that flesh back in and try again."

"Take . . . the flesh back in," I repeated in a horrified whisper.

"You recoil, sweet girl, but like the tribes of New Guinea, I have sought to ferry Catarina's soul on to another generation. I am the vessel and I carry her now within me, as I did before she was born into this world." He looked over my shoulder at the wall with a dreamy expression. That thoughtful smile soon crumbled, and he turned his attention back to me, nostrils flaring, jaw tense. "Was I wrong to take her life? I know not. Was I wrong to consume her? Who can say. . . . I regret raising her poorly. I regret taking early signs of impudence as nothing more than childish whimsy. And now I think on it, I see that I must take another for my daughter. Her soul is tainted. It was not innocent when it left her body."

Welts were rising underneath his fingernails. My leg throbbed. I felt his mood twist a moment too late and I called out, pushing at the doctor's shoulders and flinging myself away toward the other bench.

"Chijioke!" I tried to scream, but it died in my throat, a blow to the back of my head making me choke and sputter and fall to the floor. My vision blurred, the white droppings on the boards under my fingers bleeding together until the wood looked pure ivory. Scrambling, I managed to hoist myself up onto the bench and gasp for air.

He grabbed my ankle and pulled, viciously, and I flailed, nails scratching down the bench as I fought for purchase and lost. *Kick!* I commanded my legs. *Kick, damn you!* But my body was weak, my muscles responding lazily.

"Chijioke—" I tried again, but it came out as no more than a rasp.

The doctor clobbered me again with his fists, and I coughed, lashing out once more with my feet. My heel slammed into his rib cage and he reeled back, but only for a moment. His hat had fallen off in the commotion, flying out the back of the wagon, sucked into the foggy night. Merriman was upon me again, throwing me around, slamming me against one wall of the wagon and then tossing me wherever I might land.

The corpse of Mrs. Eames broke my fall, but only a little, and I coughed, feeling sick and shivery all over. I could hardly see, the punches to my head making me feel dizzy and distant, as though my thoughts and my will to fight skipped away out of reach, abandoning me to listless rolling and moaning. There had to be something I could do; I simply had to breathe. Breathe and fight. I pulled in a shuddering breath, rallying just as Merriman dropped to his knees next to me and snatched up my kicking legs, pulling off his cravat and using it to bind them together.

"It was exhilarating, I admit," he whispered, tongue poking out as he tightened the silk around my ankles. My throat was closing up with panic, Chijioke's name just a thought that I could not possibly turn into a shout. The pockmarked ground would make our struggling indecipherable from the bumpy ride. "To slice the flesh from her, to cook it, to know her taste as nobody would know it . . ."

He grunted as the cravat knot tightened, my toes going numb.

"And I confess," he said, crawling over me and staring madly and sweating into my eyes, "I crave that unholy sacrament. I crave it, dear, sweet, innocent Louisa, *and I will have it.*"

Chapter
Twenty-Seven

His horrible face was just a brown-and-black blur above me, and then I could see nothing at all, the next blow hitting my chin, rocking me onto my side.

When did I pray? Only in desperate moments. Only when I needed a miracle. Once I had been devout, as devout as my mother and father and grandparents wished, giving hours of my day to a God that never protected me. Then I grew sick of being tested. I grew sick of the excuses. I cannot say if I ever stopped believing, but I know I stopped trying to believe. But now, half-blinded by the pain in my head, tears spilling down my cheeks as I heard the soft, metallic sound of a knife being unsheathed, I prayed. Then I hoped. I kicked out with my legs, punched blindly with my arms, and I wished for someone to make this all go away.

I called over and over again for Chijioke, but blood was running down my throat and my voice was just a rattle. My teeth must have cut something in my mouth when he knocked my head around. His hot breath oozed across my face, and I fought, scratching at him, shaking when he managed to bat down my fingers and clamp my wrists in one hand. I could do nothing now but wriggle helplessly like a fish on land.

Please. Someone must be listening. Something. Anything. The good and heavenly helpers I was told about, or the dark, dangerous ones I know now to walk among us.

My eyesight was recovering, but that only made it worse. I did not want to see this monster masquerading as a man or discover that he was smiling as he hurt me. A flash of silver passed over my eyes. The knife. A sob mingled with the blood in my throat, a sad, lost gurgle that made me feel utterly undone.

Then I heard the distant thunder. He heard it, too. His head snapped up as he loomed over me, and I listened hard, straining for some glimmer of hope. Horse hooves. They were growing closer, coming upon us at a hard sprint. I threw my head back and watched, upside down, as a rider approached the wagon from behind, galloping into view with a gray cloak whipping around her head, as wind-tossed as her curly brown hair.

Mary.

"Stop the wagon!" I heard her voice cut through the painful buzzing in my ears. It was the strong, sure voice she had used when she held me during the storm. The same voice Maggie used when I was in the cupboards and needed someone to say: it will not stay like this forever.

The crack of a whip. A duo of shrieking mares. The wagon shuddered and screeched to a stop so abruptly that the back lifted completely off the ground and careened to the side. A shower of pebbles and dirt rained down on us a half second before Mary jumped from her horse. The beast stamped and circled, but I could see no more of it as Mary landed inches from my head, recovering with a hop before throwing herself at Merriman.

"Unhand me!" he thundered, the two of them tumbling over me and the widow's corpse. They struggled for what felt like torturous hours, and though I freed my hands, my limbs shook too much for me to be of use. My head pounded and my mouth filled with the tang of blood, my feet numb from the tightness of the bonds around them.

But I could see more now, my vision growing stronger with each passing moment, and I pushed myself up onto my elbows, watching as Mary jerked backward, dodging a swipe of the doctor's knife. He had been backed into a corner, but now he advanced on her. I felt her feet slip over mine before she could find better purchase, straddling both my legs and the widow's. His eyes flared and he darted forward, and I tried to brace Mary from behind to make sure she wouldn't tumble out of the wagon and into the road.

But the work was done for me. The curtain separating the wagon bed from the driver's bench tore to the side, Chijioke storming into the fray with a roar. Merriman gasped, spinning, turning into the downward swing of a club.

Thwack! Thud. The crunch echoed in my bones, sickening and final, but Chijioke hit him again with the shillelagh, sending the doctor into the wagon wall before he crumpled next to us.

"Heavens, Louisa, are you all right?" Mary turned and dropped down next to me, tearing at the cravat tied around my ankles. I wiggled my toes, feeling them gradually come back to life.

"Can you speak?" Chijioke tossed the club aside and knelt on my other side.

I shook my head, still a little dazed, my skin alive and thrumming with fear and shock. Mary took the cravat and dabbed at something on my face, blood or sweat or both. She bit her lip and looked to her friend. "Should we turn back?"

"Derridon is nearer," he replied, scooping me up and helping me to sit on one of the benches. The wrap covering the widow's body had shifted, one pale, dead hand reaching toward us. Mary kicked the shroud back into place.

"You're safe now," she assured me. "How could you let her sit alone with him?"

"I knew he was evil, but not . . . not like that," Chijioke replied in a whisper. He glanced over his shoulder, but the doctor was motionless, his face purpled and smashed. "It was just a short ride, Mary. I didn't know."

I held up one hand, trying to silence them. I coughed, and my voice felt raw and torn, but usable. "It isn't his fault," I croaked. "Tried to shout. Wheels too loud."

"What do we do?" Mary searched the wagon for answers, still dabbing at my face.

"He's gone. We take him and the widow woman to the undertaker. Mr. Morningside will just have to understand. Aye, we can tend to Louisa there. Here, Mary, give me your cloak." She untied the cozy gray cape and handed it across. Chijioke motioned for me to lean forward, and gingerly, he wrapped me in the cloak, pulling the hood up to conceal my wounded face. "Can you ride a little longer?"

"Just bruised," I whispered.

"We will need to be rid of his things," Mary was saying. She stood and scrounged up the doctor's bag from where he had stored it under the bench. Flecks of bird dung stuck to the leather. She undid the latch and peered inside, closing her eyes with a gasp. Then, just as quickly, she locked the case up tight again. "Yes, we need to be rid of it."

"What's inside?" I asked.

Mary pulled the case away from me with a worried glance to Chijioke. "It isn't important, Louisa. It only matters that you're safe."

"I want to know."

She closed her eyes again and inhaled deeply, opening the latch and showing it to us. It was too dark to see clearly inside, but there was a definite peek of white and what looked like a silky slash of red.

"Bones," Mary murmured. "And a lock of hair with a ribbon. Don't look at it, Louisa, it's too awful."

I shrank back against Chijioke and pulled my knees to my chest, holding tight. It could have been me in there. *It could have been me.*

Chapter
Twenty-Eight

erridon unfolded slowly from my view in the back of the wagon. Mary stayed with me, her horse tethered to the others as we rolled our way into the little town. It was scarcely more than a hamlet, one plaster-and-thatch chapel and a row of low, quaint buildings on either side of a main street. It was all quiet but for the soft merriment spilling out of the tavern.

Mary held my hand, or rather, she held her palm open on the bench and I perched my fingers on top of it, the occasional tremor fluttering through my body.

"How did you know?" I asked. My voice was better now, but it still hurt to speak. "I was praying . . . hoping . . . then you."

She pulled in a long, shaky breath. Now that all was quiet again, she seemed as frail and uncertain as I. The doctor's body was hidden under the widow's cover, but his fresh blood soaked the wrapping, painting a macabre mask where I knew his face to be.

"It's what I am," she said. "Ach, I might have guarded you from afar, but I was too weak from the last ritual. I could hear you calling to me in my dreams. It woke me cold out of slumber. I came quick as I could, Louisa, I hope you know that."

"Thank you."

"No thanking, please." Mary rolled her head back on her

shoulders, staring up at the ceiling. "You should never have been alone with him. I swear on my life, Louisa, I didn't know what he was, and I know Chijioke too well to think he would want you in any danger."

"He ate her," I whispered bleakly. "He *ate* his daughter."

"Devil take him, Chi should have clubbed him a dozen more times."

"What will you do with the bones?"

"Bury them, I think. Make a little marker. She doesn't belong in a bag."

I nodded and carefully massaged my aching throat. "Her name was Catarina."

"Aye. You can help me make the cross." Mary pulled her hand out from under mine and touched my shoulder just as the wagon slowly came to a stop. "But you *are* all right?"

"I will be," I managed. *I hope.*

The wagon rocked as Chijioke leapt down from the driver's box. He appeared a moment later, wreathed in the orange light glowing up and down the street. The lantern lighter passed by with his long metal rod, checking the state of the candles and tending to those that seemed low. Given the strength of the full moon, his job was almost redundant. It was a blood moon so bright it looked like a glowing ruby studding the heavens. Somewhere behind us I heard Lee chatting to his uncle. I searched the storefronts with still-bleary eyes. We had stopped at the far edge of town between the Rook & Crook Inn, labeled with the silhouette of a bird picking up a man by his hat, and a dirty, slipshod sign reading simply UDERTAKE. The *N* and *R* had been worn away to a few peeling specks of paint.

"Giles should be inside," Chijioke said, climbing up and unlocking the gate of the wagon bed. "I'll distract Bremerton and his boy while you get Louisa inside, then I can pull us around to unload."

Oh God. Lee. It would be impossible to get him to leave if he saw me in this state. He was too kind, too good to abandon me when I had just narrowly avoided death. While I refused to let a few nasty bruises keep me from rescuing us both from Coldthistle, I would need time to cover up the marks on my skin. Perhaps I might steal some of the undertaker's cosmetics to hide the welts, enough at least to fool Lee into thinking I was all right. But then . . . Mr. Morningside had been right about the widow. And he'd been right about Dr. Merriman, too. What if Lee really was hiding something unthinkable? No. The attack had rattled me, that was all. I would sit quietly for a while, perhaps have tea or a restorative, then find a way to slip Chijioke and Mary, then reunite with Lee.

"Will you fine gentlemen be enjoying a round at the Rook and Crook?" I heard Chijioke say above the rustling of Mary's skirts as she slid off the bench and held out her hand.

We stepped down onto the cobbles and Mary locked the wagon gate; then she hooked her arm in mine and led me around the far side of the cart, keeping the tall, covered bed between us and the men speaking on the other side of it. I pulled the hood close over my eyes, and we scurried by the horses and into the shadowy awning of the undertaker's shop.

As the door closed, Lee's voice trickled through the glass window. "Was that Louisa? I meant to speak with her here in town."

I'll be back to find you soon, I promise.

"Well, something hot to drink is in order for the both of us." Mary ferried me along, down a narrow passage cluttered with family portraits and potted plants. The floor was swept and clean, but the tiles were cracked and faded. The men in the portraits might have been brothers, each thin-faced and big-nosed, with pointed chins and a thatch of sandy blonde hair greased back from the forehead. The smell of vinegar was so strong my nose twitched.

"Giles! Giles? Oh, where *is* that confounded man?" Mary searched from door to door. I saw a parlor go by, and a cloakroom, as well as several closed doors with ominous labels like FUNERARY TOOLS and CHEMICALS, SUNDRIES. It was one level of labyrinthine halls and small rooms, each warmer than the last.

"You must come here often," I remarked quietly, peering into dim corners laden with homemade rat traps. One had been a success, a hairy rat nearly cleaved in two by a supper knife tied to a spring.

"Not me," Mary replied, taking me around a corner and

toward a shabby white door labeled PRIVATE. "I helped Chijioke once before, but normally he can manage on his own."

As she reached for the knob, the door swung inward with a bang. A man who might have popped right out of one of those portraits stared down at us with eyes blown huge by spectacles. He wore a smart black suit with a purple pinstripe to it and a deep red cravat. A tiny silver bird skull dotted the knotted silk. He propped one spindly hand on his cravat, while with the other he adjusted his specs.

"Good Lord. Mary! Where did you come from?"

"Giles." She blew out a breath. "We're here with more work from Mr. Morningside. It ought to have been only one body, but we . . . Well, there was a complication."

"There usually is. Come in, then," he said, sweeping us forward and into a surprisingly cheerful little sitting room. The carpets were a lively green, and the overstuffed chairs, resting on knobbly mahogany legs, were patterned with pastoral toile. "Who is this odd-looking child? A new recruit for the *armée du diable*?"

"She works at Coldthistle, aye," Mary replied, impatient. "Louisa Ditton, this is our undertaker of choice, Giles St. Giles. The tubby tabby by the fire is called Francis."

"Francis is off biscuits," the undertaker informed us gravely. "He can't jump to the bed anymore, the poor fellow."

Francis looked anything but poor; in fact, he appeared perfectly fat and happy, purring away on the rug before the hearth.

Mary guided me to one of the chairs near a small but healthy fire and removed the cloak snuggled tightly around my shoulders. "Is there tea? Louisa here had a run-in with a bad sort."

Now there was the understatement of a lifetime.

"Go on," Giles said, giddy. "I need the local gossip, you see. Business has been rubbish since that pompous idiot John Lewis set up in Malton. I say he puts far too much rouge on his corpses, makes them look like a bunch of blushing Colombinas."

"I'm sure he's nothing compared to you," Mary told him kindly. She took the chair next to mine, lifting my braid to inspect the bruises forming on my neck. "Do you have anything for this, Giles? I dearly wish Mrs. Haylam were here. Her poultice would soothe this instantly."

"My clients are already dead and unconcerned with mere bruises, but I will check the workshop. Kettle first, however, and a biscuit or two, but none for you, Francis, you greedy lump. . . ."

Francis meowed in protest and turned over, showing us his explosively furry belly.

"I can manage the kitchen," Mary said, hopping up and going to a white-painted archway across from the hearth. "Chijioke will be along any moment and I doubt he wants to tarry."

"No, he is always eager to be about his work and I am always eager to watch," Giles replied, rubbing his hands together. He wedged his tall, storklike body through a door behind me, and I heard his heeled boots clack on a set of stairs leading downward.

"How are you feeling?" Mary asked, busying herself with the range and a heavy black kettle. I watched her through the arch, reaching to scratch the tabby's neck.

"Like the apple that fell off the cart," I replied with a sigh. "My wrist was only just feeling better and now this."

Cupboards opened and closed in a flurry. I could hardly track Mary as she bounced around the kitchen gathering up tiny bottles and wooden boxes into her arms. While she busied herself in the kitchen, I glanced around for any usable cosmetics. There was nothing but books and a globe and a few framed drawings to be found. "Ah! We can see to that. Silly man. He has almost everything I need right here . . . moonwort, pigeon leaf, even baltian violets. And here I thought Giles was a hopeless gardener."

"I'm not sure I know what any of those are."

"You wouldn't. Some of these will only grow in certain soils during certain phases of the moon and wilt from the touch of humans and animals. Moonwort only grows in land fed by the corpse of a fairy," Mary explained. She opened all of the tins and bottles she had collected and began stirring in different measures of each into a miniature cauldron on the stove. She added water from the kettle and a few glugs from what looked like a wine carafe. At once, a delicious and florid scent poured out from the archway. Francis the tabby flipped onto his stomach and arched his back, sniffing. "I'm not all that talented at restoratives, but I try to listen when Mrs. Haylam teaches Poppy."

She brought me an engraved cup filled to the brim with steaming hot liquid. I put my nose into the vapor and inhaled deeply, my stomach growling from the smell. It was like buttermilk infused with violets, or the perfume of baked bread wafting through a field of flowers.

Giles St. Giles burst through the door to the cellar, a jar of ugly black leeches tucked under his arm. His face fell after catching a whiff of the concoction in my hands.

"Mary, you scamp, you sent me on a useless errand. Thought I might give her a leeching. Practically any of life's ailments can be cured with a good leeching. Except anemia, obviously." He laughed as if this was the funniest joke ever told.

"I think we might skip the leeches tonight, Giles. She's been through enough already."

"Misunderstood creatures," he moaned, lifting up the jar and stroking it. "They simply want to help."

As they talked, I sipped the sweet, thick restorative, warmth spreading through my body, all the way down to my toes. The ache in my throat and head eased, as if the pain were being drawn out of me like poison from a bite. I might have fallen asleep right there in the comfortable chair near the fire, but Chijioke peered into the parlor, pulling off his scarf and stamping his feet.

"Do any of you bother to knock?" Giles asked with a frown.

"Apologies." Chijioke did not look in the mood for an argument, going directly to the fire and holding his palms to it. Francis arched against the thick fabric of his trousers. But he ignored the cat, pulling off his coat and turning to the undertaker with a grim expression. Maybe it was a trick of the firelight, but his eyes flared crimson. "The bodies are below, Giles. We should get started. The blood moon is full and their souls are viler than most and I want to be rid of them for good."

Chapter Twenty-Nine

The cellar was cool and smelled of wet stones, and two dead bodies lay naked and washed on the table.

The scene playing out before me had the hazy quality of a dream. I drank the hot restorative and huddled under my patchwork blanket and looked openly at the face of the man who had tried to kill me. Well, what was left of his face.

My foot tapped anxiously under the blanket. I needed Lee to listen to me without worrying, and that would not happen without the creams and tinctures to cover up the last visible evidence of Merriman's attack. Unlike the sitting room upstairs, this chamber was packed with chemicals of all kinds, and I squinted, trying to find promising labels on the tins stacked throughout the place. Many of the chemicals just seemed like various perfumes to cover up the smell of rot on the bodies. Chijioke made another trip upstairs, then reappeared with the undertaker, who nattered on constantly about his new competition in Malton. Two doves cooed softly in a cage carried by Chijioke, though the birds quieted when they were brought to the table with the corpses and the cage placed there. To my right, high wooden shelves lined the wall, hundreds of tools, knives, shovels, and odd medical devices heaped in glistening rows. As upstairs, the whole room smelled faintly of vinegar.

There were two entrances to the cellar, one from the stairwell

I had used and the other from a tall, wide set of doors in an alcove behind the bodies. Scuff marks and a trickling of dirt led from those doors to the table. Chijioke must have unloaded the bodies through that back entrance.

Mary hummed as she set out a few candles around the tall, sturdy table with the bodies. Her gaze flitted to me more than was strictly necessary.

"I can hardly feel the blows now," I told her, ducking down behind the drink. I needed to get out of there, but giving all three of them the slip right that minute, when their concern was fixed so intently upon me, felt impossible.

"You're strong," Mary replied, pausing with a lit candle in hand. Some of the black wax dripped onto her skin and she hissed, shaking out her fingers and then blowing on them. "I wouldn't have recovered as quickly."

"In the last week, I've been attacked by shadows, a flock of birds, and a madman who ate his own daughter. I wouldn't call it strength so much as self-preservation. If I examine it all too closely, I'll wind up like those murderers on the table."

Mary smirked and placed the last candle, then wiped her hands on her skirts. "Still."

The undertaker loped around the room, dousing any candle that wasn't black. The flames dancing around the dead bodies burned bright purple with scarlet cores. Chijioke positioned himself between the two corpses and opened the birdcage. Neither of the doves took their chance at freedom. I couldn't blame them; the room was cold and unwelcoming, the reddish-purple flames glowing like unholy eyes in the gloom. Giles St. Giles disappeared behind the stool I sat on, rounding the corner into a little alcove separated from the larger cellar by a curtain. There was silence for a moment, and then the metallic squeal of gears grinding together, an ancient mechanism coming to life and churning. I could hear him start to pant, and pictured him laboring against a massive crank. One could all but follow the pipes and shafts that made up the machine overhead. I saw a few wheels turning, and then a trapdoor I hadn't seen before opened right over Chijioke and the table.

It did not lead above to the sitting room but straight up to the sky, flooding the cellar with scarlet moonlight.

I gasped and hunkered down farther under the blanket. It was beautiful and strange, the corpses on the table all but glowing with the intensity of that light. The screeching and churning of the machine ended, and a loud thud echoed around us as the skylight locked into position. Giles St. Giles joined us again, coming to sit on the empty chair beside me. He dropped down into it with a whoosh of excitement and slapped his hands together, rubbing them.

"My child, have you seen a ferrying before?" he whispered, as if we were about to be in for a night at the theater.

"She's very new to all of this," Mary explained. "Perhaps this will be too much."

Yes, perfect. I nodded in vehement agreement, even beginning to rise out of my seat. This was my chance to run. But Giles clapped a hand over my arm, tugging me back down again.

"Tosh! There is nothing more beautiful, more breathtaking than the ferrying of souls. Why, she should feel honored to witness it. *Privileged.* And so soon after arriving at Coldthistle! I was a trusted servant of Mr. Morningside for ten years before I was ever invited to spectate. Consider yourself beyond fortunate, young—"

"Oh shut it, Giles; all this bickering is distracting," Chijioke muttered, pushing up his sleeves and pinching his nose.

Mary came to stand on my other side, placing a gentle, comforting hand on my shoulder while Chijioke inhaled deeply and dropped his head back so he could look at the ceiling.

"When I tell you to shut your eyes and mouth," he said in a low rumble, "do it."

He himself closed his eyes for a long moment, and when he opened them again they glowed red all around, like rubies lit from within. At once, the atmosphere in the room became close, a tightness rising sharp and sudden in my chest. Mary held my shoulder more firmly, as if to anchor me there to the chair. The very air itself began to hum, a silvery miasma drifting up from the floor and gathering around Chijioke until he wore a shroud of mist.

The chill in the cellar dissipated, replaced with a wet warmth, like the first droplets of summer rain, and Chijioke began to mouth a chant of some kind. I couldn't make out the words, but I could feel their power growing, growing, until the heat in the room was almost unbearable and the swirling fog wrapped around him like a cocoon, obscuring everything but his glowing red eyes.

Hotter, hotter, and louder, somehow, a distant thunder that felt like a heartbeat filling the space around us. The doves in the cage began to hop on their perches and trill, turning this way and that as if the life was being squeezed out of them. It was becoming difficult to breathe. I held the cup of tea with one hand and touched my throat with the other. As a child I had fallen and knocked the wind out of my lungs many times, and this was similar, only it happened slowly, a deep exhalation I had no control over.

Then nothing was happening slowly—the doves flew out of the cage, just barely visible in the mist, two quick white smudges, and the bodies on the table convulsed, their chests lifting, both pairs of eyes snapping open, filled with horrible crimson fire.

The doves landed, perching on the bruised flesh of the doctor's chin and the widow's perfect white face, leaning down and dipping their beaks into their dead mouths like they were sipping nectar from flower blossoms. The instinct telling me to look away was not as strong as the raw curiosity. It was awful, sick, and yet somehow beautiful, so intricately choreographed, a sinister ballet playing out in front of my eyes.

Rapt as I was, I only then realized how short of breath I had become. Mary and Gile, too, were gasping, taking quick, shallow breaths to combat the pressure squeezing us all. Chijioke remained unaffected, chanting silently, the mist close around him falling away as the eyes of the widow and doctor ceased glowing, flaring out in the same instant the birds' eyes exploded in color.

I was choking. We all were. My lungs ached, starved for air.

"Close your eyes and seal your lips!" Chijioke's voice sliced through the heavy atmosphere like steel. I did as he asked at once and felt the pain in my chest ease. Whispers filled the room, a hundred voices, a thousand, and all of them urging me to open my eyes and drink deep of the air with my mouth. I clamped my lips together tightly, scrunching up my face, ignoring the seductive voices, the coercion, the disembodied giggles and coos surrounding us. Did the others hear it, too? Did they dare disobey Chijioke's order?

As quickly as it had commenced, the ritual was over. A single wind rushed over me, fluttering the blanket and my hair, and then the room was still and silent and cold.

"It's done. You can open your eyes."

I peered through a squint, finding the doves had returned to the cage. They preened as normal birds would, though I thought I saw a twinge of red fading in their eyes.

"What . . . What did you do to them?" I whispered.

"They can hold on to a soul and keep it safe," Mary explained. "Like wee living vaults."

The birds . . . I thought of the hundreds of them Mr. Morningside kept in the manse. Were those all holding captured souls, or were they simply empty vessels waiting to be filled? What need did a single man have of birds stuffed with human souls? A dark, dark feeling consumed me, one of foreboding and sickness. Those birds sitting passively in his office no longer seemed a charming quirk but a harbinger. I shuddered, pulling the blanket close against the returned chill. The candles had gone out. The mist abated. I glanced to my right and saw Giles with his hands clasped together under his chin, grinning from ear to ear.

"Spectacular," he whispered, flushed. "Pure magnificence."

In a way, I had to agree. I wasn't certain *what* I had witnessed, only that it was mesmerizing. He was bringing his hands together for applause when a noise from upstairs startled us all. It was the door, and someone was knocking frantically. I hopped up from the chair, leaving my cup behind on the stool and starting for the stairs. Chijioke beat me there, heading up first.

"At least *somebody* bloody knocks," I heard Giles mutter, following.

"It could be Lee," I said. It was a short journey up to the first level and the warm salon. Francis was still lounging by the fire and didn't lift his head as we passed by. "He knows I came along."

"Hmm." Chijioke led us swiftly through the maze of halls to

the front passage and all its family portraits. "It's a good thing he didn't turn up a half minute sooner."

"What happens if you're interrupted?" I asked, waiting behind the door with him. The others were crammed in behind us, Mary trying to peek over my shoulder.

Chijioke looked back and down at me, smirking. "I haven't a clue. Not keen to find out either, lass." He leaned into the door, watching through the glass peephole. "Seems you were right. It's the Brimble boy."

"Let me talk to him," I said. The astonishment of the ferrying and the shock of being attacked dropped away. The exhaustion was there, of course, just beneath the surface, but distant enough that I could shove it aside. And now here was my sometime conspirator, and we were away from Coldthistle House. Now was as good a chance as I might get to mount an escape. I had never found cosmetics, but I would just have to persuade him to leave as best I could.

"Louisa and I will step outside," Mary said. Her tone was just insistent enough to make me prickle. "The two of you can finish up here, yes?"

But Chijioke wasn't moving away from the door. The knocking persisted. He stared down at me, arching one quizzical brow. "Haven't you had enough adventure for one night, Miss Louisa?"

"I only mean to say hello," I replied. The blanket had slid down to my elbows and I folded it neatly, handing it across to

Giles. "It was a pleasure meeting you."

"Of course," he said, giving an ostentatious bow. He straightened and stuck one finger into the air. "Next time a leeching, eh? Does wonders for the constitution."

"Next time," I echoed. Yes. A leeching. A maypole dance. A swift kick in the head. I would agree to anything so long as it got me out the door.

Chijioke moved aside, slowly, sighing all the way, his displeasure so palpable that I shrank as I went by. Outside, Lee had ceased the knocking, standing back on his heels and inspecting the building as if he might find a window to tap on. He was ready with his usual explosive smile the moment he saw us.

"Thought I saw you all trot in there," he crowed. "Do you know, there was the most bizarre light flashing out from inside the place. Did you see it?"

"Perhaps it was a carriage passing behind in the alley," Mary offered. "There's a back entrance for delivering, well . . . There's a back entrance."

"Hmm . . ." The answer didn't seem to satisfy him, but he was quickly on to the next concern, my bruised face. "Heavens, Louisa, what happened? Every time I see you you've incurred some new bump or scrape."

There was so much I wanted to say, but as before, there was no telling what might endanger Lee to hear. For God's sake, I just watched a kind, gentle young man transfer a human soul into a bird! I would never be believed. The more mundane cruelty of men, I wagered, was something Lee could understand, and so I glanced at Mary, trying to ask the obvious question with my eyes. She gave a tiny nod.

"Dr. Merriman attacked me on the way over," I said. "It's a long and ugly story, but luckily he was not successful. Anyway, we have other things to discuss, Lee."

"Attacked you!? Is he subdued? I should . . . I say . . . A hundred punishments spring to mind. What possible motivation could he have?" Lee drew closer, closing one eye and examining my right temple. "The lout should rot in prison forever."

"He'll be rotting for about that long in the ground," I murmured.

"He's *dead*?" Lee considered this for a moment, grimacing. "So soon after Mrs. Eames . . ." I could see him working out the implications of this. More guests were dying, which meant he could be next.

"Try not to worry too much," I assured him. "He was an evil person. A very evil person. Not like you."

"I should have been there to help you," Lee said, lowering his eyes. "I should have insisted on having you come in the carriage with us. There was no need for you to suffer like that."

"I'm all right," I stated flatly. Dr. Merriman was dead, his vile soul locked in some poor dove's body, yet we still lived. I wondered if Mary would even mind if I asked her directly to leave us alone. I could cite the shock of being attacked. I could draw on her obvious sympathy. Would she understand if

I wanted to leave? It felt wrong to ask, considering she had just saved my life.

"Where do you suppose your uncle is going?" Mary asked, pointing along the road, tracing the trajectory of the tall, cloaked George Bremerton walking briskly to the west. We were on the very edge of town as it was, and it looked as if he stalked away toward nothing but the horizon.

"I can't believe it." Lee took a few steps after his uncle. "He wanted me to stay in the inn and threatened to box my ears if I left it. I didn't realize it was so he could go somewhere without me. This is about *my* parents; I have a right to know what's going on . . ."

"Didn't you say the address in his case was in Derridon?" I couldn't help but watch with the others. Mr. Morningside had said he didn't know what to make of Bremerton, but all his doubts seemed silly to me. He was intent on killing the man anyway. Why fuss over the ins and outs of his delinquency?

"Of course, Louisa!" Lee turned back to us, his smile as bold and bright as ever. "Well? Are you not coming along?"

I looked closely at where George Bremerton had gone. The edge of town. We could hail a wagon or simply find a good hiding spot and wait for Mary to get bored of searching. Even if she joined us, it would get her farther away from Chijioke, farther away from alerting him to the fact that we had run off.

"Won't you get your ears boxed?" Mary asked with a giggle.

But Lee was already leaving us, tiptoeing down the lane and

gesturing for us to follow. The full moonlight made his skin glow like polished bone.

"Oh, but I would suffer far worse to have this mystery solved."

I believed him, and it frightened me to my core.

Chapter Thirty

"Is this the place?" I asked as we approached a trio of cottages a half mile from the village center. They were set back from the main thoroughfare leading through town. A single unmarked dirt path led to a smattering of trees ringed like a wall around the houses. We clustered together closely as we walked, Mary's hand brushing mine as we avoided the noisier gravel of the road and kept to the overgrown grass.

"To my knowledge, yes," Lee whispered back. "Not that these homes are particularly well marked."

"How do you know of this place?" Mary slowed down a little. We were nearing the trees. The cottages beyond lay dark inside. I glanced back toward Derridon, its limits shaped roughly like a potato on its side. The inn was still lit and inviting, and the quaint homes laid out in orderly rows were so different from these homes that seemed to want nothing to do with the town.

"My uncle and I are looking into a matter of inheritance," Lee explained. He pulled back a few branches on an elm and surveyed the way ahead. "I found the directions to this place in his things."

"Why didn't he show you himself?"

"I don't know." He let the branch swing back into place and turned to us, rubbing his pointed chin. "His heart doesn't seem to be in the search. He's hardly mentioned it since we arrived. I have to wonder . . ."

I thought again of Mr. Morningside's suspicions but said nothing. What was the point in making him worry about that now? If anything, we could look in after George Bremerton and see just what he was up to first.

"Either he doesn't care or he thinks it's a lost cause," Lee concluded. He inhaled deeply, moving carefully through the trees. "We're here now; we might as well see what's what."

"At this hour? Isn't that terribly rude?" Mary asked sheepishly.

"My uncle is going, isn't he? He must know them. . . . I've waited long enough. This is my parentage, yes? I want to know what it is he's found."

I was less certain, and so was Mary, judging by her furrowed brow and pursed lips. Tarrying, I watched Lee push the branches and brush aside as he went ahead, and Mary grabbed my hand, squeezing it.

"Something doesn't feel right," she mouthed.

"Just be careful," I replied silently.

She nodded and followed almost precisely in Lee's footsteps. An owl hooted overhead, standing sentinel somewhere in the leaves above us. There was more than enough moonlight to navigate by, but that brightness made me feel naked and vulnerable as we passed out of the safety of the trees and into the void near the cottages. No lights. No smoke from the chimneys.

No signs of life whatsoever. Two homes lay before us in a pair, the third across from them on the other side of the dirt path. The third one was more recently painted, the door glistening with a fresh coat of white paint. A one-man cart leaned against the cottage with the white door, and the raspberry bushes surrounding the walk looked trampled.

Lee pushed his shoulder against the nearest cottage, peering around the edge to look at the one with the white door. We followed, waiting on him. Mary was right—something did not sit well with me. It wasn't just the darkness in the houses but the unnerving silence. No dogs had noticed our approach, and any crofter this far from the safety of the village would keep a hound on alert.

And there was something else—something harder to describe as more than an overall sense of emptiness. It was like knowing someone was watching you from a distance. You could always feel it, that tickle on the back of your neck, but you could also feel when there was nobody around at all. If you wanted to steal a loaf of bread in the market or filch from the kitchens at Pitney, you had better grow eyes on the back of your head. The houses felt lifeless. Hollow. Not safe, but not populated either.

Yet George Bremerton had come this way. These cottages were important enough to mention in his personal items. It wouldn't be right to pull Lee away now, not when he was closer than ever to some hint about his blood.

"Which one do you reckon?" Mary murmured.

Without thinking, I said, "The white door."

"Aye," she replied, too quietly for Lee to hear. "There's darkness beyond that door, that's how we know."

"We?"

A twig snapped. And yes, it was near the door we had guessed. I turned to look at her but Lee had grabbed me by the wrist, tugging me out onto the dirt path and toward that glossy white door. "Come along, that will be my uncle . . ."

There was nobody out in the lane, just us and the owl and its mournful cry. George Bremerton would have been a welcome sight, in fact, but there was nobody hiding in the shadows around the cottage. That door, however, wasn't locked; the knob had been bashed in, splinters hanging off the ragged edge.

"Careful," I whispered, tugging on the back of Lee's coat. "Look, someone's broken in."

He lifted his hand, hesitating, placing his palm on the door before making a fist. *Oh no.* Mary and I lurched forward at the same time to try to stop him from knocking, but it was too late. *Thunk, thunk, thunk.*

"Um . . . hello? Is anyone . . . There appears to be something wrong with your door."

I flinched, holding my breath, but the door didn't open on an angry, armed farmer or highwayman or anyone at all. Silence. Somehow that was worse. Lee knocked again, and again. It was polite of him, but after the third or fourth time it became clear nobody would answer.

Mary gently nudged my side. "Louisa . . . do you smell that?"

God, did I. "Copper. It smells like—"

"Blood," she mouthed.

Lee hadn't heard us. He shifted from foot to foot, weighing the options. "Then I suppose we just go in," he said in a croak. His hand visibly trembled as he took the crooked knob and pushed, opening the door onto a scene of unimaginable horror.

"Lord," he whispered, covering his nose and mouth with his sleeve. "It's . . . Dear God, it's everywhere."

Blood. Coating the floor. Sprayed across the walls. Dripping down the stairwell in slow, sticky rivers. The smell was hideous; I could hardly breathe. And it was not just blood, but all the other soft, flingable parts of a human body—guts and pieces of guts, skin and sinew, all of it hanging from the lamps, the banister, the buck's head mounted in the foyer.

In the gore covering the floor was a single set of footsteps. Large ones.

"We should go," I whispered, already backing away.

"Uncle?" Lee called out, pushing bravely or stupidly into the depths of the cottage. The foyer had three exits—the stairs leading up, a passage to the back, and an open archway to the right. He chose the room to the right, still covering his face as he picked his way through the carnage. "Uncle, are you here? Is anyone here? Are you hurt, Uncle?"

My shoes squelched, sucked down by the still-wet blood coating the floor. I followed him through the house, avoiding unidentifiable body parts on the floor. An eyeball stared up at me from under a rocking chair and I felt my stomach drop and threaten to empty. It was almost too much to take in, too violent to make sense of.

Lee no longer called for his uncle. He had frozen in the middle of what must have been the cottage sitting room. Over the hearth, suspended by two ropes around the wrist, was the pink and dripping skeleton, untidily shredded, bits of skin and muscle hanging like tattered linens from the bones.

I heard Lee vomiting and forced down my own bile.

"This isn't just a murder," Mary said, standing next to me, her voice muffled by her own sleeve. "I think it's a warning, aye? There's a message." She pointed to the splattered wall behind the hanging corpse. Someone had drawn a symbol in blood, a crude drawing of a lamb curled up and eating its own tail surrounded by a sun.

"Not much of a message if it cannot be discerned." Lee coughed, righting himself and wiping discreetly at his mouth.

"That only means it isn't meant for us," I said. But I memorized it. If George Bremerton's trip in this direction wasn't suspicious, I didn't know what was. Mr. Morningside was right—something was amiss with Lee's uncle. Even if he had nothing to do with the massacre in the house, this address had been put down in his things. I hazarded a tiny step toward the hearth and the skeleton dangling above it. There had been a fire lit recently, the ashes still giving off a subtle heat. Something curled and white winked from the otherwise black pile of burnings, and I crouched down, careful to avoid the slimy foot just above my head.

I pulled the little curl of paper out swiftly, hissing from the heat of the ashes.

"What did you find there?" Lee asked. I could hear the lingering queasiness in his voice.

"Not sure," I said. And I wasn't, until I read the single, burned line of script. It was nonsense, but I kept it, hiding it in my palm and then sliding it into my sleeve, the old grifter tricks proving useful.

The only words I could make out were the last word of a sentence and the first few of another: *traitor. The first and last children will ascend with or without your*

"It's nothing," I told them. "Just a bit of rubbish that didn't burn through."

"Shhh!" Mary whipped around, clutching my shoulder. "Someone is here."

I heard a single heavy footstep in the hall and went rigid, convinced that we were about to meet the unholy monster that had ripped this person to pieces. Turning only my head, I watched Mary dash to the archway, hiding away from the door. It was Lee who brought me out of my fright, taking me by the hand and pulling me toward a shadowy corner made by the stony bulk of the fireplace. He pulled me close to his chest, flattening us against the wall. His heart pounded against my back, his panicked breath hot on my neck. His arms folded across my stomach and held me. He gave one squeeze, and it felt paralyzingly like a good-bye.

The footsteps advanced slowly. The wooden boards creaked, then louder. They were close now. I kept my eyes half lidded, waiting, wondering if Mary would stay hidden or strike, wondering if we had any chance at all of making it out of that cursed house alive.

Then the stranger spoke and I felt all the breath rush out of both of us at once.

"Rawleigh?" It was George Bremerton. "Are you there, boy? Are you alive?"

"Uncle!" Lee shot out from behind me, stumbling to the middle of the room. The skeleton stared down at them with eyeless holes, a silent and terrible audience. "We should flee this place; the murderer could be anywhere!"

They embraced, and George Bremerton caught my gaze, his jaw tightening with anger or despair, I couldn't say. He closed his eyes tightly and held his nephew, turning them until his back shielded Lee from the corpse's watch.

"I told you not to come," I heard him whisper fiercely. "I told you not to come. Look away now, Rawleigh. By God, this is not the way for a mother to meet her son."

Chapter
Thirty-One

he ride back to Coldthistle House was long and word-
less. George Bremerton did not protest when Lee
silently signaled for me to ride in the carriage with
them. I knew it was because I had been attacked by the doctor
on the initial trip, but I also sensed he wanted me there. He
wanted comfort.

And God, did he deserve it.

I was glad that he wanted no conversation at all, for what did
one say to a young man who had just seen his mother in the most
nightmarish state? It was unthinkable. Devastating. My heart
ached for him. It ached in a way that left me deeply confused.
Was this what it felt like to really have a friend? To care almost
to distraction about another's welfare and happiness? Of course
I hadn't had the heart to speak of escape after the shock. . . .
That dream seemed distant again now, hidden behind a heavy
black curtain that I had no tools or energy to move.

Yet something had to be done. Never had so much death
descended on my life until I came to Coldthistle House.

The journey was nearly complete when Lee brought his head
away from the window. He had laid it there for the entirety of
the ride, his forehead pressed hard to the glass. His skin had left
a smudge on the foggy window. Slowly, he turned to me with

a pained, helpless expression, a smile that wasn't a smile but a buttressed door for the hurt that might spill out.

He pushed something across the seat toward me, a little shiny thing, slender and engraved with leaves.

A spoon.

"Thought it might be a funny gift," he said in a small voice. "I nicked it from the Rook and Crook. Then I felt so bad about stealing it that I left a bit of coin behind to pay for it. I thought I would feel bad about it for a while, but it's just a small thing now. Just a stupid, small thing."

"It isn't stupid," I replied. George Bremerton regarded us openly, but that didn't matter; his judgment and his opinion were irrelevant. The world outside the carriage was irrelevant, because this person who had become my friend without my wanting him to was suffering. "Thank you, Lee. I think it's perfect. And I think any establishment called the Rook and Crook should expect the occasional act of petty thievery."

He almost smiled, ducking his head before looking out the window again. Across from us, George Bremerton stared. Or rather, he glowered at me under a brow heavy with consternation, rarely blinking, hardly moving, just silently communicating his displeasure.

"Why were you at the house?" He was asking me, Lee apparently being beyond reproach in this matter.

This I could do. It was easier to make a mask of my face and respond coolly than to deal with Lee's sadness. "We followed you."

"This was your bloody idea, wasn't it?" He snorted and tossed his hair like an angry horse. "Bad influence. I knew it. Can spot a jumped-up grasper like you from a mile off."

"*Uncle*," Lee said softly, uncertainly, rousing himself as if from a deep sleep.

Bremerton smirked. "You stay away from my nephew or I'll have you sacked."

"By all means," I replied boldly. "Give it your all."

"Don't speak to Louisa that way," Lee grumbled. He crossed his arms over his chest, shifting infinitesimally closer to me on the cushioned bench. The carriage teetered on; we had to be nearing our destination. "It wasn't her idea at all; it was mine. If you want someone to blame, then blame me, but why you need anyone to blame at all right now I cannot imagine. There's been a tragedy, I've lost my mother, and all you can do is pick a fight with my friend!"

"This is not the time or place for this discussion," Bremerton began.

"And why not? Say what you will, Uncle, I trust her."

"Rawleigh . . ." He pinched his forehead between thumb and forefinger, pressing his lips together until they were white. "Very well. I hadn't gone to the house earlier because my contacts in Derridon sent a note to me at Coldthistle. It was about your mother. About her recent . . . predilections. She got herself wrapped up in unnatural practices. Devil worship. Witchery. I did not want you to think less of her. I wanted to protect you from an ugly truth."

Silence. It was not my place to speak, and instead I watched the blood drain from Lee's face. His mouth opened and closed a few times, but no words came out.

"I'm sorry—more sorry than you know—that it turned out this way," Bremerton added. "That woman did not deserve to die."

Lee did nothing but nod, over and over again, locked in a daze. "Then I suppose we shall be leaving. She can provide no proof of my parentage now."

"I will have her belongings removed and sort through them. Perhaps she left something behind to back your claim. After the burial is finalized, it will be time for us to leave," he said. "Unless of course you would rather return to the estate without me, nephew. You are not obligated to stay."

"No," Lee replied firmly. "I want to be there. I don't care what she became in the end; I belong here until she is at rest."

The carriage rolled into the drive as dawn broke across the sky. A thin blue ribbon shimmered on the horizon, ravens gathering in the trees on the lawn and the gables. I was not happy to see Coldthistle again, but I knew at least a bed waited for me somewhere. The exhaustion could not be fought any longer, and my eyes drooped with each passing moment. The rocking and warmth of the carriage might have put me to sleep if it weren't for the tense sadness hanging among us. And I felt pulled down to the ground by the weight of my failure; the night had gone completely awry. We had not escaped. I had been attacked. Lee's mother was dead, and brutally so. No matter how hard I tried, all roads led once more to the boardinghouse.

Mrs. Haylam was waiting for us outside the door, and Foster jumped down quickly to help our exit. I stood in the looming shadow of the house and watched the housekeeper take us all in, and I saw the moment she realized Dr. Merriman was no longer in our party. She did not look to me for answers, but to Chijioke, who had stopped the supply wagon just behind us. Mary trotted into the yard on her horse, diverting her course at once to the barn.

"Has the good doctor elected to stay in town?" she asked tightly.

"He preferred the comforts of the inn there," Chijioke smoothly explained. "We will not be seeing him again. I will have his things packed and delivered right away."

It was a performance for the guests, I knew, and Lee did nothing to amend the story. I wasn't even certain he heard any of it. He simply drifted into the house, as slow and pale as a ghost.

When the men were inside, I volunteered myself to Mrs. Haylam, walking slowly with her inside and into the vaulted expanse of the foyer. "He went mad after talking about his dead daughter," I told her without prompting. "I thought he would kill me; he would have, I'm sure of it, if Mary and Chijioke hadn't helped."

"How he departs is no concern of ours," she said. We paused, and I watched Lee drag himself up the stairs. Mary had already come in from the grounds, and appeared from the kitchens with a laden tea tray in hand, following the guests up. "The master told me of his crime, but we did not believe him dangerous to anyone but his own family. He would never have gone alone with you two if we did."

I nodded once. "I'm not sorry he's gone."

"Indeed?" I heard the surprise in her voice, and the not-so-subtle interest. She wore a prim white shawl over a blue dress and apron, her silvery hair braided and looped under a cap. "Indeed."

She didn't press me for more, and I wouldn't have elaborated if she had. "I need sleep. Desperately. In the morning I have something to show Mr. Morningside."

"That sounded suspiciously like a command," Mrs. Haylam drawled. Her milky eye sparkled. "But I suppose I can inquire after his schedule. Rest now, child, and fear no men. The Residents will be watchful at your door this night."

"Cold comfort," I mumbled. But I had not energy to argue. I pulled myself just as heavily as Lee had up the stairs and to my room at the end of the hall. As soon as I closed the door, I heard the scratching of footsteps on the other side. Peering through the crack, I saw nothing but a hazy black form. Sure enough, a

Resident had come to stand guard. The healing bruise under the wrap on my wrist throbbed as if in recognition, as if in greeting.

I had no idea how that made me feel. Perhaps I was simply too tired to think clearly on the subject. But rather than fear, I felt only a cold numbness. A distance. The Residents had tried to keep me from the book in the attic; they had caused me no more harm. But a man of flesh and blood had tried to kill me, and I'd seen the aftermath of true violence; when I closed my eyes I saw a dangling skeleton, the mouth of its skull twisted open in agony.

Maybe I wanted that shadow creature between me and the rest of the world. At least for a little while. At least while I slept. I vented a dry laugh and undressed, pinned up my hair, and carefully hid the scrap of paper I had taken from the cottage fireplace under my pillow. Someone, and I could guess who, had left Mr. Morningside's book on that same pillow. When I looked closer, I noticed it was not my same water-stained copy I'd left behind in the barn, but a fresh one.

I cracked the cover, finding a new inscription there, too.

Louisa,
You have questions. There are answers. They wait for you in here if only you dare to seek them out.

I crawled into bed, sighing, curling up under the welcome comfort of the blankets with the book tucked against the pillow.

Someone had left a candle burning on the table beside the bed, and I decided to let it burn a little longer, scanning the index of the book and leafing through the pages until I landed on the chapter he had suggested on more than one occasion.

"Practical Applications: Techniques for Identifying Changelings."

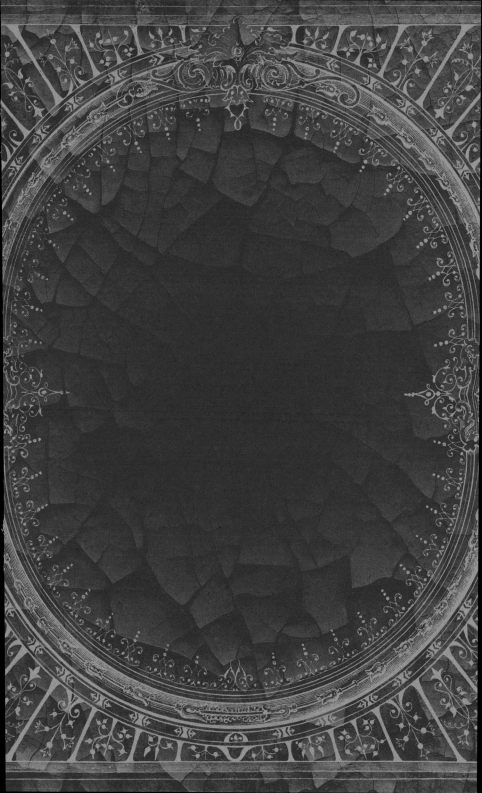

Chapter
Thirty-Two

n the early morning I dressed and performed my toilette as usual, then found my way to the kitchen. The house felt vast and empty, as it should, with two of its already few occupants gone for good. In the foyer, Chijioke was handing off instructions to Foster, who stood next to a pile of luggage monogrammed *R. M.*

Rory Merriman. I wondered briefly what any acquaintances of his might hear. The doctor had gone away to the north of England to take the healing waters and never returned. Did he have any unlucky family that would receive his things or learn of where he was buried? I watched Foster heave the bags into his arms and trundle out the door, the door that seemed to me now more like a mouth: guests arrived, knowing nothing, and were promptly swallowed whole.

"There's breakfast," Chijioke told me brightly, closing the door after Foster. "Bacon," he added with a beaming smile, "and some mutton for the morning hash from the neighboring shepherd."

"Kind of him," I remarked. Chijioke led the way into the kitchen, where, as promised, a modest spread of food waited. Poppy sat at the tall table, swinging her legs under her skirts, chatting with her hound as she ground some kind of small fruit pit with a mortar and pestle.

"Don't grind that so close to the food, girl!" Mrs. Haylam cried, sweeping in and pushing the tray to the other side of the table.

"Sorry, sorry," she said with a laugh. Then she noticed me and waved, flinging everywhere bits of the fruit pit that Mrs. Haylam swiftly tried to sweep up. "Good day, Miss Louisa. Do have some breakfast! I'm making poisons."

"How nice for you," I replied, sitting across from her and making sure my plate was free of any mysterious brown flakes before serving up a bit of food.

"Help her put that away and then roast the yams for luncheon, Louisa. Mr. Morningside will see you after."

And like that, I was a servant of Coldthistle again. It felt disconcertingly normal, like combing one's hair with an old brush or slipping on a worn pair of shoes. I knew how to put up a bit of ground pit and I knew how to roast a yam, and the knowing and the simplicity made the horror of the day before feel like a distant memory. This was what life was supposed to be like—routine, average, with no dead bodies or rituals or monsters lurking in the shadows.

The ease of it frightened me, too; I was not cleaning up a mess or cooking in a reputable boardinghouse. These people had protected me, but they had put me in danger, too, and no amount of breezy yam-baking would make me forget it.

The morning skipped by quickly, and soon the cooking was done and Poppy was chasing her hound out the door, trying to recover a piece of yam skin he'd absconded with. Her giggles flew out the door into the yard and I followed, wiping my hands on my apron and leaning against the jamb, closing my eyes against the unexpected warmth of the day and the mild breeze that wound through it. My fingers closed over the spoon in my apron pocket and I frowned, thinking of Lee and what he must be doing. Maybe his uncle was forcing him to drink some of that odious sulfurous water the widow had gone on and on about. While baking, I had watched Mrs. Haylam put together a tray for him; he was not, it seemed, stirring out of his room at all.

Still, he had searched me out so many times, perhaps it was time I did the same. I at last visited the healing waters, leaving the kitchen and winding west around the house. The gardens and barn were visible from the house, but the path between them was covered in a canopy of thick trees that leaned into one another, creating a tangled roof that shadowed the way to the water. I had thought only Bath was blessed with such a natural feature, but this was apparently a well-kept secret. It was sure to make any guests who discovered the feature even more keen to stay.

The smelly water mingled on the breeze as I plunged beneath the tree branches and took the cool walk to the water. I could hear a soft bubbling like a normal spring, but the path soon curved to the right and then dipped downward, revealing a shallow pool contained by sandy brown stones. The stones looked ancient, and they were carved with odd markings and pictures. In the wild grass lay a little tin cup and a matching dipper.

I stopped abruptly; I had not expected to actually find Lee there. His back was to me, and the occasional *plop-plop* broke the air as he chucked stones listlessly into the pool.

"I believe you're supposed to drink the water, not fight it," I said softly.

Lee paused midthrow, turning toward me with a gasp. He looked rattled and sleepless, and maybe a touch unhinged. Some of the old Lee returned as he dropped the pebble and beckoned me forward.

"Please say you came looking for me," he murmured. "I could so use the flattery."

"I did, and I hope it cheers you."

"It would go a lot further if you smiled as you said it," he teased.

"You first."

The tiniest smirk banished some of the weariness on his face. "Even when the world is crashing down around my ears, you find a way to make it easier."

I joined him near the water, staring down into it, liking the way the shifting reflections threw dancing white strands of light all around the grotto. "Imagine that; Mrs. Eames was actually right about this place. Bit smelly, but it really does feel like it could cure all ails."

"Some," Lee replied darkly. "Certainly not all."

For a long moment I had no idea what to say—what would help him or lift some of the terrible burden from his shoulders. First his beloved guardian and now his mother. I had felt loss in my life, but to experience both blows so close together?

"It isn't at all fair," I ventured, feeling an odd, girlish compulsion to take his hand. He saved me the trouble, reaching over to take mine. It burned almost as brightly as when I touched that accursed book, but it was not pain this time but comfort, a kind of paralyzing kindness that had so long been absent from my life. I didn't know what to do with the feeling, so I did nothing at all. "You're the only good person in the entire house and somehow misfortune still finds you."

"Misfortune finds us all," Lee said. He sounded older, suddenly. Wiser. "The only difference is in when and how you resolve to face it."

"And how will you face this?" I asked, growing accustomed to the shy warmth of his hand against mine.

Lee looked over at me and let his smile broaden the littlest bit. "Not alone, and for now that will have to be enough."

"Yes, but I should know what to do. I shouldn't have let you follow your uncle. Then you would have never seen . . . You wouldn't have to live with those images forever."

His grip on my hand loosened. "It isn't your doing, although I can't help thinking . . . This house, the terrible things that happen in it, doesn't it all feel connected to what we saw? To how she died? There is an evil that surrounds this place. I fear it leaks out in every direction."

I couldn't argue with that. He wasn't looking at me anymore, and he felt, disastrously, a hundred miles away. How could I blame him for associating me with her death and this bedeviled place?

My senses prickled. Pitney had taught me to know when I was being watched. We were no longer alone. I let go of his hand and turned, finding Mrs. Haylam there, watching us with inscrutably dark eyes.

"Excuse the intrusion, Mr. Brimble, but Mr. Morningside would like to see Louisa."

She was not turning to leave us, and I glanced at Lee helplessly, mouthing, "I'll find you later."

That seemed to be what he needed to hear, and he nodded, padding into the grass and picking up the tin cup that lay there. He lifted it to us both and said with a shrug, "Couldn't hurt, could it?"

Mrs. Haylam held her silence until we were just a few steps from the kitchen door. I went ahead and tried to shake off her words, though they managed to diminish the surprising lightness in my heart that had come from seeing Lee again.

"I told you not to mingle with that boy," she warned.

"I wouldn't have to if your lot would leave him well enough alone," I spat back. "I'm sure he hates me anyway, given I work with a pack of wolves."

Her response was cut short by her employer sauntering around the tall table in the kitchen and joining us in the sunshine.

"Shall we convene in my offices?" Mr. Morningside came dressed in his usual sleek suit, a tailcoat with a square cut away and well-fitted tawny trousers. His ivory cravat matched his shirt. It made me feel shabby but honest. I wouldn't know what to do with myself if offered a silk dress and slippers.

"I would rather not," I said. "Your birds are . . . I don't want to be around them."

"Ah. Yes. I heard you sat in on a ferrying. Incredible, isn't it?"

"That's one word for it." I dropped my apron and stepped out into the daylight, narrowly avoiding the pup that tore around the yard, nimbly avoiding his owner with a piece of yam flapping against his jaws. "A walk would suit me better."

"A compromise, then—the west salon. There are no birds there, to my knowledge."

I had barely stepped foot into the grand room on the first floor of the house. The guests took meals and tea there sometimes, but it was not a place the servants congregated. We crossed back through the kitchen and foyer and into the tall, overcrowded salon with its myriad green velvet couches and walls heaped with dusty paintings. It felt huge and small at once, a large space stuffed with far too many antiques and furnishings, the aged wallpaper almost unseen behind so many paintings.

Mr. Morningside shuttered the massive doors behind us while I floated listlessly in the middle of the room. I had no idea where to sit, faced with so many couches and chairs and settees. But he walked confidently to a dark wood table with curlicue legs near the side window. Two chairs were positioned at a jaunty angle and he took one, sliding into it elegantly and sitting with his legs stretched out in front of him. His feet, fortunately, were facing forward.

I took the chair opposite him, feeling awkward and out of place, like a dandelion stuck into a bouquet of roses.

"To business," he said with a clearing of his throat. "Mary tells me there was a bit of nastiness last night in Derridon. First Dr. Merriman and then a woman murdered in some cottage up the hill."

"I was nearly killed, and a woman was torn to pieces and her skeleton was strung up over the hearth," I corrected him hotly. "So, yes, a bit of nastiness did indeed occur."

"There's no need for sarcasm, Louisa, although I do apologize for the doctor. He was not your responsibility. Quite honestly I underestimated the fellow, never thought he would be so sloppy." He sighed and flicked his brows up. "You're recovering?"

"I will, yes." I didn't want to talk about Merriman. He was dead and the world was better for it, though I didn't want Mr. Morningside to have the satisfaction of knowing I thought as much. "There was something strange about the woman,"

I said, taking the little scrap of paper out of my apron pocket and pushing it across the table. "George Bremerton says it was Lee's mother. We saw him going up to the cottages and followed, but there is no way he had time to do . . . I believe it would take a very long time to completely remove someone's flesh and disperse it all through a house."

"You would be surprised," he said thoughtfully, taking the paper and studying it closely. Sniffing it. *Licking* it.

"That . . . was in a fireplace."

"Obviously." He brought it away from his face and twirled it between his fingers. "But you saw Bremerton there?"

"Yes, but only after we discovered the body. He didn't have much of a lead on us, perhaps five or ten minutes." I searched the room for a moment, finding a writing desk with quill and ink on the other side of the many carpets. Quickly, I retrieved the writing implements, then took the paper back from him, flipping it to the blank side. "There was a symbol in blood behind her. I made certain to memorize it."

"Enterprising of you," he said with a chuckle. "I knew I was right to send you."

"After what I saw, I wish you hadn't," I replied, finishing the drawing and returning the paper. "A sort of lamb or sheep devouring itself with a sun behind it."

The smile fled from his face.

"You recognize it?"

Mr. Morningside shook his head, though he wouldn't tear

his eyes away from the rudimentary drawing. "A lamb," he whispered, tapping his teeth with the nail of one thumb. "What does a lamb symbolize. . . . Youth or naïveté, though for the God-fearing it can be purity and peace, even the son of God himself. One only ever sees an Ouroboros of the serpent. A snake eating its own tail. But to exchange that for a lamb . . . What could it mean?"

"And the sunburst?" I asked. "A lamb and a sun seem awfully cheerful for a message written in blood."

"I told you, Louisa, beauty can be deceptive."

"What do you make of that writing? It looks like a masculine hand to me. Only the headmaster at Pitney had penmanship that bold." Poppy and Bartholomew passed by the window, the pup still leading her on a winding chase.

"There we agree, certainly a man's pen," he said, flipping over the paper. "Bremerton's?"

"It's possible," I conceded, "but unlikely. I took him to be genuinely horrified when he realized Lee had found his mother murdered and displayed so. And in the carriage, too, he expressed regret."

He studied me over the tiny scrap of paper, squinting his golden eyes and cocking his head. "The widow. Merriman. You know now these people are here for a reason. George Bremerton is a known thief and has killed over money and debts before. Do not be blinded to his faults because of his nephew."

"You didn't see her, sir. You . . . I cannot believe he would do such a thing to Lee's mother and then turn around and embrace the boy. And besides, whoever did the killing would be covered head to foot in blood, and he had not a speck upon him."

"That is a sensible conclusion," he admitted. Sighing, he let the paper float back to the table and pushed both hands through his wavy black hair. "This is vexing. We have far more questions than answers. This symbol, the writing you found, Bremerton, the woman . . . All of it must be related."

I was not so sure. Lee's uncle had indeed found us in that cottage, but his story made sense. Hiding Lee's mother's questionable choices seemed like the loving thing to do. Her interest in the occult, in dark things, might have gotten her mixed up with the wrong sorts of people.

The sunshine through the window next to us looked inviting, and for a while I let my mind wander, simply taking in the birds that flitted through the garden and the way the wind bent the bushes and made them ripple.

"Or it could all be a coincidence," I murmured, resting my chin on my palm. "Lee's mother made an unfortunate connection, or several, and we were there to see the inevitable conclusion of that."

"Is that what you truly think happened or what you want to believe happened?" Mr. Morningside joined me in gazing out the window, tapping his teeth again. "If I'm right, then George Bremerton is involved in this murder, indirectly or otherwise. It would mean he's not acting alone. It would mean he conspired to visit horrible suffering upon his nephew's mother. I know it sounds intolerably evil, Louisa, but we both know the world is a harsh place and unfair."

I nodded, and felt the despair of the previous day creep back in, surrounding me, dulling the pretty scenery outside. "It doesn't matter which one of us is right. Any way you explain it, it's monstrous."

The doors swung open, and Mrs. Haylam entered, expertly balancing a tray with refreshments. The crone I had met on the side of the road didn't look strong enough to lift a single teacup, and now here she was delivering a full silver service and biscuits. She swiftly laid out the tea and food, righting herself with a satisfied little *hmph*.

"Well done, Mrs. Haylam, what a spread," he said, beaming up at her. "Louisa and I were just discussing last night's excitement. Do you happen to know this symbol?"

Mr. Morningside offered her the paper and she patiently inspected both sides. "The symbol means nothing to me," she finally said. "But this phrase . . . The first and last children. Why does that sound familiar?"

"It's something of a conundrum," he said.

"I will think on it," Mrs. Haylam replied. Her eyes were already distant and thoughtful, trained somewhere above our heads as she spun and bustled out of the parlor. "How do I know that?" she was saying to herself as she went. "Where have I heard that . . ."

"So distracted she forgot to pour," Mr. Morningside said with a laugh. I reached for the pot myself and measured out tea for each of us, then settled in to not drink any. My appetite was low, and breakfast was keeping me full.

"You really should try the jam biscuits," he was saying, mouth stuffed with sweets. "Mrs. Haylam makes the apricot preserves herself."

"I'm not really one for sweets," I replied softly. "The tea will suffice."

He finished chewing, taking his time, and sipped his tea, leaning back in his chair. Then a slow, devious smile spread across his face and he picked up one of the biscuits, handing it across to me.

"Take it."

"No, thank you," I said stubbornly.

"Don't put it in your mouth yet, just hold it," he commanded. He blew out a breath that ruffled his hair, and rolled his eyes. "Will it help if I say *please?*"

I plucked the biscuit out of his grasp and held it up between both of us. "There. I'm holding it."

"What is it that you're holding?" he asked, his smile broadening.

"Don't be ridiculous. A jam biscuit. Apricot."

"And what do you want it to be?"

I frowned, sensing where this was going. Before falling asleep, I had read the chapter on Changelings. On their alleged abilities. I wanted to drop the biscuit and storm out, but I also craved the proof of his wild assumptions. That I was one of those things. That was the only thing he could mean by mentioning it so often. Wouldn't I feel special somehow? Wouldn't I sense, deep in my bones, that I had some kind of innate and magical gift? I only ever felt plain and mistrusted, not exceptional.

"Play along," he said tightly.

"Fine. I wish . . ." What did I wish for? We never ate decadently growing up. There were foods I didn't mind eating and ones I had eaten time and time again because it was all there was on offer. So what did I want? "Bread and butter."

"Bread and . . ." He shrugged and motioned me along with one finger. "You could aim a little higher, my dear, but so be it. Make the biscuit become bread and butter."

"I can't."

"You read the book?" he asked.

I nodded.

"Well then. Half of achieving a thing is just knowing you can do it."

No. *No.* I shook my head hard. The biscuit trembled in my grasp. "I'm not one of those things. A Changeling. That's not me."

Mr. Morningside's smile turned down at one corner. His golden eyes, generally bright with arrogance, grew softer. "You've been different all your life," he said solemnly.

"Yes, I have, but I don't want to be different. I've only ever wanted to feel like everyone else."

"Close your eyes," he said softly, and not knowing why, I did. But that was wrong; I did know why. He wanted me to prove he was right. He wanted me to know, really know and feel, that I was one of them. "Bread and butter. Think it. It's what you want."

I had more or less memorized the relevant passages. Very well, the relevant chapter.

If the Changeling's parentage is of sufficient dark power, they can transform objects and even their own bodies for varying periods of time. Some may turn a rope into a snake for a mere instant. Others can change their form entirely, fooling even the mimicked subject's family, friends, or lovers.

Yet I did not want that to be true. If it was, it meant that I not only belonged here with these miscreants and monsters, but that I may not fit in anywhere else. It would mean I was not human at all, that the belonging I so longed for with my mother, my grandparents, at Pitney, had been the most hopeless and impossible dream all along. My eyes were shut tight. I shut them tighter still. I could feel a sob welling in my throat, because for all I wanted this untruth of his to disappear, I could not stop thinking of bread and butter, bread and butter . . .

I knew the instant it changed. The instant it worked. The instant I was changed.

And I heard the short, delighted intake of breath from the

young man across from me. When I opened my eyes, there was a dainty piece of toast pinched between my fingers and it was shiny with melted butter.

"Louisa . . . you only ever wanted to feel like everyone else, yet everyone else can't do that."

I swallowed, hard, willing my sobs away. By God, if I could change a biscuit to toast with a mere thought, then I could keep down the cries that stoppered up my throat. I stared at the bread and marveled at the stillness in my hand—it was as if my body had known this was possible all along and it was only my stubborn mind lagging behind.

"When will it change back?" I whispered, stricken.

Mr. Morningside lowered his head, watching me through the thickness of his dark, dark lashes. "Only when you want it to or when your concentration breaks."

I let the buttered bread slip from my hand. It was a biscuit again before it touched wood.

Chapter
Thirty-Three

Chasing Canis Infernalis

No demonologist worth his salt can go a year or two in this discipline without hearing whispers of the infernal hounds, often called canis infernalis, *or otherwise referred to as hellhounds. Rumored to be dogs born of bone-crushing hyenas of Africa that mingled with unknown and terrible beasts from the darkest unmapped, unchallenged corners of the plains, I knew I could not rest until I saw one of these creatures for myself.*

It was in Marrakech that I came across a man claiming to breed these beasts. The information was bad, but meeting him whetted my appetite. *If the average market swindler knew of these dogs, then perhaps they were more than myth after all. I'm certain many a foolish wanderer was tricked into purchasing one of his inferior animals, but I lingered in the city, keeping to the least reputable establishments. I will admit with some shame that I patronized opium-addled dens of sin, crime, and iniquity, and broke bread with folk from all over the world who had come to the labyrinthine markets to escape—and for some, to simply bathe in depravity until it drowned them. Often I would sit late at night, most frequently in a place I will call The Spinning Djinn, smoking a water pipe and listening to the idle gossip, not discarding even the most witless and intoxicated babble.*

At last a pair of young ladies appeared; too young, I thought, to be alone in the darker haunts of Marrakech. But come they did, ordering simple tea from the purveyor and sitting on purple cushions to speak in low voices. The shorter girl carried a sturdy leather bag that she guarded closely. They caught my attention because the taller one wore a large necklace of teeth, and her arm had recently been injured. The wound looked grievous; even through bindings, fresh blood seeped through the linens. Veiled and quiet, they took caller after caller, speaking to adventurous sorts that came and went.

Just before midnight I approached them, offering to buy tea for us all. They agreed, though wary, and asked what I wanted.

"Those teeth you wear," I said, pointing to the taller one's adornment. "I hunt a similar beast."

"No, mister, you don't," the shorter girl replied. Her eyes twinkled sapphire behind her veil. There was no telling her nation of origin, but her accent, surprisingly, sounded similar to a Bostonian's I once met. "Thank you for the tea, now move along."

"I have money."

"Not enough."

With a shrug, I pulled what looked like a small stone from my pocket and placed it on the low table between us. The untrained eye would think nothing of it, but I suspected these travelers would know its worth.

They nudged each other, sharing a look I could well interpret. Then they leaned close and had a whispered exchange, and I enjoyed my tea, noticing that the leather satchel between them was moving. The taller girl took the egg on the table and stood, and then they both left quickly. Only the wriggling bag remained.

I took the satchel and left, not daring to open the latch until I was again in my lodgings. When I looked inside, a small brown face peered out at me, innocent and long-snouted. The fur on its neck bristled and then fell, and a wet black nose touched my fingers. It licked my palm and squirmed out of the bag.

In time it would grow big, but that would not be for perhaps two hundred years. The beasts grew slowly, but when at their full size became immensely powerful. If tales held true, a fully grown hound stood taller than two men and could snap a draft

horse between its jaws like a twig. I would never find out where
this pup had been found or from what terrible mother it had been
stolen, I knew only that in his dark eyes a low fire simmered, one
that would eventually swell into an inferno.

Rare Myths and Legends: The Collected Findings of
H. I. Morningside, *page 50*

A soul braver than I would immediately run to test the limits of this power. If I were just a common thief prowling the streets of Malton, I would have been more than happy to know of this power, but now it marked me as one of them. I wanted to forget all about the biscuit, the bread, the feeling that shimmered through me when I felt the change take place in my hand.

Mr. Morningside dismissed me after taking a tracing of the paper I had found and the symbol on the wall. He encouraged me to experience my powers but not to exhaust myself, for in his words, "The cost of such beautiful, dark magicks is time."

That meant little to me, but I remembered Mary lamenting being unable to shield me from afar after using such skill during the storm and the widow's death. Perhaps it would be hours or even days before I could use that "skill" of mine again. I pushed it out of my mind. And aye, I know how foolish that sounds, how strange. Why, if a person woke one morning to find they had wings, would they not attempt to fly? But those wings, like my power—my Changeling power—marked me as other. God, it was no wonder nobody at Pitney liked the look of me. Why strangers recoiled. Why my grandparents would rather pay the high cost of room and board rather than care for me themselves.

I fiddled with the scrap of burnt paper and watched Mr. Morningside retire to his offices. The green door guarding his sanctum still called to me, but it was quieter now, manageable. Everything, in fact, seemed quieter and less urgent now that I had the truth of my blood and my birth dangling right there in front of my eyes.

My mind was filled with cupboards and arguments as I idled in the foyer. Mrs. Haylam's voice cut through the thoughtful din.

"What do you mean another lamb's wandered onto the property?! Fetch it, Poppy! You've arms and legs that work. Fetch it!"

I dodged out the front doors, circling around to the kitchen entrance on the east side of the house, meeting up with Poppy and her pup as they tumbled out into the daylight. Bartholomew loped up to me, going onto his hind legs and pawing at my waist until I scooped him into my arms and scratched his ears.

"Has one of the shepherd's lambs wandered over?" I asked, matching Poppy's quick pace.

"How do they manage to get free?" she asked with a jutting lip. "They're ever so small, and that fluffy mutt of his ought to keep them in line."

"It's a lot of sheep for one dog to manage," I pointed out. Bartholomew seemed content to lounge in my arms, licking at my chin occasionally, his ears popping up in one configuration and then another as he eyed the fields.

"There it is!" Poppy squealed, running full tilt toward the barn.

A tiny blob of white and black paced in front of the doors. The horses inside whinnied and stamped. I bent over and let the dog jump from my arms, and all three of us reached the little lamb as it backed itself against the wood side of the barn and bleated, terrified.

"I have you now," I said softly, coaxing it into my arms. It didn't fight, snuggling under my chin. It was warm and smelled of clover, its new woolly body pleasantly scratchy against my skin. "Shall we find your mother?"

"Or we could eat it," Poppy ventured, following me as I turned toward the neighboring pasture. "Mrs. Haylam makes a lamb roast that's ever so tender."

"It isn't ours to keep, Poppy."

"You're too nice. Like Mary. I'd rather eat it."

I thought on that for a bit as we followed the fence outlining the properties until we met the road, then turned onto that, taking it east toward the shepherd's cottage. The little golden pin with the serpent was on my frock, of course, for now I was too nervous to part with it.

"We don't seem to want for food," I told her. "I used to steal quite a lot, but only ever to survive. If I had food enough for myself I wouldn't steal. Don't you think that's how it should be?"

Poppy scrunched up her chin, her arms swinging like a soldier's as she marched beside me. Her pup, of course, trotted just behind. "There is sense to that. Mrs. Haylam says the people who come to Coldthistle get here because they're greedy and cross. Maybe they take too much. Maybe they steal even when they have plenty."

I nodded, and we walked for a little while in silence, the lamb bleating occasionally, the insects in the tall grass coming to life, singing their high, reedy song.

Poppy glanced up at me now and then, chewing her cheek.

"Yes?" I asked.

"I don't mean to bother," she replied, coy.

"But?"

"But are you going to stay with us? Forever?" Both she and the puppy stared up at me. If Poppy could grow a tail right then and wag it, I'm certain she would have.

"I don't know that yet," I said. It seemed more and more like a possibility, even if Lee had to be delivered from the house before he came to harm. "Was it easy for you to decide to stay?"

"I've been here for as long as I can remember," Poppy chirped.

"The family that adopted me wanted to send me away. I wasn't normal and it frightened them. They were mean and I didn't know why. I know why now, but it was confusing before Mrs. Haylam came and helped me. The nasty brothers beat me and locked me in the attic and poisoned my food. I was sick for a long time and I think I almost died."

"God, Poppy, that's awful. I'm so sorry. What did Mrs. Haylam do?" Part of me dreaded the answer, knowing the girl would give it with her unusual directness.

"It's hard to remember now," she said, chewing her cheek again. "But I remember she came with a book and she looked funny and hunchy, not nice and clean like she does now. Mr. Morningside was with her, too, but he didn't talk much. And she said that if I wanted my family to do what I said, she could make that happen, and that it would make the book happy. It made me happy, too. Now they're all shadows, but they can't hurt me anymore and they almost always do what Mrs. Haylam wants."

I blinked down at her. "The Residents are your old family?"

Poppy nodded hard, grinning, her braids swinging. "I like them better now. Were your family like mine, Louisa? Is that why you left them?"

"In a way," I said slowly, still trying to digest the fact that Poppy's cruel parents were nothing but creepy shadow beings haunting the attic. "The teachers at my school were nasty, but at least they never poisoned me. Starved me a little sometimes, and there were beatings, but we survived."

She blinked hard, frowning. "Nobody will beat you or starve you here. Why would you want to leave?"

"Because it's scary," I told her. "It's scary to think I don't belong anywhere else. That because I'm different, my life is set on a path that cannot be changed."

"I think I understand," she replied slowly. "But I also think it is better to belong somewhere with people who like you than to spend your whole life wandering about. That would be quite lonely."

I let that lie. Solitude had never bothered me, but then I had to consider that it was because I never had trusted friends who weren't imaginary.

We reached the shepherd's cottage without incident, though I kept checking the skies for clouds of birds. None came, although the shepherd's dog did come out to greet us. The lamb kicked in my arms as the two dogs circled each other and sniffed and then growled, Bartholomew's one yip sending the bigger dog running.

The blind shepherd's laugh arrived before his body. The door to his little house opened swiftly and he chuckled, ambling out of the cottage with a cane until his dog, Big Earl, returned to guide him toward us.

"We found one of your lambs," I told him. "Poppy and I came to return it."

"Thank you, my dears, you've done a good deed this day.

Joanna!" he called, and presently the kind young girl joined us. She gave me a toothy smile and slid the lamb from my arms and cradled it, cooing.

"Oh, you sweet thing," she said with a giggle, touching her nose to the lamb's. The flock was not far away, grazing in a giant white mass behind the cottage. "Let's return you to your mum, yes? You'll both like that. I thought you might be gone for good; second wee one this week to wander away. If only we'd found the first."

"I confess I know little of sheep," I said, watching her carry the lamb away. "Can they really tell their own children from any other lamb?"

"They smell them, yes," the old man said, turning his head toward Joanna as she left. "You can see them nose the young as soon as they're born and long after. It's like a man's signature, you see, perfectly unique."

A man's signature. I smoothed my hands over my apron, feeling for the scrap of burnt paper in the pocket next to the spoon. The penmanship. I could take the little scrap and search through George Bremerton's things. . . . Lee had only checked his bags, but if he kept a journal or any correspondence, I could at least make certain he hadn't written the note in the fireplace. That would put me at greater ease, knowing that he had nothing to do with the death of Lee's mother. And if he did . . .

Well, I knew Lee needed to be away from the house soon, but that would make his leaving even more dire.

"This kindness deserves a reward," the old man was saying, turning back toward the house. "Why don't you join us for a bit of brandy?"

Poppy sighed and tugged hard at my sleeve. "Louisa, *no*. No, no! We should be going. I need to get back to the house and poison that grumpy old man with the mustache," she said in a whisper that was, quite frankly, too loud to qualify truly as such.

And I agreed we should leave, but not for her peculiar reasons.

"Actually, we're both needed back at the house," I said, giving a little bow that he would not see.

"Then you decided to stay at Coldthistle," he mused, leaning on the door frame and wiping at the sweat under his cap. "Well, my thanks again for the lamb. You ladies have a fine afternoon. It's good, strong weather we're having today. Go and make the most of it."

And make the most of it I would. I told Poppy I would race her and the hound back to the house, and she agreed. We were all three of us out of breath when we arrived. A bank of clouds had followed us over, darkening the formerly sunny skies over the mansion. Chijioke's whistle wound out from the barn, and Mary was doing a bit of washing under the overhang outside the kitchens.

Gaining access to George Bremerton's room would require

a distraction. Lee, of course, was the natural person to ask. He might be willing to draw his uncle down to the Red Room or out to the gardens for a stroll. Or, I thought darkly, he might simply want to be left alone and not pulled into a scheme to tarnish the memory of yet another family member.

I slowed down as we reached the yard, but Poppy and Bartholomew flew by, running at full tilt toward Mary and her washbasin. Poppy stopped short, but the little brown hound took a flying leap, plopping into the sudsy water and soaking him and Mary both. He barked with delight, splashing around and flinging water in every direction.

"Bad!" Poppy shouted at him, but she was giggling as she did.

"Would you control this infernal menace!" Mary screeched.

Poppy leaned into the basin, trying to fish out the slippery pup, who wriggled and bucked until at last he was on the grass and shaking away the droplets on his coat.

"Look what you've done," Mary scolded, standing up to reveal her soapy frock and apron. "Mrs. Haylam will be very cross when I tell her."

I stood back and watched, amused, biding my time while I concocted a plan to get Bremerton out of his chambers. From behind, I heard the crunch of horse hooves on the drive. Mary and I both turned to look, finding an elderly man riding in with a heavy satchel hanging from his saddle.

"That will be the post," Mary said, waving to the man. "Can you collect it, Louisa? I'm in no fit state to be seen."

She began gathering her things and wringing out the wet clothes, hurrying back inside the kitchen door. Poppy and her hound were of no use, rolling around together in the grass until both of them were covered in green smudges and dirt.

"It's up to me, then," I muttered, trotting off toward the drive. The man was balding, the naked skin on his head red from sun exposure and covered in brown speckles like an egg. He swung down from the saddle nimbly enough for a man of his age and dug in the bag tethered to the saddle.

"You're a new face, miss," he said kindly, giving a little bow.

I returned the courtesy and waited while he retrieved the messages.

"Just a few today," he added, handing across a collection of folded and sealed packets. "Please send along me apologies to the master, young miss; the rains this week kept me from my usual route. Down t'Malton there's all but a lake now formed in the south road."

"I will tell him," I said, hugging the messages to my chest. He touched his thumb to his forehead and grasped the saddle, pulling himself back up. Something prickled in the back of my mind. Messages. Rains.

I hadn't gone to the house earlier because my contacts in Derridon sent a note to me at Coldthistle. It was about your mother . . .

That lying bastard.

"One moment," I said, putting out a hand to stall him. He twisted in the saddle, regarding me with bright blue eyes. "Do you carry the messages from Derridon, too?"

"That I do, young miss."

"And are there other messengers that might have come through?" I asked, trying to keep my tone light and unsuspicious.

"I doubt that greatly," he said with a chuckle. "I'm the one knows this route best. Takes me all along the Derwent. Not much need of other riders, Derridon being as small as it is. 'Sides, I know all the men and boys that be riding this road, and the rains kept 'em all holed up in Malton this ha'week."

"Thank you," I said with a cooling smile. "You've been most helpful."

He touched his thumb to his forehead again and clucked his tongue, the horse hopping forward and carrying him off, a spray of dirt and pebbles flying up in his wake.

No riders. No messengers. I knew now what to ask Lee even if it would hurt him terribly.

Chapter
Thirty-Four

Seeking the Black Elbion

Many smarter than I have wondered at the miracle of creation, at the possibility of something appearing from nothing. In a similar vein I have wondered at the origin of the Black Elbion, a book that predates all known manuscripts and scrolls, yet I myself have seen crude depictions of it in caves scattered across Europe and Africa. In Asia. In the Americas. Beings that have not yet discovered the true nature of writing record it on their walls—a square with an eye, and a crisscross through that eye. I have seen it in France, in Belgium, in Egypt, Florence, the Levant . . .

But the mysterious how of it remains. How can this single image, an image of a book, appear again and again? Naturally, historians shrug this off as a coincidence. The symbol could mean anything. Yet I know it to be the Black Elbion. I have seen the real book. I have felt its insidious power.

The book calls to men. Its inky tendrils of sin wrap around the heart and do not let go. It speaks of power but at great cost.

I saw it first in a desert. It was luck or fate that drew me there, for I was intending to track rumors of a djinn sighted outside of Baghdad city, a diabolically tedious and ultimately futile search. Instead, I met a traveler going west, a woman swathed all in black. She went on foot through the desert, though the heat and the winds bothered her not at all. At first I thought her blind or delirious, her veiled form passing by us and into the great sea of sand, but then she stopped and turned, saw our tents, and approached. She would only meet with me and waved my guides away. In her arms she carried an immense square object wrapped in fur.

When she had taken some water, she revealed the book to me in that tent. I remember the sounds of the winds screaming against the canvas, a sudden sirocco surrounding the camp, as if the desert itself wished to shield the world from the book's unveiling. Her eyes glowed gold as she took in my reaction.

"This was pulled from the bottom of the sea before Jesus walked with his apostles," she told me. Her English was delicately accented and she must have hailed from the surrounding lands. "*The Janissaries are in pursuit. I must get it to safety. Will you help, strange one?*"

I looked into her eyes and then at the red crossed eye staring up at me from the book. Here it was. Its power was unmistakable and so was hers. I did not know if I would ever see the Elbion again if I took it and its carrier out of the desert, but of course I would have to try.

"*Will you go west with us?*" *I asked her.*

She nodded, grinned, and began covering the book again. The winds died down. "*We will go west. The Black Elbion wills it.*"

Rare Myths and Legends: The Collected Findings of
H. I. Morningside, *page 301*

---

ary stood at the deep white basin in the kitchen squeezing out her apron. She grumbled under her breath, cursing a little louder whenever Poppy's shrieking laughs traveled into the room.

"Goodness, they're a handful," I said, standing in the doorway between the foyer and her. She nodded absently and pushed a strand of wet hair out of her face.

"Aye, and I'm late with Rawleigh Brimble's luncheon. He's to take all his meals in his rooms today and I still look half-drowned. There's just so much to do. Mrs. Haylam needs me to see to at least four rooms for new guests arriving next week. Some of those floors and windows haven't been washed in years."

And thank God for that.

"Don't trouble yourself, Mary, I can do it," I offered, sweeping over to the table and hefting the tray. "It's the least I can do after your heroics."

She watched me over her shoulder, wringing out the clean white linen of her apron with a smirk. "Mm-hm. Are we sure this isn't because you want to see the handsome young man and soothe his tender heart?"

"Mary, that's outrageous." But I was already out the door, and whatever she called after me was lost to the door swinging shut. Faintly, I heard Poppy giggling her way into the kitchen behind me and her hound barking excitedly.

It was no easy feat taking the heavy tray up three flights of steep stairs, but I managed. As I went, I was struck again by the silence of the house. It might have been any family home during a quiet period of the day, with ladies sewing in the parlor and the gentlemen reading or out riding. That peacefulness would soon be broken. I needed Lee to come out of his despair, just for a moment, and distract his uncle while I conducted my search. It would be a miracle if he listened to me after the way our meeting in the grotto ended.

My palms began to sweat as I neared their rooms. It was one

thing to flout George Bremerton's wishes and remain friends with Lee; it was quite another to conspire with his nephew to reveal his dark secrets. But it had to be done. If Bremerton was lying about the messenger, what else was he concealing? Nausea rose in my gut as I considered that he might be seriously involved in the death of Lee's mother. What if he had orchestrated it? What if he had *done* it?

And selfishly, I wondered if solving the mystery *for* Lee would somehow raise me again in his esteem. *Yes, you fool, he is bound to fall in love with you after you implicate his last family member in a despicable crime.*

I balanced the huge tray on my wrist and gave a few short knocks. My queasiness sharpened when Bremerton opened the door. He glowered down at me, a vein pulsing hideously in his temple. A long pistol was tucked into his trousers, and he hastily reached for a coat on the back of the door to put on and cover up the weapon.

This would require more delicacy than I had anticipated.

"What do you want?"

"I beg your pardon; I've brought the afternoon meal as requested," I said, averting my eyes politely.

"Well, aren't you all meek and courteous. That's a change. Where's the other girl? I asked the housekeeper to only send her." He moved closer, his chest bumping the tray threateningly.

"Mary is indisposed," I murmured. "I'll only be a moment."

"Fine. Put it down and be quick about it, and then I'm

going to have a word with your employer. You're meddlesome and strange, and I don't want you anywhere near us." He gave me the smallest possible crevice to slide through with the tray. Doing so required me to brush physically against him. I felt ill, discovered, and worse, he would be watching me too closely for me to speak to Lee.

But I walked softly through Lee's rooms. The outer chamber was a sitting room area with a writing desk and a table for two. Through a small door lay his bedroom, with an armoire, screen, and window looking north out into the gardens. Lee sat on the bed, disheveled as before, his cravat hanging loose and rumpled around his neck. He stared out at the grounds, still as a statue.

"There's food here, sir," I told him gently. There was nowhere appropriate to place the service, so I diverted to the round table next to the bed and set it there. It felt bizarre to call a boy of my own age "sir," but George Bremerton was not a meter behind me, watching.

"Oh, Louisa," Lee said, standing and smoothing down his waistcoat. "You're a sight for sore eyes. It's good to see you again. I feel like we didn't quite get to finish our last conversation."

"She'll be going," Bremerton cut in, his arms folded tight and fussy across his chest.

"Don't speak to her that way, Uncle. You're embarrassing me."

Bremerton tossed up his hands and pushed by me, cornering Lee against the window. Sighing, he blew out a furious breath and jabbed a finger at his nephew's chest. "I am trying to be sensitive to your grieving, Rawleigh, but there is a limit. I will not cast aside every rule of society—"

I stopped listening. Behind me, at the open door, I felt an icy presence hovering. While they argued, I subtly turned my head, finding one of the Residents darkening the doorway, long, spidery fingers curled around the edge. It tilted its head to the side as if in inquiry, but I knew not what to do. Poppy breezed behind it, carrying a much smaller, more manageable tray, and of course Bartholomew trotted along at her heels. She didn't notice the giant black shadow creature there, and it did not acknowledge her, either. It might have been one of her cruel adoptive brothers watching me. I couldn't imagine being comfortable with such information, but Poppy was a strange creature.

Was it looking at me or the men behind me? Was it worried about me or was I under its surveillance, too?

Then, gradually, its blurry form jittering like a shape seen through fog, it lifted one hand and tapped its vacant white eye with a fingertip.

I'm watching you.

I shivered and turned back around, sensing the instant it was gone. It was Lee's turn to go on the offensive, all but screaming at his uncle, his face bright red, curls mussed and falling over his forehead.

"And you've done nothing to arrange a burial for her, have

you? You sat here all day like a hen minding its chicks. I can't even take a walk around the grounds without you having a fit. It's . . . It's stifling! Just leave me be!"

George Bremerton retreated with a snarl, but only to the writing desk. He sat down heavily in the chair and glared at nothing in particular. Only a small victory, but Lee crossed to the other side of the bed and reached for the tea, pouring himself a cup and drinking it, still defiant and angry, and heedless of the hot water. He hissed through his teeth and drank more, as if the scalding somehow emboldened him.

"Here," I said, happy for any excuse to dodge out of Bremerton's sight. "Let me set this out for you."

I slid the lid off the plate with tiny sandwiches and an array of cheeses drizzled with honey. Lee didn't take any interest in the food, still choking down his too-hot tea.

"I need you to occupy your uncle for a while," I whispered as quietly as possible. Lee leaned in close, lifting a brow. "Take him to the spa or to the gardens. Something is amiss and I need to make certain he wasn't involved with the murder."

"He . . . *What?*" Lee nearly dropped the teacup. Then he remembered himself and lowered his voice, moving so close his ear touched mine. "You have proof of this?"

"I will," I assured him. We were going to run out of time any second. "I have some new information, but I can't tell you everything right now. He's been lying to you, Lee, I know it. I'll have proof enough if you can just distract him for a while!"

"I'll do whatever it takes to find the truth, then, for my mother." Lee nodded and set his jaw, putting the teacup down on the tray with more force than was strictly necessary. "Uncle!" He gave me a confident nod and fussed with his cravat, tying it back into a presentable knot. "I think some fresh air would benefit me greatly, or we might have a dip in the waters. And we must discuss the plans for my mother's burial. . . ."

I followed him out of the room and kept walking, not sparing a glance for George Bremerton as I passed. "Will you be taking your supper in your rooms, sir?"

"No, no." Lee waved me off with admirable indifference. His uncle was rising out of his chair and buttoning his coat. "You can leave us now."

It was perhaps too callous to be believable, but I obeyed, giving a curtsy at the door and pressing through the outer chamber before scurrying out the second door and into the hall, just in time to see Colonel Mayweather stumble out of his rooms, his face purple as a plum, his huge mustachio twitching in the exact moment before he vomited blood in a spectacular arc over the Turkish carpets.

Chapter
Thirty-Five

"Help m-m-me . . ."

The Colonel fell face-first into his own sick, crawling across the floor toward me with one shaky arm extended. He flopped onto his back like a dying harbor seal, his arms twitching as he tried to form another word. His eyes were red, filling with blood that soon spilled over and ran like crimson tears down his cheeks.

His body hitting the floor would rouse others soon. I stared, helpless, watching him slither across the carpets toward me. Little footsteps pelted up the stairs, and Poppy appeared on the landing with her dog. She froze, looking, for the first time, truly dismayed.

"*What did you do?*" I whispered furiously, backing slowly away as the Colonel moaned and pulled himself toward me. I couldn't stand to look at his bloated face and the white mustache that soaked up his blood like a sponge.

"A measuring error," Poppy said, gnawing on her knuckle. "Oh dear, not enough poison in the crumpets."

"We can't leave him like this," I replied. But what could I do? Poppy seemed utterly clueless, too, pacing back and forth on the top stair while her hound sniffed at the Colonel's boot. The door to Lee's room was just behind me, and though I had closed it up before leaving, he and his uncle would be departing any moment. There was no hiding the wide trail of blood and vomit being spread down the hall.

"Help," the Colonel croaked again, reaching for me.

"Colonel Mayweather, you naughty fellow, leave Louisa be," Poppy scolded loudly.

I clapped my hand over my forehead with one hand and pointed toward Lee's door with the other.

Poppy simply shrugged. Her shout had some sort of effect, at least—the Colonel flipped around again, wheezing and crawling toward the stairs. Somehow he managed to rear up onto his feet. Unsteady, he lumbered toward Poppy, both hands extended toward her as if he might lunge for her neck. Bartholomew danced around him in frantic circles, barking and snapping. Poppy had frozen on the top step, grasping the banister. And I could hardly blame her; it was a gruesome sight, made worse by the labored breaths he kept pulling in, the blood pouring out of his mouth making each one wet and sputtering.

He had nearly reached her and the stairs when I darted forward to try to pull him away by the back of his coat. But the dog acted first, wedging himself between the stairs and Poppy, toppling the dying Colonel and sending him careening down and down, the noise thunderous enough to be heard all through the house. He fell without a word, just bones and flesh crashing and crunching, hitting the second-floor landing with so much momentum that he cracked the railing and kept going, tumbling, cartwheeling until the final bone-rattling impact on the bottom floor parquet.

The noise echoed up through the foyer to where Poppy and I stood silent, staring at the Colonel, who was splayed out and still, the last of the blood in his body seeping out around him in an ever-growing pool.

"Poppy," I whispered frantically.

"Oh, Louisa," she whimpered, gathering up her hound and hugging him to her chest. "I swear by all the saints and sinners I didn't mean for it to happen that way!"

The door behind me opened, just as I knew it would, and I heard the men before I saw them.

"What the devil is going on here?" Bremerton shouted, marching as close to the bloodstain as he dared. He gasped and turned ashen as he caught sight of the body flat and still two floors below.

Poppy ran to us without hesitation, grabbing George Bremerton's coat and tugging on it. In a blink she was a terrified innocent little girl begging for assistance. "Thank goodness you're here, sir! The Colonel became ill and I didn't know what to do. One moment he was sipping his tea, content as you please, and then he made this bad, bad sound and he . . . Oh, it's too embarrassing to say," she improvised freely, even conjuring tears for them. "He was *sick* everywhere and there was blood in it and—and—he slipped in it and fell! It was too, too horrible, sir!"

I backed away slowly but not without making certain Lee locked eyes with me. God knows what he saw there, or what he must have thought when he, too, saw the dead man in the foyer and the wet trail of blood leading from the Colonel's room to just about where I had been standing.

"He was old and infirm," I said weakly. "A man his age . . . It might have been anything. Ulcers, convulsions . . ."

"What a ruddy mess," Bremerton snarled, storming down the stairs but not before pausing on the landing, careful to keep his boots out of the gore. "Just unbelievable. Are you going to stand there or help the man? You two girls, you stay where I can see you. Two dead bodies in this house in as many days is no damned coincidence."

"Go with him," I mouthed to Lee when Bremerton had turned his back and begun descending the stairs. Then I nodded carefully toward his uncle's rooms. This was my chance. He might not be out in the gardens, but two flights of stairs would provide me enough time to search his writing desk for a sample. Lee backed away from me, but not because I had asked. His eyes were wide, suspicious, trained on me as if he was seeing me anew. Whatever he saw frightened him. And of course it would. Who wouldn't grow doubtful after so much death?

Poppy, Lee, and the dog followed Bremerton down the stairs. I made to do so as well, but turned back at the last moment, shuffling against the wall and out of sight, then doubling back to Bremerton's rooms. His voice boomed through the house, the sound echoing up in the rafters and the open galleries looking down onto the foyer. I heard the kitchen door open and shut, and then another door.

"Such commotion!" The green door. It was Mr. Morningside, come to see what all the fuss was about. At once, Bremerton exploded, scolding him for the way the house was run, and for my behavior in particular. Well, I could deal with that later. Bartholomew joined in the shouting match, barking feverishly, inconsolable.

I had stopped and faced the banister to listen, but now I whirled around to sneak into Bremerton's room. Of course I was distracted and in a hurry, and hadn't stopped to listen to my more immediate surroundings. I turned and came face-to-breathless-face with one of the Residents.

It stood sentry in front of Bremerton's door, its long, spindly feet hovering just above the floor, its clawed toes barely scratching the carpets. The huge white eyes watched me at a tilt, as if the creature was trying to make out my intentions. Every instinct within me said to flee. The shadow monster was as tall as two of me stacked, and its oddly proportioned body plucked the deepest, most primal cords of fear in my belly. But I had to fight that terror and silently shout it back down.

I approached it slowly, arms spread, hands open in a gesture of surrender. The bruise on my wrist ached blindingly for a moment, worsening as I neared the thing. I would endure. I would ignore the pain.

"I just want to look inside," I murmured. It tilted its head the other way, tenting its too-long fingers. "It's for Mr. Morningside. I'm trying to work something out for him."

The Resident floated to the side, revealing the doorknob. It did not leave or dissipate, but I had enough room at least to access the door. And I tried. Locked. Cursing, I rattled the knob, but the lock was strong.

"Like thissss," the Resident said, startling me. It crowded in close but I held my ground, watching as one of its slender black fingers lengthened, then hooked and slid with perfect ease into the keyhole. I heard a soft click and the lock released.

It withdrew its hand, holding it closely to the chest. Then it simply watched me, silent as I opened the door as slowly and quietly as I could.

"Thank you," I whispered. The cold, odd presence still unnerved me, especially knowing it was out in the hallway observing me, but at least it passed out of view as I ducked into the room. The curtains were pulled shut, the room lying in heavy darkness. It smelled oddly sweet and rank, yet it looked as though nobody had stayed in the room at all. All of Bremerton's things were stacked neatly next to the bed, as if he anticipated leaving at any moment.

The strange stench worsened the farther I moved into the room. He must have told Mrs. Haylam he wanted his room untouched, for someone would have seen to that smell by now. I pinched my nose shut and tiptoed to the desk. There was nothing on top of the desk, just an undisturbed pen and ink. A well-loved Bible was there, too, though when I flipped through it I found no annotations in his hand. The drawers were likewise barren. Nothing. I sighed and pushed through to the bedroom, swallowing a retch from the worsening smell of rot. Had he left a bit of food to molder and not known it? What could possibly cause such a stench . . .

I knew in the pit of my stomach that it was a bad omen. Only death smelled that way; the sweet yet tainted perfume of decaying flesh.

The bedroom held nothing for me, and I wondered over the wisdom of opening his bags to look inside. He might return at any moment. The argument in the foyer had dwindled, or else they were speaking more quietly and rationally now. I lingered, staring down at his bags and worrying my lower lip. The chance to poke around might not come again. I would do it.

I knelt, nearly losing my composure and the fortitude of my stomach, the reek of rot so overwhelming it made my eyes water. Reaching for one of his bags, I stopped, trembling. Something shiny and black poked out just the smallest bit from under the bed frame. Gently, I leaned closer, holding my nose, finding at last the source of the smell . . .

There was no need to touch it; I could see the dainty black hoof and a hint of pure white wool stained with old blood. It was as if Joanna's kind voice whispered through my head.

You'll both like that. I thought you might be gone for good; second wee one this week to wander away. If only we'd found the first.

Here it was. I stood, quickly, so quickly that my head spun from the smell and the shock. What was this wretch doing with a murdered lamb under his bed? I needed to clear my mind. Focus. There had been a lamb painted in blood on the wall behind Lee's mother. Could this be the connection I needed? I backed away from the bed to escape the smell a little and pace, and when I turned I saw it, plain as anything.

I hadn't bothered to look at the door after I closed it behind me, but now I had the penmanship sample I needed. Blood pounded in my ears; a shortness of breath that felt like drowning made my chest tight and clenched. Well, this was proof, but I did not want it, not like this, not when it made my flesh prickle with cold.

Shaking, I reached into my apron pocket and pulled out the scrap of paper, holding it up to compare against the words written in blackening blood on the door. The slants and loops were the same. A match.

AND THEY OVERCAME HIM BY THE BLOOD OF THE LAMB

I mouthed the words to myself with the paper still held aloft. I mouthed them as the door burst inward and George Bremerton flew at me with pistol cocked and ready.

Chapter
Thirty-Six

A scream like ice shattering across a frozen lake ripped through the room. I had never heard anything close to that pitch, so high and terrible it made my mind practically *bend*. It was the Resident outside the door. It was clawing at the air, at the open door, as if some invisible barrier prevented it from ingress.

But that was the least of my worries. Bremerton was upon me and fast, knocking his bags out of the way and grabbing me by the throat before I could defend myself. He threw me back against the wall next to the window, following up with a heavy fist squeezing around my neck.

"You did it," I cried. "You killed his mother! Murderer!"

"His mother?" Bremerton snorted and pressed his thumb into the fleshy hollow of my throat. "I have no earthly idea who spawned my nephew and I don't care. That wench was one of ours until she decided to turn her back on the cause. She was to be made an example of, nothing more."

"Then why . . . Why are you here?" If I was going to die, I at least wanted to know what had been the cause of all this suffering. All this confusion.

He rolled his eyes and pushed his thumb into my neck until I coughed. "Why, to kill the Devil, girl, what else? I didn't kill my brother, John, for my health. And now you will answer my question and be quick about it. How?" He shook me, hard, clamping down on my throat until only the lightest trickle of air got through. His eyes and nostrils bulged, spit flying from his lips as he shouted in my face. "Devious little bitch, how did you get in here? You're one of them. I know you are. So how did you do it?"

I scratched desperately at his hands, trying to pry his fingers loose from my neck.

"Uncle!"

Lee's voice rang out from the hall, and for a beautiful, shining instant I thought I was saved. But Bremerton blind fired over his shoulder, shooting the door frame. I heard Lee's cry faintly over the ringing in my ears. A thread of a whining sound persisted. Had I gone deaf? The pistol had sounded, and felt like raw fire exploding in my face.

He cocked the pistol again and turned it on me, shoving the hot barrel against my temple.

"I don't know," I wheezed, tears squeezing out of the corners of my eyes. "Please! I don't know anything."

"Lies!" he thundered, shaking me again. Through bleary eyes I could see the welts I had made on his hand, blood running under my fingernails. Nothing dislodged him. "You work for the Devil, girl, and no servant of evil is ever so innocent or naive. Tell me how you got in here!"

How . . . How . . . I scrambled for an answer that would mollify him, if such a thing existed.

"I'm not one of them!" I cried.

"Wrong again." He screwed up his mouth into a hideous pucker and nudged my head with the pistol. "One more try, and then you die."

"The p-pin," I whispered. It was the only thing I could think to say. My eyes flicked downward to show him. "Gold . . . pin."

Bremerton searched the front of my frock and with his gun hand ripped the cravat pin from my dress. His grip on my neck tightened in warning as he fumbled to tuck the pin into his pocket. There was a commotion at the door. I could see the whole of the house gathered there, trying to get in. I watched Lee shove aside first a stricken Mary and then Mr. Morningside himself.

I tried to shake my head at him. No. *No.* But he could make it through the warding on the door. *A boring human boy.* A boring human boy trying to save a dying monster like me.

But Bremerton was not taking any chances, and he was no fool. He blind fired again, and this time I felt the bullet hit. I felt it as if it had struck me in my chest, only it had struck Lee's. The bullet's discharge left me confounded and deaf for a moment, and I watched in trapped silence as Lee stopped, touched his fingers to his chest just over his heart, and pulled them away shining with blood.

Then he crumpled to the floor, a red flower blossoming across his crisp white shirt.

"You did that!" Bremerton screamed at me. "You made me do that!"

His voice was muted, and so was my own voice as I thrashed against him and shrieked incoherently, landing one blow at last, my knee slamming into his groin. He recoiled and dropped me, bending in half with a throaty cough. But the gun was still firmly in his grasp, and he blocked me completely from the door.

I looked at Lee, at his lifeless body on the floor, and groped blindly for the spoon in my pocket. There was nothing else in reach, and for now it would have to be my one and only weapon. Bremerton recovered, as I knew he would, and lunged at me again, pinning me against the wall. This time I had the desperate wherewithal to throw my arm up and grab his wrist, fighting the trajectory of the pistol before he could aim it at my head. He snapped his thumb against a latch on the pistol's handle and a short bayonet shot out toward me, missing my throat by a hair. We struggled, both of us growing damp with sweat, and just as I hoped, he paid no mind to the dull spoon in my left hand.

But it was not just a spoon. Not in that moment. It could be anything I wanted.

I closed my eyes and jabbed the spoon against his side and then his neck and he laughed me off, twisting the gun away from me. There was no more time. The pistol would need to be reloaded, and unless I could hit the latch on the handle and retract the bayonet, my moment had come. Vaguely, I heard the others screaming at one another in the hallway, disjointed voices tumbling as they struggled to find some way through the ward. I heard an ax slamming into the wall, but they would never break through in time.

It was not a spoon. It was not a spoon. Sweat ran hot and itchy over my forehead. Time slowed. It was not a spoon but a knife. *Jab jab.* It was a knife. Yes, a bayonet like the one slashing toward my neck. I wanted it to be a knife. *Jab.* Never in all of my years had I wanted anything more than I wanted this spoon to be a knife.

I felt the spoon sink in, far, and I snapped my eyes open to watch the cruel-bladed knife disappear into his throat. A gurgle of surprise bubbled out of his mouth, and his eyes now were wilder, more dangerous. It wasn't enough. He could still aim the pistol, and aim it he did, lifting it with weakening and shaky fingers and pointing it at my face.

"Mary! Quick, quick, shield them!" I heard Poppy's tiny scream pierce through the veil of dread.

It happened too quickly to feel the full meaning of it. I saw the bayonet flash toward my face and flinched, watching the blade ricochet off my cheek, the touch of it like the brush of a feather. Then there was only Bremerton's flummoxed expression and the blood pouring out of his mouth as my stab wounds disabled him at last, and then I felt the air around us deaden and flatten and I braced, knowing I was shielded by Mary but terrified all the same.

I had thought the Resident's scream horrid, and indeed it was, but this sound was the sky itself tearing in half. Over Bremerton's shoulder I saw Poppy in the doorway, her mouth wide open, her eyes black as a starless sky, as her unnatural shriek rippled toward us. It did not touch Lee and it did not touch me, but I felt its buffeting wings on my cheeks as George Bremerton's bleeding face expanded and distorted like a warmed boil and popped. I shut my eyes tight and crumpled back against the wall, blood and sinew and God knows what else showering me in horror.

My legs fell out from under me and I slid bonelessly to the floor, raking gore out of my eyes and wiping at my mouth. I spat and coughed and breathed a full breath after too long. Then the tears came, and I crawled on hands and knees away from George Bremerton's headless body to the brave young boy shot dead by traitorous blood.

Chapter
Thirty-Seven

For a long time after they pulled Bremerton's body out of the room, I sat next to Lee. There was nothing that could be done for him. The bullet had hit him square in the chest. He looked oddly untouched, the crimson stain on his shirt the only indication that something had gone terribly awry.

I wiped a piece of Bremerton's skull from his boot. It offended me that it had touched him.

"I'm sorry," I said, unable to look at his face, knowing it would undo me. "I'm so very sorry, my friend."

The bloody spoon sat in the little shallow basket made by my skirts. I held Lee's hand after making sure mine was cleaned. His skin was still warm. That made the tears come stronger, more painfully, until I couldn't see anything but a watercolor of the splattered room and Lee's fine boots.

Chijioke had finally taken his ax to the door itself, allowing the others to come in. They watched outside the mangled door frame, two Residents hovering in the very back like worried parents. Mr. Morningside was the only one brave or stupid enough to come in and stand next to me. Then, with a sigh, he sat beside me on the floor, his long legs pulled up so that he could rest his wrists on his knees.

"This is my fault," he said hoarsely. If I could feel anything but loss, I would have marveled at his taking responsibility. "The first and last children . . . I should have put it together sooner. And I definitely should have realized we had an End of Dayser among us."

I said nothing for a long time, uninterested in his explanations. When I could better manage my tears, I wiped at my face with my apron and fixed him with a stare. The black hair and golden eyes. The too-perfect proportions of his face. He stared back at me and then took a handkerchief from inside his coat. With utmost care, he reached across and dabbed at my blood-stained face.

"Is what he said true?" I asked. "Are you really the Devil?"

"Yes." He smiled wryly, exhaustedly. "Well, what he would call the Devil. What you would, too, I imagine. Most of what's put down is ridiculous, but I admit some of it is accurate. Throw darts at a dictionary long enough and you're bound to strike 'truth.' I've had many forms, many names, untold centuries to come and go as a thought or as a being."

Perhaps it was best to learn this way, while I was still numb from Lee's death. "Then you must be very powerful."

"If you like."

"But not powerful enough to walk through a *goddamned door*."

He had the good grace to flinch. Taking a measured breath, he refolded his cloth and ran it carefully down my temple. "Men like Bremerton were just a whisper for a long, long time. Their sort and others like them have always tried to eliminate me. He might have succeeded, too, if you hadn't decided to sneak in here."

"I see. I wish he *had* killed you."

"No, Louisa, you really don't." Mr. Morningside—the Devil—gave a dry laugh. "It would mean the end of the Unworld and the human world as you know it."

"Oh." I let him push the handkerchief across my forehead, trying to grasp the magnitude of this person, this *being*, sitting with me and calmly cleaning my face. Squinting, I looked harder. "You were wrong. Lee was innocent. Bremerton killed his own brother and Lee had nothing to do with it. He only *felt* responsible because he was a good person. Please, you're the Devil—I want to make a bargain. Isn't that what you do? Trick people into giving up their souls for some favor?"

He shook his head, glancing at Lee's still body. "I know what you would ask, and I cannot help you . . ."

"No," I murmured, blinking back a fresh wave of tears.

". . . but Mrs. Haylam can."

I didn't care how silly my expression was. Had I heard him correctly? Could the hag-turned-housekeeper really bring Lee back to life? I searched his face, but it was no jest. The others were still milling around in the hallway, and I could see Mrs. Haylam standing there, watching us intently.

"Mrs. Haylam, would you come in here, please?"

She approached us slowly, her hands clasped together over

her simple black frock. Her skin glowed orange in the late afternoon light filling the room. I looked up at her expectantly. Pleadingly. She fixed her gaze on where my hand held Lee's.

They began a quick conversation in a language I didn't understand. It was beautiful and guttural, and both of them spoke it with a native's ease. From her expression, I could tell she was not happy about what Mr. Morningside said.

Her silvery eyes narrowed to slits. "You don't know what you're asking, child."

"Yes, I do," I said.

"She read the book?" Mrs. Haylam asked him.

"Indeed. Ostensibly she understands the risks."

Her eyebrows twitched under her cap. "Ostensibly is not good enough, *Annunaki*. The *Da'mbaeru* could demand anything upon its return, and I will not be the one to pay the shadow price."

Mr. Morningside looked back to me, his chin still tilted up toward the housekeeper. He cleared his throat and paused. "You read the chapter on shadowmancers, Louisa?"

I nodded.

"And you remember it?"

"Yes," I said, but I was less certain now. I did remember it, and I remembered the awful things that were asked in exchange for a shadow to be brought back. At the time, it had seemed harmless, stupid, the kind of scary story used to frighten children into behaving and choosing a God-fearing path. Now I could feel my stomach tightening with dread. "I remember it."

Would Lee thank me for this? I looked at last on his face and felt my chin quiver with sorrow. Selfishly, I did not want to lose him. Mary, Chijioke, and Poppy peered in through the ragged hole where the door had been. Bartholomew stared up at his masters, his ears flattened back against his head.

Mrs. Haylam began rolling up her sleeves, her rheumy eye clearing entirely and then flashing molten gold. When I had first met her on the road, I had seen the hint of markings on her wrist, but now I saw that her arms were covered in tiny tattoos, rows and rows of little pictures. Her voice was thicker, stronger, edged with an unsettling echo. "I will ask you only once, Louisa, foolish child, and you will think carefully before you answer: Will you raise this boy and pay the price? Think before you speak; be certain you will give what is asked, even if it means your life for his."

I agreed.

If it was selfish or not, I could not say, for I felt certain that his death had been preventable, and *I* could have prevented it. I'd never told him the full truth. I'd never risked that much, and he might have saved himself in some way, been more motivated to leave, been more primed to protect himself. And as I sat on the floor, staring up at Mrs. Haylam with anticipation, the thought of losing my life for his seemed almost preferable. What was I, anyway? A monster, apparently, one that belonged among only misfits and creatures of darkness.

It was childish, to think of my own life with so little regard, but in that moment it felt like the truth. My life for his; a troubled life for an innocent one.

"I agree." That was all it took, and Mrs. Haylam was kneeling next to Lee's head, cupping her hands over his ears. Her eyes rolled back, solid, flashing gold again, and she whispered a string of words in the language she had spoken to Mr. Morningside just a moment before.

The room began to shake, subtly at first, and then it felt as if the whole roof might come crashing down on us. I gasped and inched back, watching as the sliver of Lee's shadow visible on the floor soaked into his body, disappearing, before his mouth dropped open and that same shadow emerged, floating up from between his lips until it stood, the very silhouette of the boy I knew, hovering over us.

I gaped up at it, shivering, watching as it held out its ghostly black arms and inspected them, as if trying on a new coat.

"What is the price?" Mrs. Haylam murmured, her eyes flickering like fairy lights.

Lee's shadow spun to face her, and she nodded toward me.

"She will pay the shadow price?" It was Lee's voice, but cold, emotionless, lacking the sweetness and warmth I had come to expect from him. Oh God, was this all a mistake?

"It has been agreed upon," she said.

The shadow twisted back around, its toes still dangling

inside Lee's open mouth. Its hollow eyes regarded me for a long moment before it said blankly, "Three boons I will ask. The first, a lock of your hair."

"Of—of course," I stammered. Mr. Morningside handed me a small pocketknife. I had almost forgotten his presence, as he was perfectly silent. His eyes were hooded as he handed me the knife, and again I questioned this choice. Shouldn't the Devil be gleeful to have tricked me into this course? I cut off the bottom fringe of my braid and handed it to Mrs. Haylam.

"The second, a drop of your blood," the shadow demanded.

"Done." I already had the knife in hand. Pricking my thumb, I held it up and watched blood bubble to the surface, then disappear, twirling into a mist that rose into the air and then vanished.

"The third," the shadow murmured, its hollow eyes squinting as though it were smiling, "the life of your firstborn child."

I blinked up at the thing, my heart pounding, my mouth suddenly dry. Then I looked to Mr. Morningside and Mrs. Haylam for instruction. "I'm . . . I have no child, shadow; you've made some mistake."

"There is no mistake," it hissed in reply. Then it spun slowly until it faced the door, extending one arm and pointing at Mary, who watched us wide-eyed from the doorway. "That girl is of your make, born of your wishing and your mind. I will take her now as my price."

"No!" I shook my head, going onto my knees. "You can't

take Mary; she's done nothing!"

"Louisa, you agreed," the Devil was saying, touching my shoulder gently. "There is no going back now."

"I won't allow it!" I shouted back, shoving his hand away.

Mary drifted into the room, her hands folded in front of her apron. She gave me the strangest smile, one of fondness and sadness. Of acceptance. No. *No*. This wasn't what I wanted! None of this was what I wanted. . . .

"You don't have to do this," I told her, shaking my head, tears gushing anew down my cheeks. "It should be my life, not yours! Go, Mary, turn around!"

But she simply walked on toward us, calmly, as if going righteously to an execution.

"It will be all right," she told me softly. Out in the hall, she took Chijioke into her small arms and squeezed him tight, then turned to Poppy and did the same, even sparing a moment to drop a kiss on Bartholomew's head.

"Are you sure about this, Mary?" Chijioke was asking, brushing his hand at a spill of tears.

"Absolutely" was her reply.

No . . . She was not allowed to say good-bye. She was not allowed to do this on my behalf. Mr. Morningside stood and moved to the corner and Mary took his place, kneeling and touching her forehead to mine. "I'll go, Louisa. You don't have to worry."

"No!" I looked for help, for dissension, but nobody spoke up;

they simply stared back at me. "I can't let you do this, Mary. I didn't know I made you. I didn't mean to . . . to . . ." I threw my arms around her. She was Maggie. She was Mary. I had made her and needed her and she had been my friend in the worst hours of my life. And now she would be gone. Just like Lee.

I had tried to save everyone, and instead I had led to everyone's ruin.

Mary carefully unhooked my arms from her shoulders, smiling her gentle smile, her green eyes so familiar and filled, heartbreakingly, with nothing but love.

"Don't cry, Louisa," she said, standing and taking the shadow's hand. "I'm only going home."

Chapter
Thirty-Eight

n a blink she was gone, as if she had never existed in the first place. As if my need of a friend had never manifested her into being.

And the shadow was gone, too, sucked back into Lee's mouth. The blood of his that had leaked out onto the carpets gradually absorbed back into his body until a healthy bloom of color sat on his cheeks. Then, through Mrs. Haylam's cursed magic, I saw his chest rise and fall. He lived.

"He will wake when the moon rises," she told me. Her eye was clouded once more, and she rolled her sleeves down, challenging me with a stare as she did so. I said nothing, and she and Mr. Morningside hoisted Lee up, though he did not react. They pulled him out of the room and I followed, numb and cold all over as they brought him back to his own rooms and laid him in the bed.

It took me a long moment to realize what looked wrong about him: he had no shadow as they picked him up or as they dragged him, and he had no shadow as they put him to bed. That thing that had demanded hair and blood and life of me was inside him somewhere, and the thought made me sick with regret.

What had I done to him? What had I done to Mary?

I stood over his bed as dusk slipped away to night, as a cloud of bats darkened the sky and circled the house, as the Residents came out and prowled the halls. Mrs. Haylam stayed for a while, her shoulder almost touching mine.

"I warned you," she said, and it was pity in her voice, not scorn.

"I know, and I should have listened. Will he be the same?" I asked.

Mrs. Haylam drew in a rattling breath. "Yes and no. He will be the boy you knew, but he is death-touched now, and living by the grace of shadow. There will be a greater darkness in him, and a greater capacity for malice."

I nodded, touching the blanket he lay upon. "Mr. Morningside was wrong, you know. Lee didn't belong here. He was innocent."

"Yes, and your certainty is the only reason I agreed to this," she said, gesturing to his legs. "He can never leave this house, Louisa. A shadow is not form; he is bound to the same magicks that tie the Residents here, and when his flesh has faded he will be as one of them. You will not live to see it, and he will exist here forever."

"Worse and worse," I whispered, feeling hopeless. Feeling lost. If I had bound Lee against his will to this house, then I would stay, too. It was only fair, after the mess I had caused. "I have cursed him and lost Mary in one."

"Maybe not," Mrs. Haylam said softly, placing a motherly hand on my back. "Maybe not."

"What do you mean?" I asked.

She nodded subtly to the door, and I turned to find Mr. Morningside watching us, leaning against the door frame. He was the Devil, but I did not shrink from him as he approached and held out his arm. I took it, looking up at him, not reassured by his easy smile.

The Devil's golden eyes flickered, and he patted my hand. "How do you feel about a little trip?" he asked. "To Ireland, perhaps. Waterford, more specifically. I know a well there with extraordinary power. Hold out your hand."

I did, a stirring of recognition in my head. The dream. The book. Was all not lost? Could I really see Mary again? When I opened my fist, I found he had dropped a small, warm thimble into my palm, and a familiar gold pin.

"Don't stay away too long," the Devil said, drifting toward the door. He paused and looked over his shoulder at me. "You belong here at Coldthistle House."

Epilogue

A month later I stood in the blistering cold, a woolen muffler pulled up high over my lips. Burrowing down into it, I waited outside the tavern, stamping my feet and watching my breath curl into little wisping white dragons that floated to the iron sky.

I felt like a stranger here, though Waterford had long been my home. Those childhood years felt a hundred centuries away. I was not the same miserable, shy girl rolling in the mud while my parents fought and fought. A man shouldered his way into the tavern, leering at me. I looked away, disgusted, and hugged myself to ward off the cold.

Barges drifted on the river. Workmen called to one another as they took their afternoon breaks. A few gulls floated stark and white high above me, feathers ruffled by the wind. I could no longer glance at a bird without thinking of Mr. Morningside and the multitude of souls stashed in his office. What did he need them all for? I wondered if he would ever tell me.

Sighing, I looked up and down the lane, searching every face that came and went. Would he come? Was this all just a game? No. Patience. I opened up my mitten and there it was, the promise of friendship restored. A way to make things right again.

A thimble.

Another quarter hour passed, and I decided to leave and try again the next day. That was when he appeared. He was short, with a wide and round face. His shockingly red hair stood up in every direction.

"Alec?" I asked, watching him slide up to me with a toothy grin. "I'm looking for a very special spring. Can you help me?"

His eyes twinkled and he started down the lane, beckoning for me to follow. "If a spring's your thing, I ken one fit even for a king."

I squeezed the thimble tight in my fist and followed.

Acknowledgments

I want to thank Kate McKean for not telling me I was a complete lunatic for proposing this novel in the first place. What started as a stray thought on the way back from Chipotle turned into a story that took me to places I never expected. Thanks to Andrew Harwell and HarperCollins for believing in this project, giving me an amazing amount of freedom to experiment, and to the hardworking artists who made the book beautifully sinister to behold.

My mother got me hooked on Jane Austen early in life, and I don't think this book would have come about without that nudge. I'm not sure you thought this would be the result, Mom, but I hope you're proud. I think Jane would dig it (maybe not the swear words, though). Thanks also to Pops, Nick, Tristan, Julie, Gwen, and Dom for being the most amazing family support system a writer could ask for.

To Brent and Smidge, thank you for being patient while this book took over my life and occasionally made me very difficult to live with. Thank you for your ideas and for reminding me that ye olde pistols are not like our modern ones.

A huge thanks to Tadhg Ó Maoldhomhnaigh for the

assistance with Gaelic translations. While working on the book I was fully immersed in some of Andrea Portes's brilliant novels, and her genius propelled me to try harder and think bigger.

And to the Louisa who this Louisa is named for—I miss writing with you, but thanks for lending me your lovely name.

Image Credits

Victorian border on pages ii, iii, vi, vii, 4, 16, 22, 29, 36, 43, 46, 55, 65, 78, 91, 102, 107, 110, 120, 132, 143, 156, 166, 176, 188, 195, 212, 224, 232, 242, 253, 262, 276, 282, 294, 307, 316, 325, 328, 345, 360, 372, 381, 388, 398, 402 © 2017 by iStock / Getty Images.

Wall texture on pages ii, iii, vi, vii, 4, 16, 22, 29, 36, 43, 46, 55, 65, 78, 91, 102, 107, 110, 120, 132, 143, 156, 166, 176, 188, 195, 212, 224, 232, 242, 253, 262, 276, 282, 294, 307, 316, 325, 328, 345, 360, 372, 381, 388, 398, 402 © 2017 by Shutterstock.

Rusty wall on pages 2, 3, 44, 45, 76, 77, 108, 109, 154, 155, 186, 187, 210, 211, 230, 231, 274, 275, 292, 293, 326, 327, 370, 371 © 2017 by iStock / Getty Images.

Photographs on pages 2, 3, 44, 45, 76, 77, 108, 109, 154, 155, 186, 187, 210, 211, 230, 231, 274, 275, 292, 293, 326, 327, 370, 371 © 2017 by iStock / Getty Images.

Illustrations on pages 92, 125, 177, 196, 243, 254, 346, 361 by Iris Compiet.